Immortal Allery Locke has been tasked with finding the key that opens doors to other dimensions. Find it and hand it over to the wardens for destruction. There's only one problem—the key is a woman. Whenever the key—Deni—opens a door, it allows monsters, demons, and all manner of unsavoury supernaturals to cross over and wreak havoc. Allery must keep Deni from falling into the wrong hands, because if rogue wardens get hold of her, it will cause an interdimensional war. Can Allery make the impossible decision? Kill her lover, or risk the end of the world.

LOCKE & CO.

E.J. TETT

A NineStar Press Publication
www.ninestarpress.com

Locke & Co.

First Edition, July 2025

ISBN: 978-1-64890-882-8
Also available in eBook, ISBN: 978-1-64890-881-1

CONTENT WARNING:
This book contains sexually explicit content, which may only be suitable for mature readers. Depictions of drug use/addiction, the death of a secondary character, deceased parent, abduction/kidnapping, cancer, and homophobic slurs.

Chapter One

There is no jolt. Or shock. Or sudden, great intake of breath. Your eyes don't snap open. This is no rebirth. It's like waking up but not remembering the moment you were no longer asleep. You will hurt, depending on how you went, and you will scar, but you will live again. And that's all that matters.

The whistle woke Allery from death, but it was the feeling of being smothered that made her heart hammer. She couldn't move—the new-shower-curtain smell of the body bag seemed like the only thing between her and six foot of earth pressing down around her. No, it wouldn't be six foot; they must've almost dug her out for her to have heard their signal. God, they couldn't get to her quick enough.

Don't panic. Don't panic.

The material moved against her mouth when she breathed, so she clamped her lips together and exhaled hard through her nose instead. She didn't dare open her eyes. She reminded herself she wouldn't be trapped underground for eternity. They *were* coming. There was nothing for her to panic about.

She swallowed, grimacing at the dryness of her throat. Hanging was not a pleasant way to go but it had been a necessity. The prison guards had told her the only way she'd leave would be in a body bag and she'd smiled.

She longed to be able to bend her knees and lift her arms above her head but if she moved even an inch the earth moved with her, filling the wiggle room.

It wasn't quite silent underground; if she strained her ears, she could hear a faint scratching of metal against rocks and a thumping of soil.

They were digging her up. They'd know not to keep jabbing into the ground like that, wouldn't they? She didn't know how much having a spade in the guts would hurt and she didn't like to hazard a guess. The noises grew louder, and she could hear voices above.

"...*hurry up!*" Esme, impatient as usual.

"Well, if you put your back into it..." She couldn't work out if that was Driscoll or Nick. Driscoll, probably. Nick would be on lookout, listening to the trees, checking for the guards.

The pressure eased on her chest as the soil lifted and she thrashed about to free herself. She opened her eyes though she could see nothing.

"Got her." Esme's voice again. "Quick, help her."

Somebody unzipped the body bag and she got herself out of it as fast as she could. Esme grabbed her arms and pulled her out of the grave. The early evening gloom welcomed her back to the land of the living, and she quickly relaxed—the adrenaline dropping away left her shivering and aware of the fact she needed a wee.

She stood on the ground beside the open grave and brushed dirt from her grey prison uniform. Esme leaned on her shovel, a big grin on her pretty face. Driscoll thrust out his hand.

"Good to have you back, Al," he said.

"I'm glad to be out of that place," she replied, taking his hand.

"Did you get the information?"

She smiled. "Of course." Driscoll didn't ask for it. It wasn't safe for anyone else to know; the wardens were also looking for the key, and if *she* had managed to find out about it, they would, too. Eventually.

The forest was full of unmarked graves; rectangles of fresh dirt nearby the only clues that anybody had been buried there at all. Who cared about a bunch of dead criminals? Allery frowned but Driscoll shoved his spade into the pile of earth and began filling the hole she'd climbed out of, stirring her into action. She took the shovel from Esme and helped him.

"Least they didn't cut you open to find out how you died," Driscoll commented.

Allery could still feel the rope burn around her neck. She smiled a little but didn't reply. After they'd patted the ground flat, she hefted the spade over her shoulder, aware they might have to bolt at any moment.

"So, are we going after it *now*?" Esme asked.

Allery arched her back and stretched her neck, making the bones click. "I've just come back to life after spending far too long locked up," she said. "It can wait one more day."

"I'm sure it can," Driscoll agreed, scratching his moustache with a chewed fingernail. "For now, how about we head home and have a little celebratory drink. The sooner we're away from here, the better. Nick! Get your arse over here."

It was always hard to pull Nick away from the trees once he was connected. He stood, palms to the trunk of a sycamore, his forehead pressed lightly against the bark, and Esme went to him, placed a hand on his shoulder, and put her lips to his ear. Allery dropped her gaze with a smile, imagining exactly what Esme would've said to get his attention.

"Jealous?" Driscoll teased, giving her a nudge with his elbow.

"Let's go and get that drink," she replied, hooking her arm through his. "And get the hell away from this place." She took one last look at the grey walls of the prison peeking through the trees before turning away.

*

Merrybell Cottage sat in an overgrown field at the end of a no-through road, on the outskirts of a village in the backend of nowhere. It was derelict, its roof tiles missing and windows smashed. Ivy consumed one of its outbuildings and the roof was green with moss and lichen. The other outbuilding still stood but had no roof at all, and a rotten chicken coop squatted beneath some raggedy trees by its side. It had been raining, so the ground was soft and squelchy beneath their feet, but Allery was glad to be home.

Esme and Nick practically ran ahead, giggling and flirting like teenagers. They stopped in the doorway to share a kiss before disappearing from view. Allery looked back at Driscoll locking the car and he turned to smile at her.

"Back in Merry hell," he said, throwing his arms wide. "What a wonderful shithole to bring a girl home to, eh?"

"You have no idea how much I've missed this place," she replied. "Compared to prison, this is like a palace."

"Really?"

"Well, no. It's like a slightly less shit prison. Without the bars and screws."

Driscoll chuckled. He pushed the door for her and stepped aside. "After you."

The first thing she noticed was the smell, that damp mustiness beneath the alcohol and cigarettes, as familiar as her shoes. Then she took in the mess. The empty cans of beers by the rodent-chewed sofa and the pile of pizza boxes acting as the extra leg for the three-legged coffee table. Her skin crawled but the thought of cleaning made her smile. She went inside, took off her coat, and draped it over the arm of the sofa. There was no carpet, nothing on the walls, a fireplace with broken tiles and no fire, exposed pipes, and a crack running up the back wall. A pang of something twisted in her chest and disappeared. Regret? They'd had a nice headquarters before all this, with a proper office and a sign on the door that read, *Locke & Co.*

Esme's muffled voice reached her through the ceiling and Nick's laughter followed. Allery sighed. "It's like I've never been away," she said.

"We've missed you, believe me," Driscoll said, standing at the worktop in the kitchen. "Can you believe we pulled that off? Prison break of the century. Drink?"

"I'm just pleased that tip paid off, otherwise it would've all been for nothing." She sighed. The woman she'd spoken to inside had been...insane. It should've come as no surprise—she could imagine only too well what it would be like to be trapped in that place for eternity, but the severity of the woman's delusions, her raving, her laughter, especially her laughter... Allery scratched the back of her neck and closed her eyes briefly, willing the memory away. "I want to go out."

"Out?"

"To a bar, or a club or...anywhere. I've been cooped up. I need to be out of these clothes and out of this house."

"But you've only just got here."

"I need to breathe for a bit; I need to *feel*. Do you remember my mother?"

Driscoll raised his eyebrows. "Now there's a question to come out of nowhere. Of course I do."

"You saved her life, but she was always going to die."

It was Driscoll's turn to sigh. "Yes. All mortals die at some point, though it was cruel for her to be taken so soon. I know you think you'll forget her, Allery, but you won't. Some things you don't forget." He turned to take a glass from the cupboard. "Enough of this melancholy; get a drink down your neck."

"I think I need more than one drink. Let's go to that club. I want a night of freedom."

Driscoll laughed. "Only one night? Sure, after this job, we'll all have our freedom."

"Now that's a nice thought. Come on, all four of us. Let's have one decent night together before the shit inevitably hits the fan."

Driscoll drummed his fingers on the worktop, then he snatched up the car keys. "You're on. Go get changed, fetch the lovebirds, and I'll get the car started."

*

The DJ played the dance music loud and its heavy beats pulsed through her chest, making her feel a little sick. Strobe lights flashed, people jumped up and down, and the sticky floor bounced beneath her feet. She squeezed past a group of youngsters, teens, probably not old enough to be there, their hot bodies smelling of sweat and alcohol, and made her way across the crowded dance floor to the table where the others sat. She put the drinks on the table and took a seat next to Esme.

"You all right?" Esme asked, leaning over. She wore false eyelashes, making her elfin face appear doll-like, and a low-cut top to show off her ample assets. She smelled like peaches.

Allery pulled her gaze up. "Mm? Yeah. You?"

Esme grinned. "See anything you like?"

Allery couldn't help glancing at Nick, though he couldn't possibly hear them and was deep in conversation with Driscoll anyway, before clearing her throat and looking out at the dancers. "Tall blonde," she said, "dancing with the sweaty guy."

"I think that's a man, Al."

She rolled her eyes. "No, *there*."

Esme looked again. "Oh yeah. Not bad."

"Not bad?" Allery gazed at the woman. Her curled blonde hair bounced around her shoulders as she danced and her dress was tight and short, showing off ridiculously long legs. "I'm going to talk to her," she said, getting up.

"She looks like a slut," Esme commented.

"Good!" She gave her friend a wink, and squeezed back onto the dance floor, pushing through the crowd to reach her target. The woman had stopped dancing by the time she got to her, and was leaning against the bar, laughing at some joke with her sweaty friend.

Allery rested her forearms on the bar, pretending to wait for service, and gave it a moment before saying loudly, "I like your dress."

The woman looked at her. "What?" she asked, raising her voice over the music.

"Your dress," Allery replied. "I like it. It's very tight."

"Are you taking the piss?" Then to her friend, "Is she taking the piss?"

Allery smiled and shook her head. "I'm not taking the piss. I'm Allery, by the way."

"Oh." The woman looked suspicious for just a moment longer before her frown lifted and she smiled. "I'm Caitlin. This is my cousin, Mark."

"Mark, I'm going to pinch your dance partner." Allery took hold of Caitlin's hands. "Dance with me?" She pulled her onto the dance floor before she could protest, smiling at Caitlin's confused laugh.

They danced, Caitlin's hands above her head, eyes closed. Heat radiated off the bodies around them. Allery took the opportunity to put an arm around Caitlin's waist and pull her closer. *This* was living. Caitlin's eyes opened and her arms descended around Allery's neck.

"Are you gay?" she asked.

"Little bit," Allery replied, grinning at the drunken eyes-half-closed expression on Caitlin's face. "You don't have to dance with me."

Caitlin had come very close to her, leaning in so she could hear. Allery breathed in the smell of her coconut-scented blonde hair tickling her face.

"Always wondered what it'd be like to kiss a woman," Caitlin said, moving back.

"Want to find out?"

For a reply, Caitlin's lips met her own, smooth and warm, and when she opened her mouth, Allery tasted vodka and orange on her tongue. *Love straight girls*. The kiss ended as the next track started to play. Allery lifted a hand to push Caitlin's hair from her face and froze.

Behind Caitlin, standing among the dancers, stood a warden. Though he looked like a teenage boy, his soulless black orbs for eyes and the unnatural stillness with which he held himself gave him away. Nobody else noticed him. Allery looked back through the crowd for her friends, but Driscoll sat alone at the table.

"*Warden,*" she mouthed to him, and it took only the blink of her eyes for him to disappear.

She turned back, took hold of Caitlin's arm to lead her away, but a blade burst from the girl's chest, blood red. Caitlin's brow knitted in confusion and a strangled noise passed her lips. Her fingers clutched at Allery's shoulder. She looked down at the blade, then gazed at Allery, her eyes red and teary, full of fear.

The music seemed to mute and the blood pounding in Allery's head became louder. She opened her mouth to say...to say what? The warden pulled the blade back and Caitlin crumpled. People screamed then and Allery's ears popped.

"No," she breathed, holding Caitlin as she lay dying. She looked up at the warden, heard Caitlin's cousin shout somewhere, felt him shove her aside, and she fell back onto her elbows, staring at Caitlin.

"Al!"

She came to her senses when someone grabbed her arms and pulled her to her feet, and she clutched Nick's arm and backed up with him as the warden paced towards them.

"Where's Esme?" she cried, as people scattered before the knife-wielding lunatic, bumping into one another.

A dark shape crashed into the warden, knocking him off his feet and pinning him to the dance floor, snarling over him, fur bristling.

"Oh shit, Nick!" She pushed people then, shoving them towards the exit, yelling, "Go! Go!"

Nick did the same, urging them on, and she could hear him crying, "It's all right, it's just a dog!"

A dog! Inside she was laughing hysterically. As if anyone would believe that. *A fucking dog!*

The clubbers were screaming and bumping into tables in their haste, sending glasses crashing to the floor. The bouncers fought against the tide briefly, until a howl turned them to the exit with everyone else.

Another warden appeared in front of her, a girl this time, probably about twelve years old. Clubbers skirted around her, spilling out of the fire escape into the night. The girl raised her arm; she had a gun in her hand, pointed at Nick.

Allery dived across him as the gun fired. The bullet punched into her back, and she fell into his arms. As he lowered her to the floor, she saw the wolf leap over them before the darkness closed in on her.

Chapter Two

Allery opened her eyes and blinked until her vision cleared. She was lying on the sofa back at the cottage, bloodied cotton pads discarded in front of her. Driscoll was slumped at the dining table, a can of beer in one hand and his forehead pressed into the other. As she sat up, he turned his face towards her.

"It's not your week, Al."

She stretched her back and rolled her shoulders, wincing at the pull between her shoulder blades and guessing that was where her newest scar sat. "Two deaths in as many days," she said. "It's not the best."

Driscoll picked up something from the table and tossed it to her. She caught it and looked at the little lump of metal as he said, "The bullet with your name on it."

"I'll add it to the collection," she said dryly. "How are Nick and Esme?"

Driscoll tapped his fingers on the tabletop and eyed the inside of the beer can as if looking for the answer. "Alive."

Allery picked up the cotton pads and took them into the kitchen to the carrier bag they used as a bin. "You sound pissed off," she commented.

"Do I now? Well, maybe if Esme had a brain in that pretty little head, she'd think twice about transforming in a club full of people."

An image of Caitlin's face as the blade pushed through her chest came into Allery's mind. She hoped Esme had ripped the warden's head off. She let the tap run clear before filling a glass with water, then returned to the sofa.

"How did the wardens know where to find us?" she asked.

"Don't they know everything?" Driscoll said. He knocked back whatever was left in the can. "Bastards."

"Where were you?"

Driscoll looked at her, one of his dark eyebrows raised. "Getting the car."

She nodded and rubbed her face tiredly. "Sorry. It's just... they're always going to find us, aren't they?"

"As long as we stay one step ahead, we'll be fine," Driscoll said, getting up. He pushed the chair back under the table, the legs scraping across the hard floor. "Get some sleep. We've got a busy day tomorrow."

*

Allery woke before the sun came up, took Driscoll's keys, and borrowed the car without asking. She drove for an hour through the countryside, down tiny dark lanes, until she was in the middle of nowhere, and pulled up in a layby. Light rain sparkled in the beams of the car's headlights and a badger, its eyes flashing, looked her way before trundling to the other side of the road. She switched the engine off and tutted as the wipers stuck halfway across the windscreen. Steadying her nerves, she leaned over to pull a torch from the glovebox.

The woodland beside the road was full of skinny-trunked trees that creaked unnervingly in the wind and when she closed the car door, it echoed in the distance. It was the perfect spot for wardens. All sorts of wardens.

As she stepped beneath the canopy, droplets of rain fell heavily to the earth, one catching the back of her neck and sliding under her top. She wiped it away with one hand as she directed the torchlight through the trees with the other. Ahead, a tree stump surrounded by fresh shavings caught her eye and she headed towards it. It hadn't been long felled, by the look of it, and she leaned down to touch the damp wood, wondering what she'd feel if she was like Nick. She sat down on it to wait, turned off the torch, and gazed up at the lightening sky.

She'd been waiting some time, fiddling with the zip on her coat, when a voice said, "Miss Locke."

"Jesus Christ." She flushed at having jumped out of her skin. "You scared me."

It was one of the old wardens, his hair grey and his skin wrinkled. His black eyes were dull and rheumy, and he blinked slowly at her. "You were waiting for me," he said. He had the monotone voice of all the old wardens.

"Yeah," she said, getting to her feet and brushing a hand over her damp backside.

"But you do not have the key."

"Not yet, no. Look, I'm working on it, okay? I need you to do me a favour." She expected a flicker of *something* on his face, some sort of confirmation he had felt something at her words, a confirmation that wardens *could* still feel. But he remained expressionless, so she sighed. "Open a door for me?"

"Opening a door up—"

"Upsets the balance," she finished. "I know. Sorry. I wouldn't ask, but it's important. I need to speak with my father."

"If I open a door, another will close, and some*thing* will end up trapped in your world. You ask too much, Miss Locke."

"The last warden I spoke to opened a door for me."

The warden closed his eyes and the lids flickered as he accessed the knowledge of his brethren. When he opened them, he said, "Yes. It was the price you asked for the key. You spoke with your father about the boy and yet, we still do not have the key."

"No, I know." She cursed and clenched her fist, forcing herself to calm down and not do anything stupid. "I *need* to speak to my dad or I can't do anything else for you."

Silence. She received no hint that he was thinking over her request, no hint she had angered or frustrated him. Instead, he turned from her and tore a strip from the world. It sounded like thunder, a low rumble that could've been mistaken for a passing lorry. Then, a strip of light appeared beneath the warden's fingertips, expanding as he pulled, and Allery had to look away.

When she turned back, the door was open—a rectangle of light in front of her. She nodded her thanks to the warden and stepped into it. She passed through pins and needles and into a white, square room. The door behind her closed, leaving no trace it had ever existed, and she let out a slow breath to steady her nerves, reminding herself she'd done this before.

As she turned around, he appeared in front of her. He was beautiful, as always, blond and lovely as a painting. His feathered wings flexed and folded at his back and when he smiled, she threw her arms around him.

"Dad!"

"Allery," he replied, holding her close. "If you've come about the boy—"

"I haven't," she said, closing her eyes as he ran his fingers through her hair, wishing she could stay this way for just a little longer. She pulled back to look at him. "I know who has the key. It turns out the woman in prison knows so much because the person who has it is—"

"Should you be telling me this?"

"—is her daughter!"

"Allery."

She couldn't help but grin at her father's pursed lips. "Sorry. It won't hurt for you to know that, will it? Imagine the daughter of an immortal, rare as hen's teeth. I have a name now, but I don't know where to find her and her mother didn't know either."

"Have you tried doing an internet search?"

He may have been an angel, but sometimes her dad sounded so human. She shook her head. "Not yet. If I told you her name, you could—"

"Allery, you *mustn't*. You know the wardens can eavesdrop here."

"But if you had a name, you could find her like that!" She clicked her fingers. "I could get this all over with so much quicker." She looked away from him, down at her feet and at the mud her shoes were leaving in the white room. "We could do it telepathically."

"I don't want to hurt you."

"You wouldn't." She looked at the frown marking his perfect face. "Okay, you would. But I've died way too much to let a little pain bother me."

"You've died? Allery, what have you been playing at?"

"You mean you've not been keeping an eye on me?" She rolled

her eyes. "Oh, please don't tell me you've been too busy...*forni-cating*. Actually, I don't want to know. Don't tell me. It's gross. Just promise me I've not got any little brothers and sisters running about somewhere."

Her father chuckled. "No. I've been careful."

"You know, you're never going to be allowed back into heaven." His face darkened and so she cleared her throat and decided to get back to the point. "Please, Dad. Just help me out here."

He met her gaze and gave the slightest of nods. She closed her eyes briefly, sucked air into her lungs, and let it out slowly between her lips. When she looked at him, she felt nothing at first and could hear only a faint ringing in her ears. Then he pierced her mind, the feeling as if needles were pushing through her pupils, his voice clear inside her head, pressure building in her skull as he said, "The name?"

She struggled to keep hold of herself, not to lose herself in her father's psyche, and, with a push, she let go of the name. *Deni McClellan.*

He released her and she fell to her knees, her head spinning as something warm trickled onto her lips. Blood. She wiped her nose and looked at the smear on the back of her hand before her father lifted her chin and met her gaze again.

She opened her mouth to scream as he entered her mind once more, but the information he fed her overwhelmed her senses and she could only gape as the knowledge flowed into her—a flickering map, towns and streets racing by at superspeed. When he stopped, she crumpled, and he caught her up in his arms, smoothing her hair back from her forehead.

She groaned and tried to open her eyes but the white of the room was too bright. "I'm okay," she mumbled, weakly pushing at her father's hand. "Help me up."

"Don't ask me to do that again," he said, helping her to stand. "Knowing I'm hurting you—"

"It's fine," she said. She let him go and held a hand to her rolling stomach, fighting the urge to vomit. Tentatively, she opened her eyes, blinking until everything came back into focus. "Thanks."

"Allery, maybe you should sit down for a minute."

She waved aside his concerns and moved to the wall. She gave it a knock so the warden would know to open the door. "Don't worry about me," she said, attempting a smile. "Honestly, I know what I'm doing."

A genuine smile fell onto her lips as her father embraced her and she returned the hug, closing her eyes and sinking into the warmth of him. She felt him go and when she turned around, the forest, and the warden, was in front of her.

"The key—"

"Yes," she said, rather more abruptly than she intended. "I'm getting it."

The warden said nothing. He took a single step backwards and was gone. Allery sagged. The sun was up, though pale, and birds sang in the trees. She just wanted her bed. With a sigh, she weaved her way around trees and puddles of mud and made it back to the car in the layby.

As she closed the car door, someone said, "What've you been up to?"

"Holy fucking hell!" She looked over at Driscoll grinning at her from the passenger seat, her heart hammering unpleasantly. "Don't do that! You scared the shit out of me."

Driscoll chuckled. "Sorry," he said. "Well? What've you been up to, eh? This is a strange place to meet a paramour."

"I was meeting my dad," she said, turning on the engine and forcing the car into gear. "And before you even open your mouth,

I know. It's risky."

"You're bleeding," Driscoll commented.

She cursed and wiped her nose again. "I'm taking us home." She swung the car out into the road and headed back to Merrybell.

Chapter Three

Nick's eyes closed and he forced them open, sat up in bed, and glanced at Esme sleeping soundly beside him. Her blonde hair fell over her face and she breathed through her mouth, her lips parted. Daylight filtered in through the threadbare curtains and he could hear Allery and Driscoll down in the kitchen, clunking and clattering around and probably trying to send up a hint that they should get out of bed. As he rubbed his hands tiredly over his face, Esme stirred.

"Baby, what time is it?" she asked.

The bed was no more than a mattress on the floor, and he leaned over to pick up his watch. "Ten," he said.

She groaned and laid a hand across her forehead. "Too early. Have you been up all night?"

He met her eyes only briefly. A small twinge of shame touched his guts, and he forced a smile. "Not all night."

Esme sat up, a strap from her pink vest top falling from her shoulder, and put her arms around him. "I wish you'd tell me about your dreams," she said softly. "What frightens you?"

"Nothing frightens me, Es," he replied, gently shrugging her off him. He stood and pulled on a pair of jeans, feeling her eyes burn into him. He cleared his throat and turned to offer her another smile. "See you downstairs."

"Okay," she said. "Love you, baby."

He nodded and left the room.

*

Nick washed himself with soap and cold water and dressed in jeans and a green jumper before making his way downstairs, resisting the urge to lose himself in the memories of the oak banister. Driscoll was in the lounge, sitting on the tatty sofa with a newspaper in his hands and a cigar between his lips. Allery was in the kitchen, scrubbing the work surfaces with a grey-looking dishcloth.

"Morning," he said, as he joined Driscoll on the sofa.

"Up at last," Driscoll replied, not looking up from his paper.

Been up longer than you. He didn't say it.

Allery leaned on the breakfast bar and waved the dishcloth at him. "If we stay here much longer somebody needs to go out and buy me some cleaning equipment. The thought of the germs in this place..." She grinned, dumped the cloth, and rounded the counter to join them in the lounge. "Esme ready?"

"She won't be long," Nick said. Allery perched herself on the arm of the sofa and he wondered where she'd sneaked off to in the night. "Thanks," he said. "For saving my life. Appreciate it."

"It's all right," she said, "I wouldn't have done it if I wasn't immortal."

He frowned but she shoved him playfully before getting up

and returning to the kitchen. Driscoll, next to him, rustled the newspaper and Nick frowned at the smoke wafting towards him, raising a hand to disperse it. A sudden vibration in his pocket made him start, and he leaned forward so he could pull his mobile phone from the back of his jeans. He frowned at the name on the screen.

"Your brother?" Driscoll asked, eyeing him over the paper.

"Yeah." His frown deepened as the name flashed. *Jack calling.* "I should get this."

"Ignore it."

"I can't." He got up and left the room, heading outside. He walked a short distance from the cottage and pressed the phone to his ear. "Jack?"

"You answered then."

"What do you want?" It was drizzling, the air filled with a fine spray of rain, but it wasn't cold. A pheasant kicked up a fuss somewhere off to his right and he only caught the tail of his brother's mocking laugh.

"Is that any way to talk to your brother? No 'how are you'?"

Nick looked back at the cottage and up at the window of the room he shared with Esme. "What do you want?" he asked again. "I'm busy."

"Too busy to see your sick mum?"

Something very heavy settled in the pit of his stomach. Nick swallowed. "Sick? What's wrong with her? Of course I'll see her. Where are you? Are you home?"

"I'm at St. James's. She's dying and she's asking for you. That's the only reason I'm calling. She's dying."

Nick lowered the phone, his heart beating rapidly in his chest. He pressed the heel of his palm into his left eye, then quickly raised the phone when Jack barked his name. "I'm here," he said.

"You better get here in time, Nick, or I swear to God…"

"I'm on my way." He cut the call, licked his dry lips, and glanced back at Driscoll's car. Then he shook his head at himself and hurried back into Merrybell.

"I need to borrow the car," he announced.

Allery leaned back against the kitchen worktop, cradling a mug in her hands. "You can't," she said. "We need it. What for anyway?"

"My mother's sick."

"Sick?" Esme hurried down the stairs to him, barefoot in jeans and that stupid T-shirt with the unicorns on. "I'll come with you."

"You can't take the car, we need it," Allery said again. "Sorry, but this is more important than whatever you've got going on. You'll have to visit her another time."

"She's dying," Nick said, trying not to sound pissed off or choke up. The key could wait for all he cared and besides, sometimes their personal lives were more important, weren't they? He didn't realise he'd tensed until Esme took his arm gently.

"Al, we won't be long," she said. "Please?"

"It's Driscoll's car," Allery said, shrugging.

Driscoll hadn't moved from the sofa. He looked from Nick to Allery and back again. He smoothed his moustache, tapped a finger against his chin, and said, "Take the car, but make sure you're back before noon. If you're not, I'm coming to pick it up." He leaned forward, took the keys from the coffee table, and tossed them to Nick. "You've been warned."

"Thanks." He shook his head a little as Allery turned away, then turned to leave. Esme hurriedly slipped on a pair of trainers before she caught him up.

*

It was an hour's drive to St. James's. Nick sat in the car in the car park, staring at the dreary-looking hospital building while Esme paid for the parking ticket. The double doors slid open, and a porter trundled out, pushing an old lady in a hospital-issued wheelchair and pausing to check the road before crossing over. Two men were smoking cigarettes by the ambulance bay and a nurse dressed in blue hurried past them, a phone pressed to her ear.

Nick rubbed his face and tried to prepare himself for what he might see. Would his mother be conscious? Would she look old and frail? Or would she put on a brave face and smile and tell him there was nothing to worry about? Christ, he should've *known* she was sick.

A tap on the window brought him out of his reverie and he opened the door to take the ticket from Esme and put it on the dashboard. "You don't have to come in," he told her, getting out of the car.

"I want to," she replied. "I want to be there for you both."

You've never even met her. He said nothing, simply locked the door and headed across the road to the hospital, letting her follow.

Inside, everything smelled too clean, too clinical. Unnatural. His head spun a little and for a moment he froze in the foyer until Esme squeezed his hand and grounded him. He let out a slow breath, squeezed her hand in return, then steeled himself and went to the desk.

The receptionist, an older woman with closely cropped red hair and green-rimmed glasses, didn't look up from her computer. Nick felt it polite to wait until she noticed him but Esme, impatient as ever, leaned on the counter and said, "Excuse me? We're here to see Mrs Lode."

No reply. More tapping.

"Patricia Lode?"

Eventually, she offered them a cursory glance and said, "Coleridge ward. Follow the signs, please."

"Come on." Esme took Nick by the elbow and led him down the corridor. He tried to ignore the knot of anxiety in his stomach and instead read all the signs he could see, though as he looked at the words he didn't take them in. They passed other people but he barely registered them; the smell of hospital disinfectant made him light-headed and the strobe lights were too bright.

"Es..." He reached for her hand and took it, stopping in the middle of the corridor.

"It's just here," she said, her voice soft. "Do you want to go in?"

What if she's already dead?

He swallowed and let go of Esme's hand to wipe his palms on his jeans. "Yeah," he said, stepping towards the door.

Four beds lined one wall of the ward and another four lay opposite them. Blue curtains and blue padded chairs and two wheelchairs, old people lying in the beds, a little girl wearing a pink coat standing by her mother's side, her mother clasping the hand of an older man in bed. A window at the back of the room let the light in despite the venetian blinds. Flowers and "get well soon" cards and the thought that, bollocks, he should've bought some grapes or...something. And there she was, in the bed at the end by the window. And there *he* was, sitting beside her on the padded chair.

Nick froze as Jack gave their mother a nudge and she turned her gaze his way. She smiled and he started to breathe again. "She's there," he said quietly to Esme.

They headed over. Nick didn't fail to notice how pale his mother looked, how thin. She clutched at his hand as he stood there and he leaned over to place a kiss on her cheek, her skin soft and dry.

"Hi, Mum," he said.

"You came." Her eyes were watery, through tears or illness he didn't know.

"Of course," he replied. "Mum, this is my girlfriend, Esme."

"Oh, let me see!"

He stepped back and Esme came forward, smiling nervously and leaning forward to accept his mother's outstretched arms. "Nice to meet you," Esme said.

"Nick, she is just beautiful! Jack, hasn't your brother done well for himself?"

He looked at Jack, caught his dark expression before it was masked with a smile and his brother got to his feet. "He has," Jack said, rounding the bed. "Excuse me."

"Ignore him," his mother said, waving a hand. "He's always in a bad mood lately."

"He'll be worried about you, I expect," Esme said.

"I'm just going to see what's up." Nick ignored the frown on Esme's face and turned away before either she or his mother could protest. He left the ward and caught sight of Jack farther down the corridor, filling a plastic cup from a water dispenser.

His brother, a little shorter, a little squatter, and always angrier than he was, snorted into the cup as Nick approached. "Decided to come, then."

"Of course I did. Jack...she looks terrible."

Jack drank his water and refilled the cup, the water dispenser bubbling noisily as he did so. "Maybe if you'd stuck around, it wouldn't have come as such a surprise."

"You know why I had to leave."

"Yeah, I know." Jack turned to him, gripping the cup until the plastic cracked. "I know what you are, remember? Fairy."

Nick grabbed Jack's wrist, spilling water from the cup. "Don't call me that," he hissed.

"Get your hand off me," Jack growled back.

Their faces were close, almost touching. There was an odd smell of sulphur in the air. Nick could see the venomous hatred in his brother's eyes, and he let him go with a snort of derision. "Jealousy made you ugly, brother."

"I am not your brother."

Nick stared at him a moment longer, then shook his head and walked back to the ward. Esme sat in the chair beside his mother's bed, her blonde hair glowing in the light from the window, a little ethereal halo around her head. He smiled and joined them, taking up his mother's hand once more.

*

Lung cancer. Nick sat in the passenger seat, staring quietly out of the window as Esme drove them back from St James's. How could it be lung cancer? She didn't smoke. Had never smoked. Would he see her again before she... *Don't even think it.*

He chewed his thumbnail, then clasped his hands in his lap. They were heading across open countryside now, just one long straight road flanked by hedges and huge rolling fields spotted with sheep. A tractor pulled out of a side road ahead and Esme let out an indignant curse before flying past it.

His brother's face flashed into his mind, lips curled in a sneer. *Fairy.*

Jack had always been a nasty bastard, but it was all bluster and spite. He couldn't have known how much the barb really hurt, how that, in his mind, it was more than a word now.

Warm flesh against his. Hands—

Stop, he told himself. He chewed his thumbnail again and looked at Esme when she pushed his hand away from his lips.

"Don't do that," she said.

She smiled and turned her attention back to the road, both her hands high on the steering wheel. "Es," he said, gazing at her, "pull over."

"Hmm?"

"There's a layby ahead. Pull over."

She glanced at him, then slowed the car and swung off the road. She pulled the handbrake as they stopped. "Everything okay?" she asked.

He nodded and leaned over to kiss her, putting his hand on her thigh. "I love you," he said.

"Love you, too, baby," she replied, giving him a baffled smile. "What's brought this on?"

He shrugged and kissed her again, working to remove the seat belt with one hand while sliding the other up the inside of Esme's thigh. She pulled back from the kiss a little to release her own belt. "Do you want me to come over?" she murmured.

"In the back," he said. He licked his lips and jumped out of the car, grinning as Esme giggled and hurriedly joined him on the backseat.

They kissed again, breaking apart as Esme pulled her top off over her head. He lapped up the sight of her and his lips parted in anticipation as she removed her bra. Her breasts were perfect, not too big but more than a handful, soft and lovely and... He kissed her jaw, her neck, her chest. She moaned and made to push him onto his back, but he muttered "no" and shifted her so she was beneath him instead. Their fingers worked at each other's jeans while they kissed. Nick pulled back so he could watch her expression as she freed his cock from his pants. God, he loved the way she bit her lip like that, and she knew exactly what it did to him, too.

She laughed and he grinned before kissing her again. This was what he needed, *this*. Esme. A noise escaped between his lips as he entered her, and she shifted her hips so he could take her deeper. He closed his eyes. *Forget.*

"Jesus Christ, could you not wait till you got home?"

Esme gasped. Nick's eyes snapped open. "Driscoll!" he hissed. Beneath him, Esme fumbled for her top to cover herself and he punched the back of the driver's seat in irritation. "Piss off!"

"I told you I'd come to get the car—"

"Piss. Off," he repeated. "Now!"

Driscoll shrugged and vanished. Nick looked down at Esme and she gazed up at him for a moment before laughing, her whole body shaking. He couldn't help but laugh, too.

She took his face between her hands and kissed him. "Forget it," she said.

Forget it. He kissed her again.

Chapter Four

Allery gazed out of the car window at the lake to her left, then checked it on the map. She looked up as Driscoll spoke. "Cricket St. Nicholas," he said. "Is this it?"

"This is it."

A steep hill led them up into the village, with cars parked all along one side of the road. A woman led a large piebald horse down the middle of the street and Driscoll slowed the car to a crawl, earning himself a nod of thanks. They passed pretty stone cottages with hanging baskets of pansies and the Church of St. Nicholas sitting behind its ancient graveyard. Opposite the church, a pub. The White Hart, its sign showing a white stag with golden antlers and hooves, the billboard outside proclaiming live music from the Spectral Ducks and a pie and a pint for a fiver.

The knowledge her father had given her made the sights seem familiar, and as Driscoll drove past the children's playground, she told him to take the next left up another short hill and away from the centre of the village.

"This place is so pretty," Esme said from the backseat. "Look at the tiny little houses!"

"You should live here," Driscoll said, looking at her in the rearview mirror. "Once all this shite is over."

"Twenty quid says this isn't going to be easy," Allery said. "Something's bound to go wrong. It wouldn't surprise me if the wardens were already here." She mentally took that back, not wanting to jinx it. *Everything will go according to plan.* It had to. They deserved a break; *she* deserved a break—especially after the time spent at HM's Prison for Supernaturals. Christ. "Slow down." She peered at the houses, then touched Driscoll's arm when she spotted the cottage with the blue door. "That's it," she told him. "Stop."

"You sure?"

She nodded and released her belt as the car stopped. She got out before Driscoll even switched off the engine. "Just Esme," she said, bending down to look into the back. "We don't want to cause a panic."

Nick shrugged and Esme opened the car door, joining her. The cottage was the middle one of a row of similar-looking cottages, each with a different coloured front door. A low stone wall surrounded a small front garden, and a rather green-looking pond lay on one side of the path. The gate squeaked as Allery opened it, and she glanced at Esme before heading up the path and knocking on the door.

They waited. Birds sang from a tree on the green opposite. A tractor drove round the bend and disappeared out of sight, leaving the road caked in mud and shit. Driscoll got out of the car and drummed his fingers on the roof. "Look in the window," he suggested.

Allery stepped away from the door and cupped her hands around her eyes as she peered through the front window. The room was small and dark, with a sofa in the middle and a large, boxy TV in the corner. A bookcase bursting with books and CDs stood against the back wall with a guitar propped up by its side. The carpet was hideous—dirty orange and patterned with fleur-de-lis. She could see a door just to the right, open a little, but couldn't make out where it led.

"I don't think anybody's home," Esme said.

"No," she agreed, moving away from the window.

The front door opened, and her heart skipped a beat, until she realised it was only Driscoll. "I'm not waiting all day," he said. "In you come."

Behind them, the car door closed as Nick got out and the three of them joined Driscoll inside the cottage. Allery flicked the lights and once again frowned at the carpet. "I suppose we just look for a key," she said. "Any idea what it looks like?"

Nobody said anything. Nick put his hand to the wooden doorframe and closed his eyes, and Esme wandered across the room to open the other door. "It smells funny in here," she said.

It smelled musty and old, but Allery couldn't detect anything odd about it. "Funny?" she repeated.

"Like vinegar."

A floorboard creaked above them and Allery sucked in a breath and looked up at the ceiling. "Upstairs," she said quietly.

"I'll check it out," Driscoll replied, and he disappeared.

She strained her ears but could hear nothing from upstairs. An abrupt movement from Nick caught her eye and he pulled his hand away from the doorframe. "You all right?" she asked.

"Some weird stuff goes on in here," he said. "Doors opening."

She uses the damn key. "Bloody hell," she muttered. "What if there's something *other* in here?"

They all turned as one as the lounge door opened. Driscoll held up his hands, a woman standing behind him, gripping a handful of his hair and pressing a gun to his temple. She looked young, early twenties maybe, and entirely like she'd be more than happy to shoot Driscoll in the head. Her dark hair was sweat-plastered to her face and her eyes were wild.

"Get the fuck out of my house," she growled.

"Deni?" Allery said, holding up her hands. "It's okay. We're not here to hurt you."

"I said *get out!*"

"Now, young lady," Driscoll said, twisting himself a little to try to look at her, "if you don't let me go, I'm just going to have to get myself out of this and I'd really rather not do anything that's going to make you start shooting. So, if you could do me a favour and just put the fucking gun down—"

"Shut up." Deni pushed the gun under his chin, then pointed it urgently at Allery when she dared to take a step forward. "Stay there."

"Which one is it? Stay here or get out?" Allery asked. "You'll have to let my friend go."

Deni seemed torn. Confused. Her hands trembled and her skin looked clammy. She was very pale.

"She's a junkie," Esme said suddenly. "That's what I could smell—heroin! I could smell it on my dad, too, and he ended up killing himself with the damn stuff. He was supposed to be there for me. I was his little girl, his princess, and he killed himself. I hate heroin. And junkies! She's a junkie!"

"Es, calm down," Nick muttered.

"Don't tell me to calm down," Esme continued, indignant now, "she's just a nasty little skank, she's probably pawned the key for more smack or melted the thing down and injected it into herself!"

"Shut up!" Deni screamed. She shoved Driscoll towards Allery. "All of you out, get out! I'm *not* a junkie." She gripped the gun with both hands and pointed it at Esme. "I'm not."

"Hey!" Allery said, moving towards Esme. She stopped quickly when Deni swung the gun towards her. "Calm down. Please."

"Tell her I'm not a fucking junkie," Deni said. "I've quit. I'm... I'm clean."

Allery nodded. "I know," she said, hoping she sounded convincing. "It's okay. We're not here to judge. I knew your mother, Deni, your mother sent me."

Silence. Driscoll mouthed *"Her mother?"* at her and she shrugged her shoulders a little.

"Our lead—the woman in prison," she said. "Turns out she has a daughter."

"No," Deni said, frowning. "No. She's dead... I saw her die."

She hasn't a clue. Unless the drugs had addled her mind. She was swaying slightly, the gun lowered now, hands twitching. Allery didn't know how to break it to her, so she said, "Your mother's immortal. Like I am."

Deni laughed. "She shot a cop and they killed her. I saw it. I was fourteen."

"She died, but she came back and now she's in prison. A special prison."

One of Deni's hands dropped from the gun, but she lifted it again and pointed it lazily at Nick. "Are you all immortal?"

"No, just me," Allery said, raising her hands and hoping Deni wouldn't shoot. "Only me."

"She's not going to believe us," Driscoll said. "Can you imagine? A bunch of supernaturals break into your home and tell you your dead mother's still alive? Jesus, Al, we need to get the key and stop pissing about with this one."

"I am the key."

Allery opened her mouth, closed it again, and a heavy frown settled on her brow. "Shit," she said.

"Shit is right," Deni agreed, and she ripped open a door.

The room filled with light briefly and when Allery looked again, Deni had gone. She glanced over at Nick and Esme, both gaping at the space Deni had occupied, then at Driscoll on the other side of her. Her heart thudded painfully in her chest. They had been so fucking close!

"Is she coming back?" Esme asked.

"Doubt it," Nick said. "Allery's gone and scared her off with all that talk of her mother."

Allery laughed incredulously. "*I* scared her off? Yeah, right. This isn't my fault. You know, you could've damn well warned us *she* was the one causing the doors to open."

"I told you doors were opening," Nick said, glaring at her. "How was I supposed to know the girl was the key, Allery, eh? How?"

"Did you see a key in her hand? Because if you didn't that should've given you a bloody big clue!"

"That's not how it works," Nick cried. "I'm listening to dead wood here. I don't see everything in crystal clear fucking 3D with surround sound!"

"I don't know how it works!"

"Stop!" Driscoll barked. "That's enough." He smoothed his moustache thoughtfully and sat on the arm of the sofa. "She's been opening and closing doors so why haven't the wardens found her?"

Allery sighed. "I don't know," she said. She wanted to get out of there and never think about the key again. She wanted to get in the car and drive away or... She sat down on the sofa next to

Driscoll. "Her grandfather is an angel. I suppose he could be watching out for her."

"True," Driscoll agreed.

Esme moved closer to them and tucked a strand of hair back behind her ear. "She's a junkie—"

"We know," Driscoll said.

"And you saw her. She's going through withdrawal, right? She'll be weak. She won't be able to stay long in another place and she'll be craving another hit soon so..."

Allery smiled. God, sometimes Esme was so brilliant... She looked away as Nick kissed his girlfriend.

"You are a star," Nick said. "Of course she'll be back!"

"What if she just exits elsewhere?" Driscoll asked. "She could end up on the other side of the world."

"No," Allery said, getting to her feet. "She'll come back here. She must know the wardens are after her, she'll know it's safe to open and close doors here."

Driscoll shrugged. "All right," he said. "We've got nothing else to do but wait. But...maybe it's best if just one of us stays here, eh? We don't want to scare the girl off again. I don't mind waiting."

"No, I'll do it," Allery said. "I can explain about her mother and besides, if she shoots me, it won't matter."

Driscoll's jaw clenched and he looked as if he would argue. Instead, he nodded and headed to the door, ushering Esme and Nick ahead of him. Allery sat down again to wait.

*

Allery browsed Deni's bookshelves, brushing away a fine layer of dust with her fingers before slipping out an old hardback entitled *McGinn's Guide to Demons and Otherworldly Spirits*. She sat on the sofa and flicked through it, only vaguely interested. A niggling thought persisted in her mind, and she couldn't concentrate on any of the words.

What exactly would the old wardens do with Deni once they'd handed her over? She'd never considered before what they might do with the key. Keep it safe from the new wardens or destroy it? It hadn't mattered before.

With a sigh, she left the book on the sofa and got up to look out of the window. The car was still outside, and she could just make out Nick and Esme sitting in the front, but had no idea where Driscoll was.

She tapped her fingers on the windowsill and turned back to the room. Maybe she could make a cup of tea while she was waiting…

Someone was upstairs. She hoped it was some*one* and not some*thing*. What if Deni had let something free when she'd opened a door? That was probably what all the demon books were for; she'd freed things before and had to deal with them herself.

Oh shush, she chided herself. Deni McClellan was clearly not up to much. If she'd freed a demon somehow, then she was sure they would've heard about it. Although Cricket St. Nicholas was only a small village, and it was quite possible something could've gone unnoticed. Had there been any mysterious deaths?

She shook her head at herself and crept out of the lounge and into the hallway. The stairs were uncarpeted, and she tested her weight on the lower one, practically holding her breath so she wouldn't be heard. Slowly, she made her way upstairs, found the bathroom, then peered through a crack in the other door.

Deni lay in the middle of the double bed, her back to the door. Allery pushed the door with her fingertips, gradually widening the gap until she could squeeze through. The bedroom was dark, the curtains drawn. A movement caught her eye and her heart raced until she realised it was only her reflection in the grubby mirror on the dressing table.

She slunk around the bed and froze in panic as a floorboard creaked beneath her. She stared at Deni, but the girl looked like she was sleeping. Carefully, her movements painstakingly slow, she picked her way to the bed.

What now?

She supposed she should wake her up as gently as possible. Shit. She reached out and tentatively brushed Deni's cheek, moving the hair away from her face. "Deni?" she tried. "Hey."

Allery let out a cry of alarm as Deni snatched her wrist and twisted, flipping her over onto the bed. The top of her head hit the headboard, and she winced as Deni straddled her and forced the gun under her chin.

"I told you to get out," Deni growled.

Allery made sure to keep her hands in sight and swallowed hard. Deni's weight pressed down on her and she shifted a little beneath her. "I'm not gonna lie," she said, "I'm a little bit turned on right now."

"What?"

"Uh...nothing. Sorry. Look, I told you I'm not here to hurt you and you can blow my brains out if you like —wait! Wait! I'd prefer it if you didn't... Listen to me, please. If you kill me, I'll still be here."

"I just want everybody to leave me alone," Deni said.

This close, Allery could see her eyes were bloodshot. The gun dug into the bone of her jaw and Deni had pressed her weight down onto her shoulder. She squirmed. "I can help you."

"I've survived this long without any help."

Allery decided not to point out that it didn't seem as if she had much of a life. Instead, she said, "I know, but the wardens—the new wardens—they'll not stop until they have you. They'll find you eventually. I can take you to people who will keep you safe."

Deni smiled grimly. "Your friends outside? They don't look like they're up to it."

"They're pretty kick-ass actually..." She cleared her throat. "No, not my friends. The wardens. The old wardens, that is. The good guys."

"Old wardens, new wardens." Deni shrugged. "I'm not going."

Her shoulder was aching now, and she was fairly certain Deni was sitting on her bladder, making her need the toilet. She pushed the gun away from her chin. "Do you mind? Let's go downstairs and talk. You must want to know about your mother?"

"Not really. The woman was a mental bitch." She swung her leg over and got off the bed regardless, gesturing with the gun for Allery to get up.

"She was...different," Allery agreed, thinking back to the woman she'd met in prison. She held up her hands and walked out of the room, Deni poking the gun into the small of her back as she went.

Chapter Five

Nick leaned his head back against the headrest and closed his eyes. He was aware of Esme by his side, fussing over her appearance in the sun visor's mirror. "You look great," he said, not opening his eyes.

"My hair needs dying," Esme replied. "You can see my roots."

"You look lovely." He heard her close the visor and he looked over at her. "Honestly."

"You would say that."

Anybody would say it. He shifted in the seat and nodded towards the cottage. "I wonder what's happening in there?"

"No gun shots. That's a good sign." She opened the visor again, and he watched her, bemused, as she checked her teeth. "And what's taking Driscoll so long anyway?" she asked. "He only wanted a paper."

"He'll have got *The Sun*," Nick said. "He's probably somewhere wanking over the Page Three girl."

Esme laughed and slapped him on the thigh. "Don't be disgusting!"

"It's true," he said, grinning.

He turned his attention to the other side of the road, where the village shop sat in between two new-build houses, their sand-coloured bricks not quite fitting with the rest of the dwellings. Driscoll emerged from the shop, a rolled-up newspaper under one arm and a bottle of fruit juice in each hand. "There he is," he said. "That looks like *The Sun* to me."

"He wouldn't— Nick!"

Three hooded teenagers rode BMX bikes down the hill towards the car, their wheels skidding on the road as they tore around the corner. "I see them," he said grimly, turning the key in the ignition.

The cottage door opened and Deni and Allery stepped out onto the path. Esme screamed a warning to them: "*Wardens!*" And to his horror, Deni pulled open a door and disappeared through it. Allery didn't even glance back at the car as she threw herself after Deni, the light zipping shut behind her.

Nick cursed and slammed his foot on the accelerator, aiming the car at one of the teens. Driscoll appeared in the backseat and slapped the back of his chair. "Get the bastards, lad!"

Two of the bikes and their riders swerved out of the way. The third thudded over the bonnet and smashed into the windscreen, the bike sticking on the grill. Esme squealed and Nick cried out and stood on the brakes. The body flopped off the bonnet and Nick shoved the car into reverse, looked over his shoulder, and backed up as fast as he could. He could hear the bike scraping along the ground until it dislodged.

"Look out!" Esme cried, as one of the wardens behind them raised a gun.

Nick swung the wheel, almost reversed into the corner shop, and rammed the gearstick into first before flooring it again. Guns fired and they ducked instinctively. Glass smashed. He looked up to see where he was going again and sped past the wardens and out of the village as fast as he could.

"Everyone okay?" he asked, glancing in the rear-view mirror to see the wardens coming after them, though they weren't keeping up.

"I've been hit," Driscoll growled.

Nick looked into the back. The door window had smashed, and Driscoll had clasped a hand to his left shoulder, a grimace on his face. "I'm fine," he said, "keep driving."

"We've lost Allery," Nick said, turning his attention back to the road. He checked the mirror again and slowed his speed. The front windscreen was cracked but still in place, and he winced at the memory of the teen hitting it.

"She'll manage," Driscoll said. "Get us somewhere safe."

Nick nodded. "They always find us," he said. "How do they always find us?"

"We're all cursed," Esme said, her voice sombre. "We're never going to win. We'll have to keep running or die."

Nick frowned and reached over to give her knee a squeeze. "Don't say that, Es."

She gazed at him steadily, her blue eyes wet with tears, then she turned back to the window. "I came into this because I thought it'd be fun to hunt monsters and fight evil. After I was turned, I needed to do something. I thought I'd be able to do something good—"

"You do!"

"But all this stuff with the key... I didn't sign up for that. It was Allery's deal."

Nick pursed his lips and said nothing. Their group had been together five years now, initially using their skills to stop other supernaturals, choosing which calls to take from their cosy little office. Then the new wardens arrived, and they'd had to go into hiding. When the old wardens asked for the key, saying they needed it to stop the evil, Allery had been the one who'd agreed, deciding she'd do it in exchange for a chat with her dad about that stupid kid, Dillon. The new wardens needed to be stopped; they all knew that. They caused too much carnage. If this was what it took then…well, they had to do it.

"Sorry," Esme mumbled.

"Don't be," he said, gently. He checked Driscoll and, when he spotted a turning off the main road, indicated left.

"Where are we going?" Esme asked.

"I just need to stop somewhere to check on him," he replied, turning down the lane. They passed a farm, its single-storey outbuildings close to the road. Farm workers had piled logs haphazardly on the grass verge next to the buildings and Nick slowed the car to avoid one that had spilled into the lane. Opposite the farm were fields behind low hedges, full of large pigs snuffling in the mud by their sties. Somewhere a dog barked.

Nick pulled onto the mud in front of a gate and turned off the engine. "Wait here," he told Esme.

"Definitely," she agreed, looking out of the window. "I'll ruin my shoes."

Nick went round the back of the car and opened the door. Driscoll growled something and moved away from his touch.

"Don't be a baby. Let me see."

Blood seeped through Driscoll's fingers, and as he moved his hand, Nick winced at the wound. The bullet had carved a sizable gash in Driscoll's bicep and ended up lodged in the backseat. Nick pressed Driscoll's hand back over the wound, ignoring his curse, and ducked out of the car.

"Es, first aid kit?"

She opened the glove compartment, took out the first aid kit they kept for emergencies, and passed it to him through the open window. "You'll need this too," she said, reaching for her handbag by her feet. She rummaged around inside, turfing out lipsticks and tissues, until she found a small sewing kit she'd taken from a hotel room.

Nick returned to Driscoll, opened the kit, and took out the alcohol-free wipes. "I don't think this'll be enough," he said, as blood soaked through the pad.

"You think?" Driscoll hissed. "Stay there, you great pansy."

Nick sighed as Driscoll disappeared, half-wiped blood away from his hands, then looked back into the car as Driscoll returned with a bottle of whiskey. "Ready?"

Driscoll put the cap between his teeth and twisted the bottle. He splashed alcohol liberally over his wound, crying out until he put the bottle back between his lips and took a great gulp.

Nick threaded the needle and stitched the skin together, doing his best to ignore the insults Driscoll hurled at him. Blood ran over his fingers, and he snatched the bottle and poured liquid onto the wound again.

"Go hifreann leat, fairy!"

"Call me that again and I'll stick this needle in your eye," Nick warned. "Stop shouting. You'll bring the farmer out."

Driscoll's eyes burned into him and when he glanced up, he saw the leprechaun's face was scarlet. He tied off the stitching and nodded at the bottle of whiskey. "I'll let you clean it off."

Driscoll cleaned the wound and slumped back against the seat, the colour draining from his face. "Thanks, lad."

"No worries." He used the alcohol-free pads to wipe his hands, then passed Esme her sewing kit and shoved the box of first aid equipment onto the seat next to Driscoll. "Now what?"

"I'll ring Al," Esme said, taking her phone from her handbag.

Nick exchanged a look with Driscoll. Wherever Allery was, he didn't think she'd have reception on her phone.

Chapter Six

Allery staggered and fell to her knees, grazing her hands on the ground. Mist hung all around her, so thick it seemed as if she could touch it. To her right she could make out a large body of water—a lake or a sea. In front of her, the stark silhouette of a leafless, twisted tree pierced the fog.

She swallowed her unease, got to her feet, and brushed her hands on her jeans. "Deni?" she called. She cried out when someone grabbed her arm.

"Shh!" Deni hissed. "What are you doing here?"

"I followed you," she replied. "Obviously."

The mist had been moving steadily around her, but now it stopped and filled the air like the smoke from an overcrowded bar. Tiny glittering lights, like sun on dust motes, suddenly sparkled all around them.

"Where are we?" she asked.

"Third." Deni let go of her arm. "Dimension," she added,

looking sidelong at Allery.

Oh shit. "We really shouldn't be here," she said. "This is why the wardens create rooms—so we don't go traipsing around in places we're not supposed to be."

"I don't give a toss what the wardens do," Deni said, heading off into the fog. Allery noticed how it jerked away from her, and she quickly followed.

"Well, I do. They're scary." She stopped to look at the twinkling lights, wondering what they were. Tiny little fireflies or fairies.

Deni batted her hand down. "Don't reach for them like that. They'll think you're inviting them in." She reached her own hand out to the mist, and it pulled sharply away from her touch. She smiled grimly. "One of the benefits of heroin. Demons here won't take an unhealthy body. Stay close to me, fold your arms across your chest. That's it."

Deni led her on. All around them the mist moved, pulling away from Deni and creeping tentatively around Allery. Another two trees loomed up as shadows ahead of them and Deni passed between them. Allery couldn't be sure, but she swore the mist was thickening. It seemed to be getting harder to push their way through it. "Where are we going?"

She gasped when, from out of nowhere, a tower of dark rock appeared in front of them. She couldn't work out what it was but, cloaked as it was in fog, it looked imposing. As they drew nearer, she noticed a rectangular opening in the rock that Deni seemed to be heading for. She froze, fearing a trap.

"Come in with me or stay out here and get possessed," Deni said, pausing at the doorway. "Your choice."

Lights flickered closer. "Shitting hell." Allery hurried towards the tower.

She grabbed the back of Deni's shirt, spun her around, and slammed her back against the rough wall as soon as she entered. It was dark in the tower, and cold. "Take us home," she demanded.

Deni laughed and something cold pressed against Allery's stomach. "I will shoot you in the guts, bitch."

Action beats reaction. Allery swept the gun aside and punched Deni in the face, sending her sprawling on the hard floor, the gun falling from her grip. She snatched it up and pointed it at Deni. "Get up."

Deni laughed again and pressed a shaky hand to her nose as she sat up. She pulled it back to look at the blood. "Fuck you."

Something moved outside the tower, scraping along the ground. It made the hairs on the back of her neck stand on end. She grasped Deni's arm and pulled her up anyway, pressing the gun against her ribs. "Take us home," she whispered.

"Can't," Deni replied.

Allery felt Deni sag in her grip and hiked her up. "Do it!" She looked towards the doorway, her heart thumping. "What the hell is out there?"

"Let go," Deni murmured, trying to prise Allery's fingers off. "I need a hit."

Allery pushed her away in disgust and pointed the gun at the doorway. Deni staggered away, disappeared into the darkness, and came back with a little bag of brown powder. "Thought you were clean?"

"I was," Deni replied. "For a little while. Can't open a door feeling like shit, though." She dipped a finger into the bag and rubbed it over her gums, sinking back against the wall in a stupor.

Outside, something screamed, making Allery jump. "Please, can we go?" she whispered, feeling tearful. "Deni?"

Light filled the tower and Allery had to shield her eyes. Deni grasped her arm and pulled her through the door. When she could look again, they were in Deni's bedroom. She sat down heavily on the bed, trembling. "Don't go there again."

"I go there a lot," Deni replied, crossing the room to the window. "I feel safe there." She sniffed and wiped away the blood from her nose. "The wardens are outside."

Allery joined her at the window. Four teens stood on the pavement outside the cottage, unmoving and staring at the door. Over the other side of the road, an old woman exited the corner shop and carried on her way, not noticing them.

"You should've hid there," she said. "Not came back upstairs for me to find you. I would've got bored and left eventually."

"Would you?"

Allery shrugged. *Probably not.*

"I was trying to get myself clean. I don't want to have to take the drugs all the time. I thought I'd go there and come back quickly and... I don't know. You guys might have freaked out and left. You've just seen what I had to do to get myself back this time." She moved away from the window. "Now what happens?"

Allery checked the bullets in the gun. "I guess I try to shoot the bastards."

"That's a really fucking excellent plan," Deni said.

Allery couldn't help but smile a little. Then her phone rang, and she cursed in surprise and quickly moved from the window when one of the teens looked up. She pulled the phone from her back pocket and answered it. "Es?"

"Where are you?"

"Still at Deni's," Allery replied. "Are you guys okay?"

"Driscoll got shot. He's okay, he's fine. He's just bad tempered." A pause. Allery heard her speaking quietly to the others, then, "We'll come and get you."

"You can't. The wardens are still here."

"We'll come and get you anyway!"

Allery smiled. "You can't," she said again. "Just...don't panic. I'll think of something." She hung up before Esme could argue and looked at Deni. "I don't suppose you have any ideas?"

"I could give myself up."

"No. No way. They'd use you to rip open every door to every dimension. There'd be chaos! No. I—" She stopped herself. *I would have to kill you first.* "I'll think of something." She squeezed the bridge of her nose, hoping to stave off the impending headache. "Can you open a door to somewhere else in this dimension?"

Deni nodded. "But they'd find us still."

"Go straight to a forest," Allery said. "Or a park. That's where you'll find the old wardens. They'll protect you." *Then this'll be over.* She felt a small twinge of guilt. What if the old wardens killed Deni? *Not my problem.* Her heart ached and her stomach turned over. No, she didn't mean that. She couldn't be responsible for another death. *Not that Dillon died.*

"Wait. Go to Bristol," she said. "I'll get my friends to meet us there. They'll pick us up before the wardens can do anything."

"Anywhere specific?"

"The Hippodrome." She closed her eyes and mentally cursed herself for saying it. The theatre held too many memories. The smell of velvet and ice cream and too much perfume. Stolen kisses backstage and the feel of bare wood beneath her naked feet.

Get over it. She sent a text to Esme and looked at Deni. "Let's go."

Chapter Seven

Nick checked the wing mirrors before pulling out to overtake a van driving at fifty miles an hour on the M5. It was silent in the car, tense. For some reason, the damn radio wouldn't work, and he wondered if something was damaged somewhere. He looked in the rear-view mirror, paranoid a police car would follow them and pull them over for having smashed windows, then glanced at Driscoll.

"How are you doing?" he asked.

"Just dandy," Driscoll muttered.

Nick pulled back into the inside lane. "You know why she wants us in Bristol, don't you? Because her bloody ex-girlfriend lives there."

"Maybe she has a plan," Esme said.

"Yeah, I bet she has a plan," Nick said darkly. "She's planning to meet up with her ex and have a quick shag while the rest of us work out what to do."

Driscoll shifted on the back seat. "I doubt Sophie wants anything to do with her after what happened to the boy."

Nick grunted a response, unconvinced. They were silent a while, and he paid attention to the road, keeping an eye on the overhead signs and getting into the right lane to take him into the city.

"She fancies you," he said to Esme. "She thinks I don't know, but I do."

"No, she doesn't."

He glanced at her. "She does. I've seen the way she looks at you." He drove across the bridge over the river Avon, inwardly cringing at the great ugly pylons beside the river and the huge, grey office blocks over the other side.

"So what if she does?" Esme replied. "She knows I'm straight."

I don't like it. Nick knew better than to say it aloud. He kept quiet and drove on into the city.

*

From the outside, the theatre was an unassuming building sitting between a pub and a fancy-dress shop. A large poster advertising the musical *Hairspray* hung over the entrance and the word *Hippodrome* was emblazoned across a red-tiled arch over the glass doors.

Nick pulled into the taxi bay right outside and tapped his fingers on the steering wheel, looking down the street to the tall, modern glass building towering over the road. He turned instead to the trees on the other side, pale-leafed London planes, uniformly spaced and surrounded by concrete. A bus drew alongside the car and blocked his view. He rubbed his forehead.

"Is she in there?" he asked. "Can somebody go in and get her? I can't wait here all day."

"I'm sure she'll be out in a second, baby," Esme said. "She..."

Nick didn't hear the rest of what she said. Farther down the street, waiting to cross the roads at the lights, stood a man he recognised. Tall, with dark hair and a long straight nose. He was dressed in a suit and carried a briefcase, and as the lights changed and he walked across the road, Nick panicked. He slammed the car into gear and swerved out into the road, causing the car behind to blast its horn. He did a U-turn and drove in the opposite direction, glancing back in the rear-view mirror as he went.

When the blood stopped pounding in his ears, he heard both Esme and Driscoll shouting at him. Driscoll demanding to know what the hell he was playing at, Esme berating him for almost getting them killed.

"What?" he muttered. "No, I saw someone." He managed to prise one hand from the steering wheel to wipe his clammy palm on his jeans.

"Who?" Driscoll asked. "Unless it was a warden, you'd better turn around and get us back to the theatre right now. You don't just pull out into traffic like that!"

"Who was it?" Esme asked, her tone gentler than Driscoll's. "Nick?"

"Uh." He frowned. It was nobody, probably. A businessman. The damn city was messing with his senses, the air too full of the smell of pollution. "A demon. I thought I saw a demon."

"You thought you saw one or you did see one?" Driscoll growled.

"I'm sure I saw one." He sounded uncertain, even to himself. He had no idea where he was going now, simply following the rest of the traffic. A roundabout lay ahead and he paid no heed to the road signs, instead driving right the way around it to take them back the other way. "I'm sorry," he said.

Esme reached over and squeezed his thigh, offering him a concerned smile when he looked at her. He couldn't tell her. He couldn't.

*

Allery stepped out of the theatre just in time to see Nick swing the car out into oncoming traffic. Certain he'd seen a warden, she snatched Deni's hand and pulled her back into the building.

"What the hell?" Deni exclaimed, shoving Allery off once they were inside.

People milled in the foyer, looking through leaflets and collecting their tickets ready for the evening's show. Nobody gave them a second look, but Allery tugged Deni's arm and indicated they should move on. She headed up the stairs and into the bar area, squeezing her way through the few people already there to go and look out of the window.

She cursed when she spotted the car driving away. "I think something's spooked them," she said.

"Now what do we do?" Deni asked. "We can't hide in here. I'm surprised we haven't been kicked out yet as it is."

Allery turned and gazed at the room. People chatted quietly among themselves, laughed over shared jokes, and sipped wine or beer. There were a few furtive glances in their general direction, but nobody looked as if they'd approach them and demand they leave. She wondered if they could sneak into a show without a ticket and decided that, if there was a warden around, a packed theatre really wasn't the best place to meet one.

She caught sight of Deni disappearing through the crowd and she hurried after her and snatched at her arm. "Where are you going?" she hissed.

"I need the loo, all right?" Deni said. "Bloody hell."

She let her go. "Right. I'll come with you."

They made their way out and found the ladies. Allery pretended to wash her hands so she could keep an eye on Deni when she came out of the cubicle. She had a sneaking suspicion the girl was taking drugs in there, but she said nothing. Briefly, she thought Deni might escape through a door and she looked urgently in the mirror, though no bright light engulfed the room and all she saw was a little old lady who smiled at her and left without washing her hands. Allery screwed up her nose.

"You done?" she called.

"I'm having a crap!" Deni called back impatiently.

Allery rolled her eyes. She turned and leaned back against the sinks, taking out her phone to dial Esme's number. She was just listening to it ring when the door opened and a familiar face greeted her.

"I thought it was you." Sophie had dyed her hair red, and it was styled in cute curls that framed her face. She wore a blouse with the buttons straining at her breasts and a pair of very tight skinny jeans.

Allery licked her lips, heart fluttering. "Hi."

Sophie arched a perfectly plucked eyebrow. "Is that all you have to say for yourself?"

"I didn't know you'd be here..."

"I popped in to see Helen. Not that it's any of your business."

Helen. Sophie's older sister. She worked as the box office manager and used to be one of Allery's best friends. *Years ago. Too many years ago.* She nodded. "I'm just...here with a friend."

Sophie approached her and jabbed a finger at her chest, her nails sharp. "Funny you have time for the theatre when you promised me you'd get my son back."

"I'm trying, Soph, I'm really—"

A toilet flushed and Deni emerged from the cubicle. She looked at Allery and Sophie, ignored them, and instead picked up Allery's phone from where she'd placed it beside the sink. "Hello? Yeah, sorry. She's busy having a chat with some tart... You're outside? Okay." She put the phone down and washed her hands.

Sophie laughed. "What did you call me?"

"Nothing," Allery said, placing herself between the two women before things could escalate. "She didn't mean it. Soph, please, can we go somewhere to talk? I spoke to my father about Dillon—"

"Don't even say his name," Sophie growled, her eyes blazing.

"Sorry. I spoke to my father, and he says there's nothing we can do. Once someone becomes a warden—"

Sophie lashed out and slapped her hard. Allery held a hand to her stinging cheek and looked at her ex-girlfriend in surprise. "Don't start with that," Sophie warned. "He joined that stupid gang because of you." She laughed. "I used to put up with your stupid stories because I thought it was quirky and I loved you. Now...now I just think you're a crazy, deluded bitch who I should've stayed the hell away from. Leave me the fuck alone, Allery. If I see you here again, I'll call the police."

Allery didn't know what to say. She stood there with her hand to her cheek, her mouth slightly open and tears in her eyes, willing herself not to cry. Sophie glared at her with such hatred written all over her face.

Deni pressed her phone into her hand and moved towards the door. "Your friends are outside."

Allery swallowed and averted her gaze from Sophie, looking instead at the phone. She pushed it into her pocket and followed Deni out.

She barely noticed the state of the car, or the people gawping at it, taking photos with their mobile phones. She waited for Driscoll, then Deni, to budge over and got in beside them. She fastened her seat belt without a word.

The indicators ticked as Nick pulled out into the road, and she watched as they left the theatre behind. She closed her eyes.

"I'm Deni, by the way," Deni said. "Sorry about the whole gun thing. We probably got off on the wrong foot."

Allery opened her eyes and sat up, supposing she should introduce everyone. "I'm Allery," she said. "This is Esme, Nick, and Driscoll."

"And very pleased we are to meet you at last," Driscoll said. "We've been looking all over for you."

"Should've made myself harder to find," Deni said. "So, you're all...creatures?"

"Supernaturals," Nick said, glancing in the rear-view mirror.

Allery smiled. "Supernaturals," she agreed. "I'm like your mother. The daughter of an angel and a human—an immortal. Esme's a werewolf, a very pretty werewolf. Nick's a f—" She caught herself quickly and said, "Drus. A tree spirit. And Driscoll's a leprechaun."

"A very fine and handsome leprechaun," Driscoll said. "Who almost got his arm shot off by those bastard wardens."

"And what, you fight crime or something?" Deni asked.

"Something like that," Allery said.

"Are we going to the nearest woodland?" Nick asked, stopping the car at a set of lights and looking into the back briefly.

"No," Allery replied, getting in there before anybody could say otherwise. "Not yet. Take us home."

Nick nodded and as the lights changed and they drove on, Allery relaxed a little.

Chapter Eight

Later, at Merrybell, the five of them ate pizza and drank alcohol together, chatting and laughing like old friends, all pointedly ignoring the fact they had the key and should give her up. Driscoll lounged on the sofa, smoking a cigar and weaving a story about an old friend of his who outwitted a human king and became the richest leprechaun in history.

Esme sat with her back comfortably against Nick as he wrapped his arms around her and playfully dabbed tomato sauce onto her nose.

From the kitchen, Allery watched. Jealousy and alcohol stirred in her guts, and she turned away, smacking open another bottle and pouring the sweet liquid down her throat. Forget Esme. Forget Sophie. She would outlive them all anyway. There was no *point* being attached to anyone.

Give Deni to the wardens.

Her attention shifted to the girl, sitting cross-legged beside the pizza box on the floor, her face bright with laughter. She was attractive, in an angular sort of way. A little too slim, a little too world-weary. The shakes and the sweats had gone, and Allery wondered how long it'd last before she had to take the drug again. She dribbled booze down her chin and turned to get a kitchen towel. When she turned back, Deni had joined her.

"Missed a bit," Deni said, wiping a thumb over Allery's chin before reaching past her for a bottle.

Allery's heart raced. Deni was standing close, moving slowly. Was she...? Did she...?

"You coming?" Deni asked, heading back to the lounge. "Come on."

Allery followed and gulped back another mouthful as she sat down. Nick was talking now, banging on about his brother and how sick he'd looked upon seeing Esme. She rolled her eyes and took another swig.

When Esme pushed her for a story, she shook her head. "Deni doesn't want to listen to anything I've got to say," she said. "I always end up getting killed."

"Only to protect us," Esme said. "You're very brave."

Hardly brave when you know you can't die. She picked at the edge of the pizza box, peeling away a strip of cardboard.

"Tell me more about this prison then," Deni said.

Allery glanced up and saw the others looking at her expectantly. Driscoll leaned forward to stub out his cigar in the ashtray, then sat back and folded his arms. They all waited.

"What's to tell?" she asked. "It was boring." She didn't want to tell them about the screams or the sadistic guards or the fact that most of the other inmates terrified her. "I went in, got the information off your mother, and then got the hell out. That's it."

"How did you even know about my mother? How did you get

in? How did you get out?" Deni asked. "Christ. My mother murdered someone; tell me you didn't do the same?"

Allery shot a look at Driscoll, and he nodded to say it was okay. "We'd had an anonymous tip-off, a note suggesting we look up your mother if we wanted information about the key. As for the how I got in… We'd had a run-in with the wardens and I'd sort of…grabbed one and jumped off a building with her. It was an accident, really. Anyway, of course, the girl died, and I didn't…" She sighed. "We knew it was an opportunity we couldn't afford to lose, so I went to the police and handed myself in. Told them I'd pushed the girl."

"And you ended up in this special prison," Deni prompted.

Allery nodded. "HM's Prison for Supernaturals. Once you're in, you don't come out."

"Not unless you're in a coffin," Driscoll said, grinning. "Which is why our Al was perfect for the job."

"They take your blood for testing," Allery said, "to check what kind of supernatural you are. We couldn't have them find out I'm an immortal or they simply wouldn't have buried me."

"We used Esme's blood," Driscoll added.

"Driscoll switched the samples at the lab," Allery explained.

Deni laughed. "That's fucking brilliant." She lifted the bottle to her lips. She swigged her drink and said, "So you died, the prison buried you, and your friends came and dug you up?"

"Yep," Allery said, touching her neck, knowing the faintest of scars remained. "Hanged myself."

"Wow." Deni gazed at her with what looked like admiration in her eyes. She nodded appreciatively, finished her drink, and changed the subject.

Later, after Esme and Nick had gone to bed and Driscoll had also retired to his room, Allery collected the empty cans and bottles and stashed them away in a bin bag. She was just shoving a pizza box into the bag when she felt Deni's hand on the small of her back.

"Leave that," Deni said.

"I can't. It irritates me," she replied, tying up the bag before turning to Deni.

"When you die," Deni said, taking one of Allery's hands and brushing her thumb over her wrist, "does it hurt?"

"Every time."

"What do you see? When you're dead."

Deni's touch was making her skin tingle. She moved her hand away and shrugged. "Nothing."

"God, that's depressing."

Allery nodded. Deni stood very close again, their bodies almost touching. Allery gazed at Deni's lips, then, when Deni put a hand to her waist, she kissed her. Deni returned her kiss, tasting of alcopops and the puff she'd taken of Driscoll's cigar. Allery kissed her harder, hungry, aware of the sound of her own breathing. She moved to kiss Deni's neck, one hand pulling her close, the other fondling her breasts. In return, Deni slipped a hand into Allery's jeans and when she felt her touch, she moaned and pushed herself closer still.

"We should go upstairs," she mumbled.

"No," Deni replied, undoing Allery's jeans to give herself better access. She grinned wickedly. "I want you here."

Allery could only steady herself against the worktop, all rational thought gone, as Deni pushed the jeans down her legs.

*

Allery awoke with a start when a hot hand pressed over her mouth. She breathed in hard through her nose and looked at Deni. In the half-light she could see the girl had dressed and, catching the look she gave her, quickly leaned over the side of the sofa to grab her own clothes.

"What is it?" she whispered.

"I think there's someone outside," Deni whispered back.

Allery pulled her T-shirt on over her head, indicated for Deni to stay where she was, and crept to the window. The moon was a thin sliver glowing dimly through a grey cloud, and drizzle misted the outside of the window, making it difficult to see. She could hear nothing outside, and she glanced back at Deni, thinking she'd been mistaken.

"There!" Deni hissed, jabbing a finger at the window.

Allery turned back and the breath caught in her throat. Beneath one of the trees, a large, dark shape rooted around by the old chicken coop. It was bigger than a dog, bigger than Esme when she changed, and when it lifted its head, its eyes flashed red.

Allery gasped and pressed herself back against the wall beside the window. "It's a wendigo," she said quietly.

"A *what*?"

"Flesh-eating monster," Allery said. "Human flesh."

"Oh, well, that's all right then," Deni said. "What the fucking hell is it doing outside?"

"Uh..." Allery didn't have a bloody clue. Unless it had become trapped when she'd asked the warden to open a door for her. She cursed inwardly and chanced a look out of the window again. "Go upstairs and wake the others, will you? I'll keep an eye on it."

Deni did as she told her and while she was gone, Allery went to retrieve the gun she'd stashed in the cutlery drawer in the kitchen. Heart pounding, she stood beside the window again and chanced a quick peek outside.

The wendigo had disappeared from view and all was quiet.

Driscoll, followed by Nick and Esme, then Deni, came down the stairs and Allery indicated for them to stay away from the window.

"Big one?" Esme asked quietly.

"Too big for you, Es," she replied.

"Why can't we all just hide until it pisses off?" Deni whispered.

"Because it'll kill people," Allery said. "We either kill it now or lead it to a forest and hope the wardens deal with it."

Driscoll joined her by the window and looked out. "I'll take the car and lead it away," he said. "Where is it?"

"I..." Allery grimaced. "I don't know."

He gave her a look that let her know he was unimpressed by her inattention. "Well, I—"

Something large and dark crashed through the window with a shattering of glass. Esme and Deni screamed, Nick yelled something, and Allery gasped and pressed herself back against the wall as the wendigo stood in the middle of the lounge, shards of glass glittering in its fur.

Nick grabbed Esme and tackled her to the floor behind the sofa as the wendigo lashed out with its hand, tearing into the cushions. Deni stumbled back and fell, looking up at the creature in terror as it bore down on her. Allery remembered the gun and fired it, shooting the beast in the flank. It flinched and turned back towards her and Driscoll, its eyes sparkling.

"Outside!" Nick shouted. "Now, everyone out!" He bustled Esme and Deni up and towards the door and as the wendigo turned in the direction of the movement, Allery shot it again.

"Time to get out, Al," Driscoll said, before he disappeared.

She cursed, shot the wendigo in the shoulder, and scrabbled out of the broken window. She jumped down onto the wet grass. Her hands bled. She picked a shard of glass out of the heel of her palm, adrenalin numbing the pain, and ran.

Behind her, the beast leaped through the window. It roared—a high-pitched wail that set her teeth on edge—then it came after her. She ran onwards, chancing a quick look back and wishing she hadn't. Then headlights appeared, blinding her momentarily, and she dived towards the car. She pulled the back door open and slid in beside Deni and Esme.

"Just fucking drive!" she cried.

The wendigo leaped at the car as Driscoll slammed his foot on the accelerator. It landed behind the car, corrected itself, and came after them. Allery watched out of the back window, her eyes wide. "It's catching up!"

"I can see that," Driscoll growled.

The lane ended at a T-junction and Driscoll stood on the brakes and yanked the wheel to get them to take the corner, making the tyres screech. The wendigo skidded into the hedge, pushed itself free, and came after them again.

"What happens if we meet someone coming the other bloody way?" Deni hissed. The road wasn't wide enough for two vehicles to pass by.

"We won't," Allery said. She hoped they wouldn't.

By her side, Esme had twisted in her seat to look out of the back window. "It's gone!" she cried. "It's not following us any more!"

Driscoll didn't slow down, and Allery saw him glance in the rear-view mirror. Her heart was in her mouth. Out of the corner of her eye, she saw it. The wendigo burst through the hedge alongside them, its arms outstretched, and crashed into them.

The car's back end spun, everybody screamed, then they were upside down, the car on its roof, rolling over and through the hedge and into the field where they came to a standstill.

Horrible silence. The car was on its wheels, but the roof was crumpled. When she could breathe again, Allery looked over at Deni and Esme. They were slumped together, Esme's face bloodied from a gash on her head. Deni groaned and lifted a hand to pull the seat belt away from her neck. In the front of the car, the men were silent.

"Shit," she whispered, voice shaky. "Es? Nick?" She fought to release her own belt but couldn't unbuckle it. "Driscoll?"

"That thing," Deni said, pushing against the door. "There it is!"

Allery followed her gaze and looked out of her window. The wendigo was in the middle of the field, sprawled on its front, dazed only, as it started to bring its arms back under itself. Deni was frantically trying to open her door now, but it had twisted out of shape.

"We're trapped," she said.

"Mine opens," Allery replied, shoving the door open. "But my belt's stuck. Can you get past?"

Deni was already crawling over Esme and squeezing awkwardly past Allery to get out of the car. "Get Esme," Allery said, taking Esme's belt off and pulling her towards the door so Deni could grab her. She looked past them to the wendigo. "Quickly!"

"I'm trying to go fucking quickly," Deni snapped, dragging Esme out.

"Nick!" Allery shouted, hoping to wake him. "Nick!" She kicked the back of his seat, knowing it would harm him if he were injured, but knowing that death by wendigo was probably a whole lot worse. He groaned and she once again pulled at her seat belt.

"Get out of the car," she told him. "Nick?"

"What happened?" he muttered.

"Get out!" Deni pulled his door open, released his belt, and pulled him out.

The sight of the recovering wendigo quickly brought him to his senses, and he helped Deni carry Esme around to the other side of the car. "Get Driscoll out," Allery cried to them.

Nick opened the driver's door and hooked the leprechaun's arm around his shoulders. "Come on, Al," he said to her.

"I'm stuck. I'm trying!" She looked at the wendigo and realised it was hurt. It dragged its rear leg and limped on its front, but it still came towards the car. She pulled at the belt, trying to make it longer so she could escape, but it wouldn't budge.

"Hey!" Deni rounded the car and placed herself squarely between Allery and the beast. "Eat me!"

"What are you doing?" Allery practically screamed it. She could only watch, helpless, as the wendigo pounced.

Deni sidestepped, pulled open a door, light glaring, and the beast sailed through it. She closed the door.

"Shit," Allery breathed. Then she laughed. Her heart beat painfully, but the relief flooded through her. Calmer now, she was able to extend the belt and clamber out of it. When she emerged from the car, Deni leaned against it, shaky and pale.

"I'm fine," she said, waving a hand. "See to your mates."

Allery walked around the car to see Nick tending to a now-awake Esme while Driscoll lay flat out beside them. "He's not...?"

"Dead?" Nick finished. "No. He must've hit his head." He returned to tenderly checking Esme's head wound while Allery crouched beside Driscoll.

She checked the pulse in his neck for herself and looked him over for obvious wounds or broken bones.

"We need to take her to the wardens," Nick said quietly. "As soon as possible. We need to end this."

Allery glanced back at Deni leaning against the car. "Yeah," she agreed. "I'll deal with it."

Chapter Nine

They abandoned the car in the field and, when Driscoll came to, he waved them away and vanished. Allery and Deni trudged along the lane in silence, while Nick and Esme walked behind them. Allery was sure she could feel Nick's eyes burning into her and wished he'd just give her a break. She needed time to *think*. If Driscoll had hung around, she could've consulted him, asked him what he thought it best they do. Although, by his disappearing act, she presumed he'd already decided and had gone to fetch the wardens. *We've done our part, hand her over.*

The road was muddy and gravelly, and a small stone had lodged itself in the tread of her trainers. She scuffed her foot along the ground to try to remove it, then stopped and hooked it out with her finger instead.

"So, we're going to a wood or something?" Deni asked. "Or a park or whatever it was. You're turning me in."

"It's not like that," Allery said. "The wardens will look after you."

"And I always thought my life couldn't get any better," Deni said sarcastically. "You should've left me at my house; I was safe there until you lot showed up. If the wardens want me so badly, why didn't they come for me themselves?"

"Nobody knew where you were. And anyway, they can't leave the woods—the new wardens, the teens, they've restricted their movements."

"Old wardens, new wardens. You need to rename one of them. Call the teens drifters or something 'cause they can't stay in one place."

Ahead, the road dipped, and in the distance a coppice perched on the hillside like cress-hair on a potato head. Allery rubbed the bridge of her nose, glanced back at Nick, who nodded, then pointed out the trees. "We'll head there, the wardens will pick you up and then—"

"Then you can all go home and abandon me," Deni said. "Thanks."

Allery sighed. She had to do this; she'd made a deal with the wardens. But that was before she knew the key was a person. It was one thing handing over a piece of metal...

"Where did Driscoll go?" Esme asked.

Allery looked back at her. Dried blood matted in Esme's hair and her left eye was bloodshot. She held Nick's hand and clung to him as if she'd fall over if she didn't. Allery wanted to pull her into her arms and protect her.

"Sulking somewhere, I imagine," Nick said. "Or he's gone ahead to tell the wardens to expect us."

Wish he'd spoken to me first.

They continued on in silence. The sky brightened and wispy

clouds drifted on the breeze. A car passed, and they all moved over to the side of the road, traipsing in single file. In the hedge, sparrows twittered, and a hawk circled over the field to the right. Allery wrinkled her nose as she caught the scent of the local farm, the smell of pig shit filling her lungs.

She'd just covered her nose with her hand when she noticed Deni shake her head. Unease stirred in her guts, but before she could do anything, Deni pulled open a door. The flash of light blinded her, and she screwed up her eyes. Someone grabbed her arm and yanked. Nick shouted out, then his voice ended abruptly, and her head hit something solid.

Groaning, she opened her eyes and squinted at grey cobbled streets. There was an odd rattle nearby and a juddering in the ground. She pushed her hands underneath her body to heave herself up, when Deni snatched at her arm and pulled her upright and to one side as a horse and cart rumbled past. The driver, a dark-skinned man wearing a straw hat, swivelled in his seat to frown at them as he went.

"Where are we?" Allery asked. Black-and-white Tudor houses flanked the street and chickens clucked noisily as they pecked in the dirt nearby, picking bits from between the cobbles. A woman walked by, wearing a red, woollen dress. She carried a wicker basket in the crook of her arm, filled with bread and objects wrapped in brown paper. Overhead, a sign bearing the picture of a tree creaked and swung in the wind and Allery stared at it, not quite sure she was seeing what she was seeing.

"Have we gone back in time?" she asked.

Deni laughed. "No! This is another dimension. I'm not sure which one, you tend to forget which is which after a while."

Allery held a hand to her head and gaped. There was an uncomfortable pressure behind her eyes and a sick feeling in her stomach. Before she could do anything else, Deni gave her hand a tug and disappeared into the building with the tree sign.

Shit. Allery followed, pushing the wooden door and stepping inside onto a floor strewn with rushes. It was a tavern...or something like a tavern. There were no tables and no patrons. The only people there were a red-faced man standing at the back of the room, wearing a white apron over his fat belly and a frown on his face, and an unnaturally tall woman whose blonde hair was pulled up into a tight bun on the top of her head.

"Uh..." Allery stepped back as the woman stepped forward, but Deni put a hand to the small of her back to stop her from going farther.

"It's okay," Deni said. "I've seen this sort of thing before."

The woman reached out, pointing with her thin index finger, and touched first Deni then Allery on the forehead. Allery felt an odd pull as the woman removed her finger.

"Welcome," the woman said. "I am pleased we may talk now I have learned your language. I am Poedan. This is Poedani." She swept her arm out to indicate the man, whose expression hadn't changed since the frown.

"Hi," Allery said. "Deni, I think we need to—"

"I need some of that orange stuff," Deni said to Poedan. "The sap."

Allery realised Deni was shivering and that her skin had washed out. She watched, eyes narrow, as Deni pressed a hand to her stomach as if in pain.

Poedan inclined her head. "Payment will be two memories."

Deni shrugged. "Fine."

"No, what do you mean, 'two memories?' I think someone needs to—"

But Poedan touched Deni's forehead again and Allery realised nobody was going to pay any notice to anything she said, so she folded her arms and waited. Poedan released Deni and before Allery could stop her, her finger pressed against her skin and she suddenly remembered the smell of popcorn and sitting with Esme in front of a TV, Esme's head resting on her shoulder. When she blinked, it had gone and Poedan had pulled back.

A strange feeling of having forgotten something washed over her and Allery balled her hands into fists. "What did you do?" she demanded.

"Two memories," Poedan said, smiling. "Nice memories."

"I didn't give you permission to take one of mine! What did you take?"

The room began to shake. Deni grabbed her arm and pulled her back, and the hot anger filling Allery's chest quickly dissipated as a tree pushed its way through the floor. A thick trunk, growing leafless branches as it moved upwards, emerged from the centre of the room, pushing poker-straight until it touched the ceiling, then it turned and grew horizontal until it hit the wall and headed back to the floor.

The tree wrapped three times around the room. Allery could no longer see the man, Poedani, and couldn't see Poedan until she stepped over the trunk to approach them again. Poedan studied the branches, selected one, and snapped it off. She brought forward a small glass and filled it with the thick golden liquid seeping from the trunk.

As Poedan passed the glass to Deni, Allery caught the smell of vinegar. "What *is* that?" she asked.

Deni knocked back the liquid and gave the glass to Poedan. She stopped shivering, and the colour returned to her cheeks. "Discovered it a while ago, somewhere like this," she said. "You should try it."

"I'm not giving up any more memories. We need to go." Allery took hold of Deni's hand and pulled her out of the tavern back on to the street. "You need to open a door and take us back."

Deni pulled her hand free and started off down the street. "No, I don't."

"Yes. You do." Allery caught up with her and snatched at her arm. "Nick and Esme are on their own. God knows what could happen!"

"I don't care."

"Take us back."

Deni stared at her. Allery noticed the line of gold around her pupils, complimenting the chestnut of her irises. "I'm not going to the wardens," she said.

Allery let go of her arm. "I won't make you."

Deni looked away first, scratching her forearm. She turned and walked down the street, chickens clucking and pecking around her. "I should open a door for you."

"You should," Allery agreed, hurrying after her. The town—village—wherever they were, was strangely deserted. She noticed the colour of the sky for the first time, oddly blue-green, and a creeping sensation ran down her spine. She turned but there was nobody behind them.

Deni turned down another street, stopped, and sat down on the ground, leaning back against one of the houses. Allery stood over her. "Will you open a door?"

"I don't want you to go," Deni said.

Allery sat beside her. "Come with me." Farther down the street, a top-floor window opened, and a woman leaned out to overturn a chamber pot. Its contents splashed unpleasantly on the cobbles before she disappeared back inside. Allery cringed. "Please, let's go."

"Your friends want rid of me. I'm not going." Deni leaned forward and pulled her jumper off over her head. She picked at the black vest she wore, her skin shiny with sweat. "Hot," she explained. "Are you hot?"

"Not particularly." Allery frowned. "Are you okay? Is it...withdrawals?"

"Shouldn't be." She laid her hands on her knees, palms up, and Allery noticed for the first time Deni's lack of veins. The track marks she'd seen and tried to ignore out of some ingrained politeness, but the startling, unnatural white of her skin... Allery reached out and touched Deni's forearm, feeling the heat beneath her fingers.

Deni shifted and folded her arms. "Don't."

"We can't stay here," Allery said, getting to her feet. "There could be creatures here. Poedan wasn't human."

"Nobody here's human," Deni said. "Even us. We're just diluted versions."

Allery held out a hand and Deni took it. She pulled her to her feet, and they stood very close to each other. Deni leaned close and her lips brushed Allery's in the lightest of kisses, as if she wasn't sure of herself.

Don't. Don't get involved. Allery closed her eyes. Her heart thumped, and the heat radiating off Deni's body warmed her. A rattling along the cobbles stopped her and she pulled back as a horse and cart rumbled past the end of the street.

"Sorry," Deni said. "I thought maybe you were... It doesn't matter."

Allery swept Deni's jumper up off the ground and passed it to her. "Thought I was what?"

"Gay. Or bi, you know, I'm bi so...whatever floats your boat."

Allery blinked. "What?"

"I get it, I've made a tit out of myself. It's fine." Deni tied her jumper around her waist and set off down the street.

"No…" Allery hurried after her and walked by her side. "Didn't last night give you a pretty big clue?"

"I thought you were staring at Esme, I didn't realise it was Nick!"

"Nick?" Allery grabbed Deni's hand, and they stopped walking. "We slept together."

"Wow. Poor Esme. She'll probably find out, you know. If she hasn't worked it out already."

"What?" Allery's headache was threatening a return. "Not me and Nick. Me and you! You weren't *that* drunk."

Deni glared at her for a moment, then her shoulders sagged. "Shit. Must've been a good memory."

"Poedan," Allery said. She didn't know whether to be upset that Deni couldn't remember and someone else now shared the experience or be pleased it was nice enough for Poedan to want to take it.

"I have hardly any good memories as it is." Deni raised her hands in the gesture that Allery recognised meant she was about to open a door.

"Wait!"

Deni paused. "If I don't open one now, I'll be too weak to open one later."

"Don't take us back to Nick and Esme."

Deni grinned. "I wasn't going to."

Chapter Ten

Nick stared at the space where Allery and Deni had disappeared and threw his arms in the air. "I don't know why we bother!"

He gazed down the road, first one way, then the other. As soon as another car came, he'd flag them down. He'd had enough—screw Allery, screw Driscoll. He'd go away with Esme and they could start a new life together. They could get new jobs, rent a flat...

Esme pushed her hair out of her face. "Now what?" she asked. "Baby, I'm tired. And my head feels fuzzy. Can we go home?"

Concerned, Nick took her face between his hands and looked at her eyes. He gently pulled down her eyelid to see if she had anything in the left one to make it so red, but she pushed his hand away. "We should get you checked out," he said. "You could have concussion."

"Can we go home?" she asked again.

"Back to Merrybell? I don't think it's safe there any more." He held her close, and she leaned into his chest, clasping her hands behind his back. She heaved a miserable sigh and Nick smiled a little. "I'll stop a car," he said. "We'll head to the nearest town and work out what to do from there, yeah?"

"Okay."

She let him go and they walked side by side. Nick thought about calling Jack and asking if they could stay at his for a while but quickly dismissed the idea. His brother would accuse him of only calling when he wanted something and, to be fair, that would be exactly what he was doing. Plus, he couldn't handle the jibes or strained talks about Mum.

Guilt twisted a knot in his stomach. He *should* be with his mother, not gallivanting across the country on some stupid mission. It wasn't anything to do with him any more anyway. Allery had the key, and it was her job to take it, *her*, to the wardens.

He could hear a car approaching so tugged Esme's arm and she joined him at the side of the lane. When it came into view—a red Mini with a white roof—he raised a hand to flag it down. Only when it was close did he notice the driver was very young and had very dark eyes.

"Wardens!" he hissed. "How the hell?"

He placed himself between Esme and the car, then backed up. The Mini stopped and all four doors opened. Two girls and two boys, all in their teens, got out of the car and each closed their door in unison.

"We haven't got it," Nick said, raising his hands. "Allery has it—"

"Nick!"

He ignored Esme. A dark-haired girl, wearing what looked like a school uniform, took a step towards him. He noticed the gun tucked into the waistband of her skirt. "Allery has it but she's not here, okay? We don't know where she is."

Behind him, Esme muttered a curse and, cold washing through him, he half-turned to see the start of her transformation. "Es, no!"

Her clawed hand knocked him into the hawthorn hedge as the wardens raised their guns. She leaped, guns fired, and Nick pushed back into the branches, heart hammering. Shaking, he pressed a hand into the dirt and felt for the roots.

Wake up.

The werewolf jumped onto the roof of the Mini, ripped the gun from the hand of the nearest warden, and threw the boy over the hedge. She was bleeding—dark red glistened on her flank.

Nick pulled his awareness away and forced it into the roots. Hawthorn and fairies often went hand in hand, and he could hear the echoes of his people. Things stirred beneath him, the ground trembled, and with a great *crack* the earth splintered. Roots pushed up through the road. Somebody fell into the hedge beside him. Esme snarled and howled.

Through a haze, he could see roots reaching up and wrapping around the legs of the schoolgirl. Bullets fired, thudding into the ground and echoing around the hills.

"Stop this."

The voice sounded too deep to come from any teenager, yet it was the girl who'd spoken. Nick's vision cleared and he released the roots. They loosened from the girl's legs and sank back. Esme lay in the road, chest heaving, fur spiked and staring. A boy stood over her, his gun aimed at her head. The body of the other girl slumped, twisted and broken in the hedge beside him. Dead.

"Esme!" Nick cried, forcing himself up. He stopped short of going to her when the schoolgirl turned her gun on him.

"I said, stop." She cocked her head. "You've killed two of us today."

"You're already dead. Or as good as," Nick said, his eyes flicking to Esme again. "Let me go to her. She's hurt!"

"No silver bullets," the girl said. "She'll heal. We're not your enemy, Nicholas Lode."

Bullshit. Nick frowned but the word wouldn't leave his mind. Esme stirred, moving a clawed hand to dig a bullet from her thigh. She snarled at the warden when he came too close. Nick went to her side, figuring if the warden was telling the truth, then she wouldn't shoot him. He parted the fur on the wolf's flank and breathed a sigh of relief at the already healing wound.

"What do you want from us?" he asked. He looked at the girl briefly, then turned back to Esme and pushed his fingers into another wound, wincing in sympathy until he found the bullet and pulled it free.

"Balance," the girl said.

Nick snorted. "You want chaos."

"Come with us."

Esme started to change, her bones shifting and scraping, her claws receding, jaws reshaping. Nick pulled her into his lap and held her. "Don't trust them," she whispered.

"We could have killed you," the girl said. "We choose not to."

"You're going to use us as bait or something if we go with you," Nick said. He helped Esme to her feet and held her hand. She gripped him so tightly it hurt.

The boy lowered his gun and turned back to the girl. Nick couldn't decipher the look that passed between them. The girl inclined her head. "We'll leave you, Nicholas Lode. We're only interested in the key."

Both wardens returned to the Mini and the girl opened the

driver's door. She paused. "The offer to come with us is always open."

"Just leave us alone!" Esme snapped.

Once the wardens had got into the car and reversed back down the lane, Esme fell into Nick's arms and sobbed. He held her close, running his fingers comfortingly through her hair. "They're gone now," he said. "Are you okay?"

She sniffed and nodded and wiped a hand across her eyes. "I hate all this. I hate the fighting and the being shot and the creepy teenagers and...and Al's gone and Driscoll's gone and—"

"Shh!" Nick kissed the top of her head. "It's all right. It'll be over soon."

Birds twittered in the hedges again. Roots had settled back into the earth, but the road was churned up and splashes of blood marked the ground. There were two dead wardens to deal with and Nick reluctantly let Esme go.

"We'd better bury them," he said. "Or find a river to throw them in."

The state of the road could be blamed on the weather and the blood would soon disappear. Two bodies were more of a pain. He approached the girl in the hedge and sighed at how young she looked. Thirteen maybe? She was Asian, with large lips, perfect skin, and long dark hair tied in a tail behind her head.

"I wonder what her name was."

"It doesn't matter," Esme said. Her tear-stained face was expressionless, though her voice was barely more than a whisper. "Whatever her name was, that person disappeared when the wardens got hold of her."

"I know." Nick kneeled in front of the girl. The werewolf had clawed her chest open, exposing the glistening bones of her ribcage.

"Nick."

Esme had her arms wrapped around herself and her lower lip trembled. Nick left the girl and went to her. "You saved her," he said. "The wardens turned her into a monster, and you set her free."

"It's just...hard." Her voice broke with a sob, and she stared at the body. Usually, she didn't get much involved with the clearing up, though she generally created the most mess. Or rather, the wolf did. It helped both of them to think of the wolf and Esme as separate entities. Esme was sweet and loving—not a sharp-toothed murderer.

As he turned back to the body, Driscoll appeared in front of him, making him jump. "Where the hell have you been?" he asked.

"Waiting for you guys up on the hill," Driscoll said, looking around. "Jesus, you've had a spot of bother here by the looks of things. Everyone okay?"

"Fine," Nick said. "Brilliant." He marched up to the girl's body and took hold of her arm to drag her out of the hedge. "Help me out here. There's another one in the field."

"Where's Al?"

"Your guess is as good as mine."

Esme joined him and helped him move the body without a word. They carried her the short distance down the road to a gate and took her into the field. Driscoll was ahead of them, standing over the boy's corpse. He smoothed his moustache and looked up at Nick and Esme. "We need that key," he said.

"She has a name," Esme said, lowering the girl's legs to the ground.

"We need Deni," Driscoll corrected himself. "And Al. If either of you have any idea where they are—"

"They just vanished," Nick said, laying the girl next to the boy.

"Deni opened a door and off they went." He scratched the back of his head and looked at the bodies. He could use the roots to rip a hole in the ground and cover them over, he supposed.

"You didn't get a look at where they were headed?" Driscoll asked. "Did you see anything familiar through the door?"

"You know what happens. There's a flash of light and you can't see anything," Nick said, starting to get annoyed. "Thanks for just leaving us to face these bastards on our own, by the way. We could've done with your help."

"Yeah. Sorry about that. But look, I didn't know the wardens were going to show up, did I? I'm here now."

Nick shook his head. He knelt on the ground and pressed his hands into the grass, feeling for the roots.

Chapter Eleven

Cricket St. Nicholas was not a village Max cared for. The locals were mostly old, or ugly, or both, and there was nothing to do of an evening except sit in the local pub and drink cider with Whippet Bill. The pub—The White Hart—had carpets darkened by spilled beer and floorboards stickier than he left most of his victims. The soles of his shoes peeled off the floor as he crossed to the bar. Whippet Bill got up from his usual spot and headed outside for a smoke, so Max ordered drinks for them both. He turned and leaned on the bar as he waited, eyeing the traps and various hunting and farming paraphernalia hanging from the ceiling and decorating the walls. He liked the look of the scythe and wondered if anybody would notice if it went missing.

"Old Rosie for 'ee, Max, and one for Bill," the barman said, placing the glasses on the bar.

"Cheers." Max handed over the money and his mind wandered as the barman counted his change. He could just imagine somebody waking up in the night to see him standing over them with a scythe.

"You look 'appy," the barman commented.

"Yeah?" Max pocketed the change and picked up his cider. "Happy thoughts."

"Ah. Off out tonight, be 'ee?"

"Oh, I dunno. I might prop up your bar all night, John." Max swallowed a mouthful of his drink, relishing the apples on his taste buds. He licked his lips. "I'll probably head out after this. See if I can find someone to warm my bed for the night."

John chuckled. "You'll be lucky." He turned away to serve someone else and Max smirked to himself.

I'm always lucky. He might even go for John's wife. Shag her brains out while she slept and come all over her back so she'd blame John when she woke. The thought almost made him choke on his cider and he swallowed his laughter.

Whippet Bill was taking a bloody long time to return. Perhaps the old feller had wandered into the road and been hit by a tractor. Max gulped down his cider and headed outside.

The village was quiet, though wind rustled the leaves of the trees on the green. The moon shone brightly over the church and a couple of stars dotted the sky. In the park, the swings creaked as they moved on their own. *So. Fucking. Dull.*

"Bill?" he called.

He could hear something. Muffled voices. He crossed over the road and opened the gate to the church. "Bill?"

A winding path led up to the church, illuminated by orange lights. Gravestones and bulky sarcophagi were all around, in no apparent order. A spindly tree creaked in the breeze and Max glanced at it briefly.

He was about to turn back when somebody cried out. Muttering a curse under his breath, he hurried towards the sound. As he rounded the church, he saw Whippet Bill. The old man cowered in front of a gravestone, surrounded by four hooded teenagers. As one of them pulled his foot back to kick Bill, Max ran in and yanked him away. Without thinking, he spun the kid around and punched him in the face.

The teen's head snapped back. When he recovered, Max noticed his black eyes. The boy showed him a bloodied grin and, angry, Max smacked him again.

"Get out of here!" he yelled, shoving the boy away. "Go on!"

He ignored the teens as they backed off and congregated beneath a tree and went to Bill. The old man's breathing came in rattled gasps, and his face was cut and bloody. Max reached out and Bill gasped at his touch, his eyes widening in horror.

"It's all right, feller, it's Max."

"Demon," Bill whispered, staring at him. "Demon!"

"Shit. Bill, it's just me. Remember Max? Your drinking buddy." He hooked an arm around Bill's shoulders, but the old man struggled and pushed him away. "I've got you a pint of Old Rosie waiting at the Hart. Let's get you up."

"Max?"

"Yeah, pal, it's me." He noticed the glisten of blood on Bill's jumper and, spinning to look at the teens, spotted the blade in the hand of one of them. Bill clung to the front of his shirt, but his grip weakened and fell. Max tapped Bill's cheek, gripped his chin, and gave him a little shake. "Bill?"

Blood running cold, heart pushing through his breastbone, he checked Bill's neck for a pulse. But Whippet Bill was dead. With a sigh, Max closed his friend's eyes and laid him gently on the ground.

Then he stood up and turned to face the teens.

"Warden bastards," he said. He spat on to the ground. "What

do you think you're playing at?"

"We're *bored,* Max," the boy with the knife said. "The women aren't coming back to the cottage. We've waited long enough."

"Do you think the boss'll be happy with you lot drawing attention to yourselves?" Max asked. "Fucking idiots."

The boy sneered and pointed the knife at Max. "Not like you've done nothing while you've been here either, is it? Don't think we don't know about you screwing half the village."

"Sticking my dick in someone while they sleep and sticking a knife in someone's guts is *a bit fucking different,*" Max snapped. "Jesus." He looked at Bill's body, then away. "All we had to do was stay here, keep our heads down, and wait. What do you think the boss is going to say, eh?" The boy shrugged. Max snatched him by the neck and dragged him close. "Bill was my *friend.*" He applied a little pressure, ignoring the boy scrabbling at his wrist.

"You don't have friends, incubus." One of the girls stepped forward, sweeping down her hood to reveal a blonde pixie-cut hairdo. She looked the oldest of the four of them. Seventeen or eighteen, perhaps. She closed her eyes and, as her lids flickered, Max realised she was talking to the boss. He kept hold of the boy's throat, giving him a sharp shake when he struggled.

The girl opened her eyes. "Jacob says you can have me as an apology for the old man. Once you're done, the four of you are to head back. The key is no longer in this dimension."

Max grinned and dropped the boy. "I can take the whole of you?"

The girl nodded and her face, and dead black eyes, remained expressionless.

Max laughed. It had been a while since he'd last fucked someone to death. He held out his hand and smiled when the girl took it.

Chapter Twelve

A brief tingling sensation passed over Allery's skin as she crossed through the door. The next thing she was aware of was the cold wind pulling at her hair and clothes. She wrapped her arms around herself and squinted into the wind. They were in a valley, surrounded by rocky green mountains. Grey clouds rolled across a blue sky, forming moving shadows on the grass that shimmered like waves. Further along the valley she could see a few trees but there were no houses, or roads, or anything that gave her any idea of where she was.

She turned to Deni. "Where are we?"

"Earth."

Allery frowned. "Can you be more specific?" She had to shout to be heard over the wind.

"I dunno. Norway maybe. Scotland. Somewhere like that."

"Can you take us somewhere else? A town?"

Deni raised a hand and shook her head. She turned aside,

doubled over, and vomited. Then she groaned and sunk to her hands and knees before curling up into a ball.

Allery cursed quietly. She glanced behind them, then up at the mountains, flicking the hair out of her face. It was just the sort of place the wardens would love and if she didn't move Deni soon, they'd surely come for her. She crouched by Deni's side and rubbed her back. "You okay?"

Deni trembled beneath her fingers. Her eyes were tightly closed and sweat shone on her forehead. Allery touched her brow. "Den?"

"Dying," Deni muttered. "Kill me."

"Bollocks. Get up." Allery pulled Deni up into a sitting position, away from the puddle of vomit. She brushed the hair out of her face and tilted Deni's chin to get a good look at her. Her skin was hot and clammy, though she shivered violently.

"Need a...hit," Deni said, pushing Allery's hands away. "Please."

"Yeah, I'll give you a hit all right." She hooked Deni's arm around her shoulders and pulled her to her feet, ignoring her cries and feeble protests. "Come on, we need to get out of here."

She half-dragged, half-supported Deni along the bottom of the valley, glancing up at the hills and back the way they'd come. When she couldn't pull Deni any longer, they both stumbled and dropped heavily to the ground. Allery, breathing heavily, made an attempt to pull Deni up once more.

"Just leave me to die!" Deni protested. Her eyes were wet with tears, and she pushed Allery away before curling up in a ball, shivering.

"You're not dying," Allery said. "You'll be dead if the wardens show up, though." She sat by Deni's side and brushed the hair away from her face, frowning at the clamminess of her skin.

"Old wardens or the drifters?" Deni asked.

"Either would be bad." With an effort, she managed to get Deni to sit up and wrapped her arms around her to try to stop the shivering. She rubbed Deni's back while she tried to work out what to do next. There was nothing around for miles—the landscape stretched on and on, and the mountains loomed over them. She let go of Deni with one hand to pull the phone from her pocket.

No signal. Not that there was any point ringing anybody anyway, she supposed, putting the phone away. She didn't know where they were so why would anybody else? At least she still had the gun pushed through her belt. She might be able to shoot one warden before they took Deni away.

Or shoot Deni.

"Why wouldn't you kiss me?"

Allery pulled back to look at her. Deni met her gaze only briefly before looking at her trembling hands. "What?" Allery asked.

"You say we slept together," Deni said. "But you wouldn't kiss me earlier." She thrust her hands beneath her armpits and met Allery's gaze again.

Allery sat back on her heels. "I can't get involved."

"Right. So, sex is okay but kissing...?"

"I shouldn't have slept with you. Can we just forget about it?"

"Already have."

Allery sighed. "I'm sorry." She rubbed her hands together to try to warm them up, checked Deni was okay, and got to her feet.

The wind made her eyes water, and she wiped them on her sleeve before squinting into the distance. Something shimmered up ahead, almost like a heat haze, but confined to a small area as if it rose from a campfire. When she realised what it was—*a door!*—her heart raced. It couldn't be the wardens coming for them already?

She waited, frozen, but nothing came through. Doors opened independently sometimes, giving creatures who knew about them the opportunity to pass through. Her father would visit women via such doors, the horny bastard, but he'd managed to visit her a few times, for which she was grateful.

She returned to Deni and crouched by her side. "There's a door down there!"

Deni didn't reply. Her eyes were closed and her forehead furrowed as if she was in pain.

"Den?"

"Need some gear." Deni groaned and curled up in a ball. "Please. I can't—"

"I haven't got anything to give you. You can't be going through withdrawals already! What was that stuff Poedan gave you?"

"Opening doors makes me weak." She was sobbing now, still curled on the ground. "Please help me! It hurts."

Allery pulled Deni's arm around her shoulders and hauled her to her feet, ignoring her groans. She dragged her towards the door, fighting to keep Deni upright and not let her weight pull them both down. "I don't know where we're going to end up," she said. "So, cross your fingers."

"No!" Deni wrenched her arm away. "We're on Earth *now*. We need to get to a town!"

"We can't stay here." She looked at the door shimmering in front of them. *This is crazy!* She had to risk it. They couldn't stay. The wilds of Scotland...Norway...wherever the hell they were, were too much of a warden's stomping ground. But she hesitated, torn. If they kept walking, they might come across a road, or a house, though Deni didn't look like she could make it very far.

She swore silently and was about to move away when a flash of light on the hillside caught her eye. A figure dressed in white paused and scanned the bottom of the valley until he spotted them. Then he started towards them.

Allery grabbed Deni's arm and shoved her through the door. She followed without looking back.

*

Wherever they were, it was nighttime. And raining. And a city. Deni pulled Allery back from the road as a car drove past, blaring its horn, and they both pressed themselves against a wall.

Buildings towered over them—modern office blocks and flats—and bright lights dazzled them. Allery lowered her gaze and watched as people—*people, we're on Earth!*—hurried by with their heads down and umbrellas up. The place was bustling with activity, cars, so many cars, tourists and shoppers and...it was overwhelming. She reached for Deni's hand and held it, swallowed hard, and tried to control her nerves, taking slow breaths.

"Hear the accents?" she asked. "We're in Australia."

"They might be tourists," Deni said.

Allery shook her head and pointed out the building across the road. "Bank of Melbourne." She laughed a little. She'd always fancied a trip Down Under, but maybe somewhere quieter—the outback perhaps. Though there would be no wardens in the city. No old wardens anyway, and the new ones wouldn't know they were there. She hooked her wet hair behind her ears, squeezed Deni's hand, and gave her a tug to indicate they should move.

"We need to find a hotel," she said.

"No, I need to find a dealer." Deni's voice was hushed but had a crack to it, and when Allery looked at her, she noticed the way her eyes moved, searching the faces of the people they passed as if any one of them might have what she was after.

"I'm not going to help you buy drugs," Allery hissed.

Deni gripped Allery's arms tight. "Look at me! I *need* something."

"I thought you were going clean. You can start now." Spotting a gap in the traffic, she held Deni's hand and hurried across the road with her. Down from the bank, at the edge of the crossroads, was a tall building with a neon-green sign at the top. *The View Hotel.* If it was cheap, it would do.

She stopped at the ATM and took her wallet from her back pocket, then she inserted the card into the machine and withdrew five hundred Australian dollars. She stuffed the cash inside the wallet and back into her pocket, all too aware of Deni watching her every move.

"Where the hell did you get that much money from?" Deni asked. "I've seen that shitty cottage you live in."

"Merrybell was a safe house," Allery said, setting off towards the hotel. She didn't mention the money wasn't exactly *hers*. Deni caught her up and held her arm, walking just a little too close, and Allery could feel the warmth through her jacket. Someone barged into her, knocking her shoulder, and she turned to glare at the man. He was too busy stuffing a burger down his throat to apologise. She wondered what time it was. She wasn't tired and neither was half of Australia by the look of it.

"Why are we bothering with a hotel?" Deni asked as they stopped outside the building's glass doors. A porter lingered nearby. He eyed them but said nothing.

Allery made her way inside and headed to reception. "Because we should both get some sleep—you especially—and I need to work out what we're going to do next."

She ignored Deni's groans and smiled when the receptionist

acknowledged her. After booking a twin room, she hauled Deni towards the lift. They stood in silence, Deni leaning against her, and Allery put an arm around her waist.

"We'll be all right," she said softly.

The lift came to a stop and a woman's voice announced the doors were opening. Allery slipped her arm free and stepped out into the corridor. The red carpet had blue spots and the walls were cream. There were only doors along the corridor, no windows, and Allery scanned each one until she spotted room 208. She swiped her key card and ushered Deni inside, closing the door behind them.

The twin beds dominated the room, filling the space along one wall and separated only by a single cabinet with a lamp on it. Opposite the beds was a dressing table and wardrobe squashed into the space next to the bathroom door, and at the back of the room the window gave a view of another skyscraper.

"It's cosy," Allery commented as Deni went to lie on one of the beds. "It'll do."

"Just as well we have no luggage," Deni said. "It'd never fit."

Allery investigated the bathroom—just a shower cubicle, toilet, and small wash basin, but it was clean and there were complimentary soaps and shower gels. She knew she'd have to go and buy them each a toothbrush and maybe a change of clean clothes, depending on how long they'd have to stay. Her stomach growled, reminding her she hadn't eaten for a while.

"I'm going to head down to reception and see where I can get something to eat," she said, going back into the room. Deni had curled up on the bed now, hands covering her head. "Can I get you anything? A drink?"

Deni shook her head and said nothing. Allery went to sit by

her side. She brushed strands of greasy hair away from Deni's forehead.

"I won't be long, okay? Sit tight." She waited but received no indication Deni had even heard her.

If prison had taught her anything, it was patience. There was no point getting stressed about situations she had no control over. She squeezed Deni's hand and left the room.

Chapter Thirteen

Old-fashioned Tudor houses lined the cobbled street, making the place look like it'd been lifted out of a museum. Max scratched his chin and folded his arms. Wherever they were, it was even quieter and even more boring than Cricket St. Nicholas. Chickens clucked and scattered, flapping in a panic, as a small human-looking child ran past and disappeared around a corner.

"You sure Jacob got the right place?" he asked. "Oi. Kid?"

Two of the wardens, the girl and oldest boy, had disappeared into an inn to question the patrons, while the youngest lad lingered outside with Max. The boy was a scruffy-looking little sod—skinny with hair so blond it was almost white. His pale eyelashes clashed oddly with his black eyes. Max found him creepy.

"I said, you sure Jacob got the right place? There's nobody here. Boy? I'm talking to you!"

The warden moved away from the pub's door. "Course he got the right place," he said. "Don't call me Boy."

Max snorted to let the little brat know he'd call him what he liked. "What were you, nine?"

"Ten."

"Ten!" Max said, raising his hands in mock surprise. "Blimey, sorry, big man. Ten years old. Bugger me backwards." He fetched a kick at a chicken which came too close to his boots and went to the door to peer inside. The wardens knelt over a fat man on the ground, silently plunging bloodied knives into him over and over again. Muttering curses, Max pushed the boy aside and went in.

"All right, all right, I think he's dead already. Well done."

The room was large and empty but for bloodstained rushes on the floor. The wardens looked up from the corpse, their faces splattered red.

"They were here," the girl said.

"Yeah? And now they're not?" Max rolled his eyes. "I could've told you that. Come on, kids, I think we've murdered enough locals for one day."

He ushered them out of the inn, feeling far too much like their minder, and walked back out into the street. He waited while the girl felt for a crack in reality's seam so she could open a door.

Doors opened by wardens were pretty rubbish, in Max's opinion. They didn't stay open for long enough and he had a bad feeling that one day one'd snap shut while he was only halfway through and his arse'd end up in another dimension. That's why old Jacob wanted the key, of course. The doors would stay open, unless closed by the key, and it'd be a lot less of a pain for everyone. Well, everyone interested in cross-dimensional travel. Which wasn't *exactly* everyone—humans, rubbish as they were, tended to die either passing through the door or not long after. Some demons were a bit crap in certain dimensions, too. But that was their lookout.

"Come on, come on." He hurried the girl and two boys through the door.

He'd just taken a step when there was a high-pitched scream from the direction of the inn. No sooner had he formed the thought, *someone's found the body*, than something snatched at his ankle and pulled. Instinctively, he grabbed hold of the nearest thing—the blond boy's hood—before he was hurled backwards. The boy fell back, the door slammed shut, and Max hit the ground. He scrabbled at the cobbles with his fingertips as something dragged him along the street.

To his credit, the boy ran after him though he was too slow. Max yelled as he was lifted off the ground and pulled through the inn's doorway. He found himself dangling upside down in front of a very tall, very angry-looking woman. The room seemed to be full of tree now, and when he looked, he saw a root grasping his ankle. Blood rushed to his head and his T-shirt rucked up around his neck. He didn't struggle, but he spat the filthiest curse he could come up with.

The boy appeared in the door and the roots snaked towards him. They grabbed him just as he turned to flee. Max waited, hanging like a worm on a fishing hook.

"You killed my male," the woman said. She sounded calmer than she looked, though her voice was deep and malevolent.

"*I* didn't," Max said. He curled up to try to free his ankle, but the root held firm. When he flopped back down, he noticed the man's corpse amidst a tangle of branches and thin, tendril-like roots pushing into the body. He screwed up his nose.

"Then, the boy," she said, pointing a finger at the warden.

"Nope. He was with me." He made an attempt to free his leg again. "Look, you're gonna have to let me down before I pass out here."

His eyes widened as the root loosened around his ankle and before he could cry, *"Wait!"* he fell and hit his head on the floor. He groaned and sat up, probing his skull tentatively for damage. Roots entangled the boy in the doorway or he might've tried to make his getaway. Instead, he pushed himself to his feet and faced the woman. She was at least three heads taller than him and Max didn't think he could take her in a fight.

He smiled. "There's been a bit of a misunderstanding. Your old man's dead, and I'm sorry for that, really, I am, but it's got nothing to do with me and the boy here."

"Show me."

"What?" He took a step back as she approached him, then pushed her hand away when her finger came towards his head. "Gerrof." Roots wrapped around his ankles, preventing him from stepping back again, and he raised his hands, a little slither of worry pinching his chest.

"Let me see what you know." Her finger came at him again and he screwed his eyes shut. Her touch was warm and firm at the centre of his forehead.

Thoughts came unbidden into his mind, disorientating and strange. When the woman released him, he blinked hard to try to clear the feeling. Roots loosened and shrank back. Max rubbed the spot on his forehead and glared at her. "Well?"

"You spoke truthfully."

"I did." Max marched towards the boy and pulled him out of the tangle of roots. "Now then, if you don't mind, we've got things to do."

He shoved the warden outside and was about to follow when the woman called, "Wait! The two who did this"—she swept a hand back at the corpse—"they should be punished."

Max sighed. "I'm not their bloody father. Or their boss."

"Jacob—"

"Yes, Jacob." Max frowned, wondering how much information she'd taken from him, wondering if it mattered. If perhaps he should silence her. "I'm sure he'll kick their arses when I tell him what's happened, all right?"

"Jacob's looking for the key."

Something about the way she said it made him pause. "That's right."

"She was here. With a friend."

"Yeah?" *Give me more than that.*

The woman smiled but her eyes were cold and hard. "The enemy of my enemy is my friend, incubus. After the attack on my male, I will stand against Jacob."

Max laughed. "I'm sure he's quaking in his boots. No offence or anything, but I don't even know who you are."

"I am Poedan," she said, as the tree creaked and moved, retreating from the room—the corpse no more. "I am Life and Death. I am the Creator. I am a Goddess in this realm. I am—"

"I'll tell him," Max snapped. "Poedan's his enemy. Got it loud and clear. Look, if you're after a new male, I can't promise to marry you or anything, but I can give you a good shag or three."

Poedan walked towards him and he backed up until he'd stumbled out of the inn and into the street. He glanced back to see the warden waiting for him.

Poedan stopped in the doorway and bared pointed teeth at him. "Your power does not work on me."

"Well..." Max scratched his cheek and thought about it. "We could shag anyway. I'm pretty good, you know. Lots of practice."

"If you, or your boy, enter this realm again," Poedan said, "I will break you in half." She took a step back and the door slammed shut.

Max turned to the warden. "That went better than I expected."

The little brat just rolled his eyes and turned to open a door. So, Jacob had yet another enemy, so what? It wasn't Max's fault. There was a flash of light, and he hurried into it.

Chapter Fourteen

Nick put an arm around Esme as she leaned against his shoulder. Behind them, the rain pattered against the glass of the showroom window. In front, Driscoll laughed with the car salesman, before scratching his moustache and nodding appreciatively at the red Ford Focus.

Just get any one. Cars were all the same—noisy and smelly and ugly. He flicked through the messages on his phone again, once more feeling royally pissed off that Allery hadn't bothered contacting them to let them know what the hell was happening. He typed in *Where R U???* and pressed send.

Just as he was about to put the phone away, the screen flashed with a new message. From Jack. It read: *Mum's not getting any better.*

Nick could imagine his brother's sneer as he'd typed the message—it came across beautifully in the words. He hit reply, his thumb hovering over the keypad, wondering what he could say.

"You should go and see her." Esme's voice was soft, and she lifted her head from his shoulder.

"But you're—"

"I'm fine. All healed." She smiled at him, and he relaxed and kissed her on the forehead. "Go and see her. We're going to be stuck in here for ages."

Driscoll *was* taking his time choosing a car. Nick didn't know why he didn't just get them a banger; it would probably only end up destroyed like the last one. He drew his attention back to Esme as she pulled her purse from her handbag and handed him some cash.

"Take a taxi," she said.

He took the money gratefully and pushed it into his back pocket. Then he got to his feet and headed outside to call for a cab. The car park was devoid of people, the rain keeping them away, and all the cars were closed up so the interiors wouldn't be ruined. A Ford flag hung wetly at the top of a pole and slapped against it in the breeze. Opposite the showroom, buildings loomed grey over him, making him turn away with a shiver. Rain dampened his skin, and he ran a hand over his face as he listened to the phone ring. Eventually, a woman answered, and he called for a taxi to take him to the hospital.

Inside the showroom, Driscoll wandered about with the dealer and Esme twisted in her chair to give him a little wave from the window. He smiled back at her. He'd go and see his mother. Everything else could wait.

*

Outside the hospital, Nick glanced back over his shoulder to make sure nobody was watching before bending down and scooping up a handful of wet mud from the beds in front of the building. He smeared dirt over his wrists and rubbed his hands together until the rain had washed them. Then he tugged at his sleeves to cover his wrists and headed inside. The sterile environment made his head swim, despite the earth against his skin, and he kept his gaze down as he made his way towards his mother's room.

His heart thumped as he pushed open the door and he tried not to look at the other occupants in the room as he walked over to his mother's bed. He sat in the padded chair and tentatively took her hand—it was warm and dry, and the veins were raised beneath his touch.

"Nick," she said. She smiled though her voice was weak. "Jack didn't say you were coming."

"He didn't know." He lifted his gaze briefly to meet her eyes, but guilt made him look away. "I'm sorry I don't visit enough."

She touched his face, smoothing his cheek. "I know you're busy with work. And your lovely girlfriend. She's not here today?"

Nick shook his head. "She's with a friend." He chanced a look at his mother as she settled back in bed. She seemed thinner since the last time he'd seen her. More frail. Her lips hung open as she breathed lightly and her brow creased in a permanent frown. "Is Jack still here?"

"Hmm?" She pulled her eyes open. "I think he went to get a bite to eat. He should be back before you go."

Great.

He sat, holding his mother's hand and trying to think of something, *anything*, to say to her. The dried mud on his wrists tugged at his skin, bringing some small comfort. He shifted in the chair and said, "My friend Driscoll's buying a new car."

His mother smiled. "Oh? Any particular kind?"

God love her for pretending to be interested. He spoke to her about cars and told her a story of the time he'd given Esme a driving lesson before she'd passed her test. Every time his mother smiled or squeezed his hand, his worries melted away a little more. For once, in a very long time, he felt normal. When the conversation ran dry, he kissed her on the cheek, promised to visit again soon, and made his way out into the corridor. He *could* have normality. It was easy, really.

As he stood out in the car park and pulled his phone from his pocket to call for a taxi, footsteps coming up behind made him turn. His shoulders sagged when he spotted Jack.

"Not even going to speak to your brother, eh?" Jack demanded, stopping short of Nick and opening his arms wide in a challenge.

"I was hoping not to," Nick muttered, scrolling through his phone for the number of the taxi firm. Jack smacked him on the arm, and he looked up with a frown. "Hey!"

"Well, look at me when I'm talking to you," Jack snapped, eyes wide. "You think you're so much better than me. I'm the one who's been caring for Mum, I'm the one who's been here for her. You're a waste of space, Nick."

Nick shook his head and turned away with the phone pressed to his ear, hoping his brother would get the hint and bugger off.

He didn't. Jack walked round to face him again. "Where's your pretty girlfriend? She had enough of you? Or has she found out you're a *fairy*?"

Nick shoved his brother roughly, fury burning inside his chest. Jack retaliated, swinging his fist. The blow struck Nick's jaw, making him bite his tongue and sending the phone spinning from his grasp to hit the ground with a crack. Adrenaline smothered the pain, and he turned and punched his brother as hard as he could, watching as blood burst from Jack's nose.

They grabbed each other, wrestling, pulling at each other's

clothes and landing blows on ribs and stomachs and backs. Nick kicked Jack's legs and Jack punched him in the ear. At some point, Nick must have received a blow to the face as blood dribbled into his right eye.

Hospital staff pulled them apart. The pounding in his head subsided and Nick blinked until his vision cleared.

"Fuck you, Nick!" Jack was shouting. "Fuck you!"

Nick watched, wiping a hand across his eye, as Jack was taken back inside the hospital, flanked by two orderlies.

"You, too." A woman's voice. "That's a nasty cut; you might have to have a stitch."

He looked at her, then at the blood on his hand. "I'm fine," he said, though his voice was faint.

"Mm." The woman took his arm and guided him towards the hospital. "You two know each other?"

"He's my brother," Nick said. "He's just...scared for Mum."

And he hates you. Always has.

*

Nick's head spun as a nurse cleaned and stitched the cut above his eyebrow. He blinked slowly and attempted to return the nurse's smile. He wondered vaguely if Driscoll had bought a car yet, and what Esme was doing. She'd have to give him some sympathy, he thought, grinning woozily.

He hadn't realised he'd passed out until he opened his eyes to see the nurse leaning over him, a concerned frown on her face.

"Mr Lode?"

"I'm fine," he muttered. *Damn hospitals.* He heaved himself into a sitting position and rubbed his face. "Where's my brother? Jack. Is he okay?"

"One second." The nurse retreated behind the curtain and left him alone on the bed. He could hear muttered voices and the nurse's footsteps as she walked away.

He felt his pocket for his phone, then remembered he'd dropped it outside. Hopefully somebody had picked it up and handed it in at reception. He twiddled his thumbs, probed tentatively at the stitching above his eye, then looked up as the nurse appeared again. She gave him a smile that made his stomach turn and his world narrow.

"What is it?" he asked.

She turned from him briefly to draw the curtain around them and his heart thumped. "Mr Lode, I'm sorry to have to tell you this, but it's your mother—"

He stopped listening and stared as her lips moved. *No, no, no, she was fine!*

"—passed away. If there's—"

"She was fine!" Nick yelled, suddenly angry. "Mrs Lode. Patricia Lode. Are you sure? Check again."

"Mr Lode—"

"I'd just come from seeing her! She was fine!"

"I'm sorry, she—"

Nick got up, barged past the nurse, and ran, ignoring someone shouting after him. He just needed to get out of there. He needed air, earth. The automatic doors opened with a soft *hoosh* and he hurried outside. He fell to his knees in the car park.

"*No, no!*" He slapped the concrete with his palm, then pressed his forehead to the ground, shaking with silent tears. "No."

Somebody touched his shoulder, and he lifted his head to see an old woman give him a concerned smile. "Are you all right?" she asked.

He shook his head. "Mum," he said, sitting back on his heels. "My mum, she's..."

The old woman rubbed his back, comforting him though he was nothing but a stranger to her, and the gesture made him cry harder. After a while, she managed to usher him towards a bench located beneath the shade of a whitebeam tree beside the hospital. He reached out to touch the trunk, relaxing at the feel of the bark beneath his fingertips.

"I've come to see my husband," the woman said. "My Arthur."

Nick blinked. He wiped his tears away with the back of his hand and sniffed. "Is he okay?"

"Hm? Oh, he'll be all right. Routine hip operation, he'll be home in no time."

Nick nodded. *Jack. I need to find Jack.* Cars came and went, moving slowly as their drivers looked for spaces to park. People wandered back across the car park, laughing, talking. A teenager trundled by on a skateboard, continuing on down the road and out of sight. The old woman carried on speaking, but Nick had stopped listening. His limbs were as heavy as his heart and his thoughts sluggish and hard to get hold of.

He attempted to focus when the woman gripped his hand. "I have to go now," she said. "You'll be all right, won't you?"

He nodded and offered a faint smile. She patted his hand, got up from the bench, and strolled towards the hospital doors as if she had all the time in the world. Nick leaned forward and rubbed his face. *I should see Jack.*

Instead, he got to his feet and started walking.

Chapter Fifteen

Deni tossed and turned all night, groaning so much that Allery was sure somebody would come to investigate. She held on to her until Deni pushed her away, then she sat by the window, knees to her chin, watching and wishing she could do something to help.

Deni moved again at midnight, staggering to the bathroom where she stayed for an awful long time. Allery pushed the window open a crack to let out the smell of vomit and shit and tried to distract herself by reading the messages on her phone. Nick sounded pissed off mostly. Esme concerned and also angry: one text read, *Driscoll nos u took money from acc. Tried 2 by new car. Where r u?* Another said, *hes gunna check wiv bank which atm u took money frm.*

She sighed. *We'll have to move on again, soon as we can.* She put the phone away and dozed with her head against the wall until Deni shook her awake. Sirens sounded outside.

"There's something under my skin," Deni hissed, pinching at her arms.

Allery pushed hair back from her face, frowning sleepily. "What?"

"Under my skin," Deni said again, her voice a harsh whisper, her eyes wide and staring. "*Living.*"

"Let me see." Allery took hold of Deni's skinny wrist and rubbed her arm. "There's nothing there, darling, it's just the withdrawals."

"Not your darling." Deni snatched her arm away and paced the small room, scratching her hands frantically. "It's beetles."

Quickly, and wide awake now, Allery got up and took Deni's hands to stop her scratching, concerned she'd keep going until she'd ripped into skin. She could feel Deni's nervous energy through her palms. "You'll hurt yourself," she said softly. "Try to get some sleep."

"Need a hit," Deni said, vainly trying to pull her hands away. "Please, Allery, please! *Please.*"

Allery pulled her into a hug and held her against her chest, heart breaking at Deni's sobs. "It'll get better, I promise. You can do this!"

"Please, please," Deni muttered, voice small and broken by tears—breath hitching at the back of her throat. "Please."

Allery held her and said nothing, closing her eyes against the pain until Deni pushed her away, her eyes flashing hate.

"You can't keep me in here, you bitch."

Deni lunged for the door. Allery snatched her around the waist and pulled her back, trying to be gentle, but Deni struggled like a wild cat, scratching, kicking and screaming so much that Allery wrestled her to the bed and pressed her weight down on her, a hand over Deni's mouth.

"Shh!" Her heart raced. Someone would've heard that. A member of staff was bound to come up soon. Deni screamed beneath her hand, the sound muffled. Tears streaked her face.

Allery didn't release her until she saw the fight leave her. Deni dissolved into quiet sobs and curled up, facing the wall.

"I'm sorry," Allery said. *I'm doing this for you.* She sat beside her on the bed, arms wrapped around her legs.

After a while, Deni said, very quietly, "Let the wardens kill me."

"No."

Deni didn't reply and neither of them spoke again that night.

*

Max decided that what Jacob didn't know wouldn't hurt him, so he didn't bother telling him about the encounter with Poedan. Besides, it was getting dark in... He scratched his head and prodded the boy in the back.

"Oi, kid? Where are we?"

They were walking along a street lined with terraced houses that could've been almost anywhere in the world—except Max recognised the British number plates on the cars parked along the road.

"Brislington," the boy said.

"Brislington... Bristol, right? So, we're back in the southwest." Once they'd left Jacob, the boy had opened a door, and Max had quickly followed him through it. Jacob had given them no more instructions and until they were called upon, they were free to do whatever they liked. Max cleared his throat nosily and spat onto the pavement. "Any particular reason?"

The kid shrugged. "Used to live here."

"Oh." Well, that was weird. Wardens usually lost every sense of their self after Jacob turned them, but this particular nuisance seemed to be clinging to his past like a limpet. "You remember your name, don't you?"

"Dillon."

Max snorted. "Poncey-arse name if ever I heard one."

They continued walking in silence. Somewhere in the distance, cats screamed, setting off all the local dogs. Max debated telling Jacob he hadn't turned the boy properly but then decided that if Jacob was losing his touch, it was nothing to do with him.

"Tia remembers her name, too."

Max looked up as Dillon spoke. The warden continued walking ahead, not turning back to him. "And who the hell is Tia?"

"The girl who killed Poedan's male."

Maybe he should tell Jacob after all. He couldn't be dealing with wardens knowing their own names and having personalities and things. That was far too human. They were probably all reverting, then what would happen?

He reached out to tug on the kid's hood, telling him to stop. "Can you open a door back to the boss man for me, eh? There's a good lad."

Dillon turned around and blinked his black eyes slowly, as if he hadn't understood. "We're on free time."

"I know—"

"Don't you need to go and do your thing?"

"I don't *need* to do it," Max said, annoyed. "It's not like my bollocks'll explode if I don't get my leg over one night."

"What am I supposed to do?"

"I don't bloody know, you're on free time. Do whatever the hell you like. Just don't kill anyone." He waited. The boy looked all around before pulling open a door and Max hopped through it before it had a chance to close in his face.

Darkness surrounded him, pitch black. It was only the feel of something solid beneath his feet that told him he wasn't falling, or on his arse, or stuck halfway through a bloody wall. Grumbling obscenities, he moved forward, holding his arms out in front of him as if he were a zombie. Jacob liked to move around, varying his position so he'd be harder to find. The kids always knew where he was, as he knew where they were, so despite the fact he couldn't see, Max knew he had to be around somewhere. Unless the stupid kid was messing with him.

Max.

The voice made him jump and curse. He stopped walking. "Boss man? You couldn't turn the lights on, eh? I feel like a right dickhead stumbling round in the dark."

The lights came on too suddenly and Max had to screw his eyes shut. They watered unpleasantly when he opened them, and he blinked several times until he could see properly. The ground stretched away all around him, flat and white and featureless. Ahead, sitting upon a white throne atop a dais, was Jacob, also dressed in white, his grey hair and black eyes the only colours on him. Max forced himself not to roll his eyes and approached the warden.

No key? Jacob's lips didn't move, and his voice sounded all around.

"We're working on it. Look, there's something you should know. Are we on a private channel?"

Jacob's eyes closed for a moment. *Yes. You may speak.*

"Great, listen." Max came as close to the dais as he dared and looked up at Jacob. "One of your kids, the scrawny one—Dillon— he's remembering who he is. You might want to give him another zap and make him all cold and dead again."

I need the key.

Max held up his hands. "I know, boss, I know, and you'll get it, I promise, but if you could just sort these kids out, I'd be grateful. It's really hard to concentrate when they're being all snarky and teenage."

Jacob didn't blink. Max shivered as the warden stared at him and wished he hadn't bothered. Jacob obviously didn't seem that worried; he could probably just change some new kids and replace the defective ones.

I need more power.

Max arched an eyebrow. Now that was interesting. Was Jacob admitting to weakening? Or was he just a greedy, impatient, power-hungry bastard? "Yeah," he agreed, "and for that you need the key, I know. So, um, in the meantime...?"

Jacob rose to his feet in one smooth movement and Max took an involuntary step back. *Father a child for me, incubus.*

"Wh—"

Father a child. Impregnate a woman and bring her to me. There is power in the children of incubi, more so than in the children of men. I will drain it from her.

"Okay. Good." Max didn't want to father a child. To do that meant he couldn't just shag any old woman, it had to actually *mean* something. Bloody rules. He scratched the side of his face. "And this extra power will stop the wardens reverting, will it? It's just that—" His eyes widened as his throat tightened, and he choked and lifted his hands to claw at his neck. Jacob hadn't moved, but his eyes had narrowed and that was enough for Max to know he'd stepped over the line and was probably about to have some of the power drained out of *him*. He tried to speak, and spit flecked from his lips. "I know...you're not...weak," he managed to gasp.

Jacob released him and Max dropped like a stone, spluttering and coughing on his knees. Jacob returned to his seat and turned the lights off, leaving Max wondering how the hell he was meant to find his way out.

Relax, incubus.

A door opened and Max crawled through it. He flopped out onto the pavement back in Brislington. He lay on his back, gazing up at the grey sky. Dillon's face appeared above him and he groaned.

"Thought you wanted to speak to the boss?" Dillon asked.

Max frowned. "I did." He picked himself up and brushed down his clothes before grabbing Dillon's arm and tugging him with him down the street. "Come on, kid. Free time's over."

Chapter Sixteen

Nick had walked numbly onwards. The world became little more than a blur around him. He tried not to think, because his mind wanted to show him his mother and so he pushed all thoughts gently aside so that he didn't grab on to them. A familiar tug in his chest made him move his feet, a feeling that drew him nearer the trees, a feeling he could ignore, usually, but which he gave in to now. In the early evening, he stumbled into a lifeless children's play area. A huge oak tree, its roots bulging through the earth around it, sat in the centre of the park, calling to him. He rounded the swings to reach it, dried bark chippings—repulsive to him, like hard skin foot-shavings—pressed into the ground under his shoes. He reached out to the tree and joined with it the moment his touch connected, and he almost laughed in relief as he pressed his forehead against the rough trunk.

Two hundred years of history flooded his senses, an overwhelming cacophony of noise and images, until he passed it and reached the heart of the tree. Its roots plunged deep into the earth, warming and grounding, their glacial movements instantly calming. With a deep sigh, he raised his awareness up through the trunk and into the branches, smiling at the wind whispering over the leaves. He didn't know how long he listened to that, but he stopped when it began raining and pushed back down and forced himself to not seek out the network of other trees but to pull himself free.

He opened his eyes and stared at the furrows and valleys of the bark, brushing his fingertips lightly over them. Blinking, he moved back, wiped moisture from his face, and wondered what the hell the time was. He wasn't wearing his watch, and his phone was gone. Esme would be worried and if she rang the hospital to find out if he was still there, then surely she'd discover his mother had died and only worry more.

It was nighttime, but streetlights glared, and Nick found himself glaring back at them, hating everything manmade and unnatural.

They caused her cancer. The thought sprang to him before he could stop it. All this manmade shit? Evil, *cancerous* shit. He reached for the tree again and stirred its roots into action, forcing it to wake up, to rise up... Wood creaked and groaned and the ground beneath his feet began to split. Nick clenched his jaw, stared past the swings and the streetlights to the road beyond, and pushed the roots deep underground, forcing them to change direction. He would *destroy*—

"Stop this."

The voice startled him. Nick stopped and turned like a guilty teenager caught reading pornography. A warden stood behind him, an old warden, tall, with white hair and paper-thin skin.

"They will only fell the tree if it causes damage," the warden said. "You know this."

Nick folded his arms. "What do you want?"

The warden smiled. "You work for Locke & Co?"

"I don't work *for* them, I am them. The co bit, I mean. And anyway, I never thought we should've been called Locke & Co. If anything, Locke & Lode is much better—at least it's amusing! But oh no, we have to do what Allery says, just because she's going to live forever and has to put up with it for longer than the rest of us. Well, she can shove her immortality up her arse."

"Do you have the key?"

Nick frowned. "Not yet." He didn't want to let on to the warden that they'd had the key and had lost her. He backed up. "I'm just going to go, okay? It's late. My girlfriend will be worried about me."

"We are patient, Mr Lode," the warden said. "But only for so long."

Nick walked away, scowling to himself. He buried his hands in his pockets and kept his head down, looking up whenever a car passed in case he had the chance to flag down a taxi. Esme would shout at him. She'd probably cry. He wouldn't tell her about his mother, though; he couldn't handle the sympathy. He lifted his gaze as a car drove by again but it wasn't a taxi and so he walked on.

*

Allery had risked leaving Deni alone in the hotel room while she nipped to a supermarket and bought them something to eat. She'd rushed around the shop, spending more than she'd intended and fighting visions of returning to find Deni gone—either taken by wardens or snuck off to score a hit. She was in the hotel lift, cursing herself for buying loo roll, when her phone beeped. She took it from her pocket and read the text from Esme.

Nick's missing. Where r u? Pls answer my calls!

The lift doors opened but Allery barely noticed until somebody squeezed in beside her and she had to lurch forward to stop the doors from closing. She pushed her phone back into her pocket, grabbed her bags, and headed out of the lift. She wandered down the hallway back to their room. Nick probably wasn't *missing*. He'd probably got stuck listening to a damn tree and was standing on his own somewhere zoned out like a right idiot.

She swiped the card at the door, struggled with the bags and the door handle, then entered the room. Deni sat in the window, gazing out over the city, and didn't turn round.

"I've got us lots of food," Allery said, taking the bags to the dressing table and pulling out a multi-pack of crisps. "So, we can stay here until you're all better, okay? And I've got cleaning stuff and toilet rolls and tampons and all sorts of things."

She looked at Deni. She had showered, at last, and her dark hair was damp on her shoulders. "Den?"

Her phone buzzed again and, annoyed, she took it out.

Driscoll gone 2. Dont no if looking for Nick. Didnt say. Worried.

"I don't know why you don't turn it off," Deni said, not turning away from the window. "Your friends keep contacting you and you keep ignoring them, yet you keep the phone on."

"That's because..." *They might need me.*

She sat on the bed and read the text again. Nick missing and now Driscoll too? Esme was probably overreacting. Nick was late home or something and she was being impatient as per usual. Driscoll had probably gone to look for him and the pair of them would be home soon. She sighed.

Deni moved from the window, approached Allery, and took the phone from her hand. Allery opened her mouth to protest, but this was the most active Deni had been in a while, so she said nothing and just watched as Deni lifted the phone to her ear before passing it back to her.

"It's ringing."

Allery took the phone. "You called Esme?" She listened to the ring. She had no idea what time it was in England now. Maybe Esme had sent the texts and fallen asleep, maybe she'd sent the texts hours ago and they'd only just come through.

The ringing stopped and Esme answered, her voice excited. "Al! Where are you? Are you coming home? You've got to get here quick. I don't know where Nick is. He went to see his mum and didn't come back! And now Driscoll's gone, and I can't get any answers from anybody! Where are you?"

"I'm..." She rubbed her forehead. Driscoll would find out where they were anyway after she'd withdrawn the cash. What was the point in lying? "I'm in Australia. What time is it there? Where are you?"

"Two in the morning," Esme said. "Couldn't sleep, too worried! I'm back at Merrybell."

"I thought we decided it wasn't safe there any more?"

"I don't know! I don't know what's happening any more. Nick's gone, Al, he's gone, and his phone goes straight to voicemail. I'm on my own."

Allery cursed softly and gazed at Deni, who shrugged at her and went to pick out a packet of crisps. Esme sucked in a sob at the other end of the line.

"Don't worry, okay? Just stay put. Driscoll's probably gone to find Nick; they'll both be back soon."

"Are you coming back?"

Allery watched Deni as she shoved a handful of crisps in her mouth. Her hands were steady now, at least, but her skin was still deathly pale and clammy. She looked away. "I don't know. Deni's...not well still and I can't just hand her over to the wardens. I can't."

"Not well," Esme scoffed. "She's a junkie."

"I know." Allery lowered her voice and turned away, though Deni could still hear her. "We're working on getting her clean. She's clean now."

There was a thump at Esme's end as if a door had closed, then Driscoll's distant voice, "Esme? Can't find the lad. Esme? Are you asleep?"

Allery cut the call before Esme could try to talk her into coming home. Driscoll was with her now. She'd be safe. *But where's Nick?*

Deni sat on the bed by her side and offered her a crisp. "You should go home."

"And leave you?"

Deni shrugged. "Why not? You're not going to turn me in."

"No." Allery took a crisp though she wasn't hungry. "But I can't just leave you on your own. The wardens could find you. I need to make sure you're safe."

Deni smiled and gave Allery a little nudge. "That's sweet. But I'm a big girl."

"Mm." Allery decided not to mention that she thought Deni would be back on the drugs as soon as she took her eyes off her. She squeezed her knee instead. "You look better."

"Every now and then it feels like something crawls across my skin," Deni said, rustling in the crisp packet. "But yeah, I've felt worse." She licked her fingers, screwed up the packet, and threw it across the room.

Allery got up to retrieve the empty packet and put it in the bin.

"Wardens won't get me," Deni said. "They don't even know where I am."

"No," Allery agreed. *Not yet anyway.* She returned to sit on the edge of the bed and stared at the wall opposite.

*

Allery was weird about germs and bugs, she knew that. She understood other people's frustrations when she tidied up after them or wiped down the surfaces they claimed to already have cleaned. Esme asked her once what she was worried about—*"it's not like it'll kill you"*—and yes, of course she was right. It wouldn't kill her, but she didn't fancy spending an eternity blind, say, after a bout of granular conjunctivitis or, as was her current worry, paralysed from Australian encephalitis.

So, the buzzing she'd heard at night, when she laid awake thinking about Esme, had convinced her there was a mosquito in the room somewhere. She'd got out of bed and cleaned the room as quietly as she could, hoping to eradicate any nasties it'd left behind as well as eventually coming across it to kill it. Deni had woken up and scowled at her and eventually managed to convince her to go back to bed with the promise that they'd buy some insect repellent in the morning.

Allery woke early, thought about heading out on her own, but eventually waited for Deni with the decision that it would be good for her to get out of that stuffy room. Plus, she could keep an eye on her if they were together.

They left the hotel and headed into the city. The weather was warm enough that Allery rolled up her sleeves and vaguely pondered the notion they'd need to buy summer clothes at some point, while Deni didn't seem particularly bothered. Sunlight reflected off the windows of the skyscrapers, reminding her of Nick, and how much he'd hate it, and a pang of guilt touched her chest before she pushed it away.

She spotted a chemist over the road and was just about to point it out to Deni when a figure standing very still among the crowds of people-traffic caught her eye. Her heart thumped and she clutched at Deni's arm so tight it caused Deni to curse and pull away.

"It's a warden—a drifter," Allery said, keeping her voice low and her eyes on the teen girl. "How the hell did they know?"

Wardens were very good at staying unnoticed unless they did something that attracted attention. Allery knew the girl wouldn't rush them unnecessarily, so she stayed put and tried to work out what to do. She couldn't ask Deni to open a door, not right in the middle of the street.

"She's tiny," Deni commented. "We could take her."

"Not here we can't. Come on." She turned and headed back the way they'd come, glancing back over her shoulder to make sure the girl was following. "We'll lead her somewhere quiet."

"And then what?"

"Find out who sent her, how she knew where we were, and convince her to leave us the hell alone."

Allery had to walk some way before the city even began to become anything close to quiet. The skyscrapers disappeared and the crowds of people dwindled but traffic still passed them by. When Allery passed a row of bikes, she briefly thought about taking one and losing the warden, but she *had* to find out what the girl knew. The warden followed them at a distance, alone, and seemingly not caring that they knew she was behind them. In one way, she wished the girl would act.

Deni lagged behind, grumbling about her feet. She heaved a loud sigh as they passed by an empty playing field behind a wire fence. "Let's just go in there. It's a cricket pitch; there's nobody playing cricket now." She didn't wait for Allery's reply. Instead, she turned to the fence and began hauling herself up it.

"There's barbed wire on top of that," Allery said. "You'll cut your hands open, get down." When Deni ignored her, Allery marched over to her and grabbed her by the hips to pull her back down. The warden had stopped by the bikes. Deni squealed in protest like a naughty toddler.

"Over the road," Allery said, pointing. Trees grown too large burst out of the pavement like stakes out of a vampire's chest. The analogy made her smirk—it'd been a while since she'd staked a vampire, bloody things, and she quite fancied having another go. A boarded-up building, the door covered in graffiti, lay behind the trees and she grabbed Deni's hand to pull her across the road towards it.

After waiting for a lull in the traffic, Allery yanked the board away from the door and went inside. Broken boards at the windows at the back of the building let in just enough light to see rubble, broken glass, cigarette butts and, worst of all, condoms on the ground. Allery shuddered.

"Surely she's not stupid enough to follow us in here," Deni commented.

"I'm hoping she is, but she might have back-up. Can you fight?"

"No."

"Right. Okay." Allery grabbed a piece of rubble and passed it to Deni. "Hit her with this if she tries to touch you. If all else fails, open a door and scarper."

"Open a door?" Deni laughed. "Yeah, 'cause it's that easy."

Just as Allery opened her mouth to reply, the warden squeezed through the door and stood opposite them. She didn't say a word.

Unsettled, Allery clenched her fists. "Who sent you? How did you know where to find us?"

The girl smiled. "Jacob," she said. Her accent hinted at South Africa.

Allery didn't know a Jacob, but she presumed he was the leader of these teen wardens. That was good information to have, she supposed. She wondered if her dad would know the name.

"How did you know where to find us?"

The warden laughed. "We have a spy, Miss Locke. We know everything. We will always be one step ahead. Now." She held a hand towards Deni. "Hand over the key."

Deni hurled the piece of rubble and it glanced off the girl's chest, causing nothing more than a grunt. Taking advantage of the momentary surprise, Allery rushed the girl and forced her back against the wall, pressing her arm across her throat. "Tell me more about this spy," she demanded. "Now!"

"No, we need to go," Deni said, her voice urgent. "I can feel doors—"

There was a crack in the air and a flash of light as a door opened in the room and two teen boys, both taller than Allery and Deni, stepped out. The door closed as quickly as it opened, and the gloom settled around them. Allery ignored them and instead bared her teeth at the girl as she pushed harder with her arm. "Tell me."

"Shit." Deni dodged as the boys made to grab for her and ran down the length of the room to get away.

Annoyed, Allery pushed the girl aside and ran after the boys. *God, I need Esme.* Deni feinted, switching direction to run back towards Allery. Allery kept going and as Deni passed her, she dropped down and kicked out, knocking one of the teen's legs out from under him and sending him crashing to the ground. She got up, snatched a piece of rubble, and hurled it at the second boy. It smacked him squarely on the back of the head.

As the boy hit the ground, she turned her attention back to the girl just in time to see her pull a door open and allow two more wardens to enter.

"Den," she called. "Time to get out of here. Open a door!"

Deni had stopped running and now stood with her hands on her knees, gasping for breath. "I *can't.*"

Cursing inwardly, Allery joined her and backed up, away from the approaching wardens. She glanced back to check how close they were to a window. "Go," she told Deni. Then she ran at the wardens.

She kicked the first in the stomach even as the second passed her. One of the tall boys had recovered, the one she'd knocked off his feet, and as he came at her again, she smashed her fist into his face with a yell. Then she jammed her elbow into his stomach for good measure and looked back to see the other two wardens pulling a struggling Deni away from the window.

She ran, pulled the South African girl away, and punched the other warden in the face. Deni scrabbled uselessly at the boarded window again and stomped on the girl's hand when she grabbed her ankle.

Allery was pleased she wore her heavy boots. She kicked the board from the window with a shout and practically shoved Deni through it. The warden she'd hit with the rubble still hadn't risen, and she briefly wondered if she'd killed him, but the other four were made of tougher stuff. The lead girl lunged at her and grabbed her around the waist, holding tight as she barked orders at the others to get after the key.

"Run!" Allery yelled, just about catching sight of Deni racing across the scrubby waste ground. She elbowed the girl in the ribs and managed to pull the final warden away from the window, though the other two had escaped.

"Give it up, Miss Locke," the girl said, as she and the boy closed the space between Allery and the window. "The key is ours now."

Shit. Allery dragged a hand through her hair. *I've fucked up royally.*

She turned from them and ran for the door.

Chapter Seventeen

Good news. Allery strode along the pavement, her gaze flicking towards any sudden movement. *I've lost the wardens. Bad news, I've also lost Deni.*

If the wardens got hold of her... No, she just had to hope Deni had escaped, and she had to find her again quick. She stopped walking, pulled her phone from her pocket, and flicked through the contacts. Her finger hovered over Driscoll's name. No, he couldn't teleport that far. He couldn't help. Shit. No good contacting Esme, and Nick wouldn't be any help either, especially not if he was still missing. They should've all stayed together, then none of this would've happened.

You shouldn't have panicked about the bloody mozzie.

Angel. Now there was a name she hadn't thought about in a while. Her name was ironic, given that Angel was in fact a demon, and not just any demon, but a direct descendent from Asmodeus, king of demons. She also happened to be an ex-girlfriend. They hadn't parted on bad terms—they had both simply been too busy for a relationship. Allery had just set up Locke & Co and Angel had a hell of a lot of wrath to dish out. Animal abusers were her thing.

Unable to come up with a better idea, Allery sat on a bench by the side of the road and dialled Angel's number. It rang six times before she picked up.

"Allery?" Angel's voice was loud. A man screamed in the background, Angel grunted, then there came another shriek which cut off with a gurgle.

"You're working," Allery said. "Sorry. I shouldn't have bothered you."

"No, no! Don't worry." The sound of pitiful begging followed by a meaty thud. "I haven't heard from you in ages. How you doing?"

"Uh. Yeah. Not bad. Well—"

"*Por favor, Dios, no. ¡Tener compasión!*"

Allery frowned. "Where are you?"

Another scream. "Spain," Angel replied. "That was the last one, fucking bastards. We can talk now."

"Great." Allery rubbed her head. "I need help, Angel. I didn't know who else to call. I've lost something...someone, and I'm on my own here. The wardens—"

"Put the phone down, Al. I'll be right there."

Allery placed the phone on the bench. Smoke rose from the screen, then, in the blink of an eye, Angel was sitting beside her. She lifted her backside and passed the phone back to Allery. Their hands touched, Angel's skin black and smooth and beautiful, and Allery swallowed and quickly pushed her phone back into her pocket.

"You missed me, I can tell," Angel said, smiling.

Angel looked like an African queen, no, a goddess, dressed in jeans and a tight T-shirt. She wore an ornate scabbard at her hip, which concealed a silver dagger.

As Allery stared, Angel moved her hand and placed it on Allery's thigh. She leaned close, as if to kiss her. Allery jerked back. "I haven't got time." *God, I really haven't got fucking time.* "This is important. I need your help."

Angel sat back and folded her arms, watching the traffic pass. "You can't blame me, Al. Lust is in my DNA. Lust. Revenge. Wrath."

"Yeah. Listen, have you heard of a Jacob?"

"I have heard of many Jacobs," Angel said with a sigh. "I have probably killed many Jacobs. Are you looking for a specific one?"

"I think so. You're aware of the new wardens, right? These kids that just appeared out of nowhere. Well, one of them mentioned a Jacob to me. I think Jacob's their leader. Maybe he's another warden, or a demon."

"Jacob the demon." Angel looked thoughtful as she gazed across the street. "I know a Justin. You sure it wasn't Justin? He is one sick fucker."

"It wasn't Justin."

"Then I can't help you, babe." Angel got to her feet. "Was that all you wanted me for? Would've preferred a booty call."

Allery smiled a little. "I'll keep that in mind for next time," she said. "No, it wasn't all. The wardens are after a friend of mine—we had a run-in with them a moment ago and they took off after her. I need to find her before they do."

"A girlfriend?"

"A friend friend. She's *really* important. I'm talking she-could-bring-about-the-end-of-the-world important if I don't find her."

Angel sat by her side again. "You're close to her. That's good. It means I can get the details I need." She smiled and leaned close once more. Their lips touched and as Allery opened her mouth, Angel literally sucked information from her. It passed from her lips in a shimmering blue mist.

Angel sat back and swallowed. "Deni McClellan," she said. "Scrawny-looking thing." She laughed. "You've got better at controlling what you share, Al. You won't tell me why she's so special, eh?"

Allery shrugged. "Sorry. You've got enough to go on, though, right? You can find her?"

"In a heartbeat." Angel sat still and settled her hands on her knees. Her eyeballs turned very white very quickly and Allery suppressed a shudder. Still in her trance, Angel reached for Allery's hand and held on tight. "Are you ready?"

"Nobody's going to notice this, are they?"

"Have some faith, Al."

Before Allery could protest further, black smoke enveloped the pair of them, writhing around them as if it were a living thing, filling Allery's lungs and making her cough.

When the smoke cleared, Allery still coughed for a moment. Then she straightened up and eyed the veil of grey mist surrounding them. Lights twinkled.

"Fuck," she breathed. "We're in the Third."

"Looks like it," Angel agreed, drawing her dagger. Lights approached, shifting in the mist. Angel slashed with her blade and they retreated briefly before creeping closer once more.

A scream pierced the air and Allery's heart jumped. "That was Deni. Den!"

She ran towards the sound, the lights in the mist recoiling and pressing forward again around her. A dark shape caught her eye, sprawled on the ground. Angel ran by her side, swiping at the lights.

"Deni." Allery dropped to the girl's side and took in the state of her. Deni had her trembling hands pressed over her face and she'd curled into the foetal position. She sobbed and let out another pained scream.

Angel stood guard over them, dagger ready. "What is it? What's happening?"

"I...I don't know." *It's like she's going through withdrawals.* Allery fought with Deni's hands to remove them from her face and get her to look at her. "Den. Deni, it's me. You're safe."

Deni's chestnut gaze met hers, then she sat up and flung her arms around Allery, squeezing her tight. "Kill me. Kill me."

"No!" Allery stroked Deni's hair and shot Angel a worried look. "What happened? I thought you said you couldn't open a door?"

"Can't," Deni whispered, trembling, her voice muffled by Allery's shoulder. "Shouldn't. It uses *so* much energy. Had to... Had to..." She pulled back and stared at Allery, her eyes blown wide. "It feels like I'm being ripped apart!"

Then she screamed again.

The mist and the lights jerked back from them and even Angel, standing over them, looked spooked. Allery grabbed Deni and pulled her close again. "It's okay. You're safe now! What do I do, Den? How do we get out of here?"

Deni sobbed and shook her head. "I have to do it again."

Allery rocked her in her arms and looked at Angel. "Can you get us out of here? Take us to...to Esme."

"Can't take the both of you, Al."

"Bollocks." The violence of Deni's shaking worried her. Allery chewed her lip and looked around. She could just make out a tower of dark in the mist. She turned back to Deni.

"Don't hate me," Deni said, wiping her eyes messily on her sleeve. "Take me there."

Cursing inwardly, Allery lifted Deni in her arms and, looking to Angel for her to protect them, headed to the tower. The lights shone brighter and grew bolder around them. Something *snarled* in Allery's ear, setting her teeth on edge.

They made it to the tower's opening and Allery hurried inside, where she lowered Deni to the ground. She recognised the place from when they'd been before, and the pleading look in Deni's eyes told her what she was after.

"I'm sorry," Deni whispered, her voice echoing in the chamber. "I need it."

Allery hesitated. "We can wait. We'll wait it out, wait for you to get stronger."

Deni groaned and curled up. Allery looked at Angel standing in the doorway, her dagger still held ready. "Can they possess you?" she asked.

"Yeah. A demon-possessed demon. Let's not try it, eh?"

"God." *Father, help me.* Allery moved away from Deni and felt around in the dark, the stone beneath her hand damp and cold, her eyes wide as she tried to see. She touched a little bag and brought it forward to reveal Deni's stash of heroin. Again, she hesitated.

Deni cried out in pain. Something outside the tower roared.

"Whatever it is you're going to do, Al, you damn well do it!" Angel shouted.

Allery thrust the packet into Deni's hand and closed her fist around it. She turned away so she wouldn't have to watch, forcing down the guilt, the disgust, the pain, and joined Angel in the doorway.

"They're coming," Angel said.

"Maybe I should let one take me," Allery said. "Then you can kill me. That'll keep them busy for a bit."

There was a ripping sound and a flash of light. Allery turned to see Deni had torn open a door. She swayed on her feet but smiled grimly. "Go," she said. "Go!"

Angel needed no second telling, and she disappeared through the door first. Allery followed and, just in case, she grabbed Deni's hand to pull her with her as she passed.

They emerged into the living room of the cottage in Cricket St. Nicholas.

Chapter Eighteen

Nick woke with a gasp. He frowned, wiped drool from his chin, and pulled himself upright in the car seat, tugging at the belt. He blinked out of the window, realising he was in a layby in a lane…somewhere…and looked over at the driver.

"Good morning, Mr Lode." The warden, a boy in his late teens, didn't even look up from the newspaper he was reading.

Nick suppressed a groan. Last night it had seemed like a good idea to take the offer of a lift. This morning, not so much. "Where are we?" he asked.

"Heading home."

"My home?"

The warden folded his newspaper and smiled. He looked past Nick out of the window and Nick followed his gaze to see two more wardens, a young girl and another lad, heading back towards the car. They got into the back seat and clipped their belts.

"We're so pleased you decided to join us," the girl said, as the driver started the engine. "You'll be a great asset to our cause."

"Mm." Nick folded his arms, wishing he had his phone so he could text Esme. "Look, what you said last night, about the whole being evil thing being a lie. I was pretty cut up, I would've believed anything. You've could've told me the sky was green!"

Nobody seemed to care. He looked at the driver, then at the two in the back. The girl smiled at him.

"Hey, how about we go and pick up my girlfriend? She can join us too, right?"

"All in good time," said the driver.

Nick drummed his fingers on his knees. *How are you going to get out of this one?* He looked out of the window again, at the beech and whitebeams standing tall behind the hedge, and decided it definitely didn't look like the road back to Merrybell.

"Will I get to meet Jacob?"

"Of course." The driver glanced over at him briefly, his black eyes unblinking. "You'll like Jacob."

Nick wasn't sure. To be fair to the wardens, they hadn't harmed him or forced him to go with them. They seemed like nice kids, really, if it wasn't for the spooky eyes. Maybe they weren't so bad after all.

"Are you really sure opening up all these doors is a good idea?" he asked. "You know it lets all sorts of undesirables through."

"That is why Jacob needs the key," the girl in the back explained. "With all doors open, supernaturals will be able to come and go as they please. They won't end up trapped here."

"Yeah, but..." Nick frowned and crossed his arms again. Would that be a bad thing, really? If creatures could return to their own dimensions, then surely they'd be more likely to leave this one alone? "I'm not sure—"

"I can pull over," the driver said. "You're not a prisoner. You can leave whenever."

Nick twisted to look at the two in the back. The girl sat up suddenly and closed her eyes. Her lids flickered.

"We have a situation," she said. "Cryptid trapped near Bishop Sutton. We're the closest team—Jacob wants us to handle it."

"What do you reckon, Mr Lode?" the driver asked. "Want to come and help, or shall I drop you off?"

This is a trick. They were tricking him into making him think they were the good guys.

Or they were the good guys.

"Okay," he said. "Sure. I'll come with you."

*

Nick's apprehension grew as the driver pulled off the road and stopped the car in front of a gate. He could make out the top of a dilapidated farmhouse over the hedge and, after he'd taken off his seat belt and joined the others outside, he spied a lake adjacent to the farm. The teens climbed over the gate and dropped down into the field, and he followed them. The four of them were silent as they scurried across the grass. Nick had thought the farmhouse abandoned until he heard a dog bark. He wondered if the animal had spotted the cryptid. Since the teens were making towards the lake, and seemed to know what they were doing, he presumed they had some sort of intel to which he wasn't privy. So he didn't question them when they crouched beside the reeds and looked towards the water.

He looked back at the farm and saw the dog—a white bulldog, rather than the collie he had been expecting—pacing up and down behind a chain-link fence.

"Do we know what it is?" he asked, keeping his voice low.

"Hodag," said the oldest teen, the driver.

Nick had no idea what a hodag was. He couldn't recall the name, either, and was just about to open his mouth to ask another question when the driver shushed the group.

Something splashed in the lake. Nick had been on too many outings with Locke & Co to be foolish enough to believe it was just a duck. He pushed his hands into the earth as he crouched beside the wardens, grounding himself for a fight.

"It'll be after the dog," the girl whispered, after a few painful minutes where nothing had happened. "They eat bulldogs."

Weird.

The driver shushed the girl. Nick pushed his senses through the grass roots, extending outwards until he met with the reed beds and other plants going into the water. Something *dark* sped through the lake and he gasped and pulled back, heart thumping.

The creature burst out of the water and sailed over the top of them, spraying them with water. It landed and ran, a great lolloping run, towards the farmhouse and the dog. Two of the teens raced after it. Nick stared.

The creature was barrel-chested with short, thick legs like tree trunks, an odd frog-like head, and the spiked tail of a stegosaurus. He'd seen some things in his time but this... It hardly seemed real.

As he watched, the teens reached inside their jackets and drew forth short sticks, which erupted into long staffs at the press of a button.

"Can you help, Mr Lode?" the driver asked, still crouched by his side.

"I'll try."

"Good. Help my friends lure it back to me. I'll open a door, and we'll send this thing home."

It sounded easy. There was a strange sense of disconnect about the whole thing—he'd never worked with anyone other than

Locke & Co. Could he work with anyone else? The hodag, a head taller than the wardens and three times as wide, had stopped its charge and swung its tail, knocking the girl's staff from her hand. Behind them, the bulldog barked and barked.

Nick ran for the beast. He pulled up short when it turned to grin pointed teeth at him. He dropped to his knees and touched the ground. An oak grew alone in the middle of the field and its roots spread and stretched away beneath the earth. He reached for them, asking them to wake up and rise.

The other teen menaced the beast with his staff, only to have it pulled from his grip and tossed aside. It lashed out with its claws and knocked the boy to the ground.

Nick gritted his teeth. The ground trembled beneath his hands and roots burst forth, wrapping around one of the hodag's back legs. Meanwhile, the girl snatched up her staff and smacked the creature on the head and neck until it began turning back towards the lake. It roared in frustration and ran for Nick, ripping tree roots from the ground.

Nick cried out and dived aside. The hodag swung its tail and Nick grunted as it struck his lower back, sending him flying forward. He picked himself up and turned to see the wardens brandishing their staffs at the hodag once more.

"Nick!" the driver called. "Bring it this way!"

He glanced back at the boy standing by the lake and nodded. With a cry, he dashed behind the hodag, clapping and stamping, until it turned and flashed him its teeth.

"Chase me," he goaded it.

The hodag charged and, cursing, Nick turned and fled towards the lake. "Open the door," he shouted at the warden. "Open it!"

He'd almost reached the boy when the hodag swept him aside with a clawed foot, hooking him up into the air like a ragdoll. His eyes widened, and he plunged into the lake. The cold took his breath away, and he thrashed and swallowed water until he surfaced, coughing and gagging and slapping the lake's surface as he tried to keep afloat.

He wiped his face and blinked at the wardens watching him from the lakeside. The driver waved at him. "Good work!"

"Has it gone?" Nick called. "You sent it back?"

"It's gone."

Nick swam towards the wardens, then stood and waded out onto dry land, shivering. It was only then that he realised the beast had caught him with its claws and he was bleeding from a wound on his right arm. It throbbed dully.

"We'll get that cleaned up, Mr Lode," the girl said. "Don't worry."

"Right," he agreed. He thrust his hands under his armpits and followed them back to the car.

Chapter Nineteen

Allery wandered out of the kitchen with a cup of tea for Angel and passed it over as she joined her on the sofa. Deni snoozed opposite them, curled up in the armchair.

"There wasn't any milk," Allery said. "Well, there was milk, but it had lumps in it so…"

Angel smiled. "Vegan, remember?" She sipped the tea and eyed Deni. "Can you take care of her?"

"I think so."

"Do you want to take care of her?"

Allery gazed at Deni, at the worry lines creasing the girl's pasty skin. "Yes," she said. There was an ache in her chest she hadn't felt for a little while and she pulled her attention away as Angel leaned forward to put her mug on the carpet.

"I have to go," the demon said, getting to her feet. "Work calls."

"Oh." Allery stood, a little disappointed Angel wasn't sticking around but thinking maybe it was for the best, really, if she and Deni were on their own. She saw her friend to the door.

"If you ever need me, babe, just call, okay?"

They kissed and Allery watched as Angel walked down the garden path and set off down the road towards the centre of the village. She lingered for a moment, half-expecting wardens to appear, when Deni stirred and she closed the door and turned back inside.

"I've always been safe here," Deni said, her voice soft. "It was my granddad's house."

"Your granddad the angel," Allery said. She supposed the wardens wouldn't come looking for them there, thinking they'd fled the place. For now, at least, they were safe. "Are you all right?"

"Tired," Deni murmured.

Allery picked up Angel's mug and sat on the sofa, torn between taking it back out to the kitchen to wash up, and watching over Deni. "Go to sleep, if you want."

"I wish I wasn't like this," Deni said.

"The key?"

"A junkie." She covered her mouth with the back of her hand as she yawned. "It's my stupid mother's fault."

"Your mother made you a junkie?"

"Mm."

Allery raised her eyebrows. Deni had closed her eyes and seemed about to drift off again, but she chuckled softly and muttered, "Bitch. Her and her stupid boyfriend."

"We can talk about it," Allery suggested. "If you want."

Deni pulled her eyes open and gazed at Allery, her face expressionless. "I wish she was dead. I wish she had died and stayed dead." She shifted in the armchair, sitting up and pulling her feet up beneath her. "Her and her creepy boyfriend, they gave me the drugs—all sorts of drugs, we worked up to heroin—they said it'd help me control my powers. They wanted to control me, that was all."

"Arseholes. They can't hurt you any more. Your mum's never getting out of that prison."

"Good." She held out her hands and smiled a little when she realised they weren't trembling. "Wish I knew what happened to Jacob, though."

"Jacob?" Allery's blood ran cold. She put the mug back down and sat forward, her heart thumping. "It can't be. No, it is. Of course it bloody is. Jacob! He's the guy who's after you now."

"What?" Deni looked unsettled, glancing towards the door as if Jacob might suddenly appear, and Allery wished she hadn't said anything.

"We'll stop him," Allery said, getting off the sofa and kneeling in front of Deni. She took her hands. "He won't get you, I promise. Do you remember what he looked like? If he had another name?"

Deni shook her head. "Just Jacob. I don't know. I was young, I didn't pay much attention. He was...ordinary looking." Her eyes flicked to the door again.

"He doesn't know we're here."

"How did they find me? After all these years. I was safe here. I was safe until you showed up." She pulled her hands from Allery's and clambered over the arm of the chair to get away from her. "Granddad was keeping me safe, and now they *know* where I live. You led them to me, Allery!"

Allery stood up and swallowed. "I don't know... I didn't mean..." The tip-off... What if it'd been Jacob all along? Had he led them to Deni's mother thinking she'd reveal the whereabouts of her daughter? She dragged a hand through her hair. Dillon had been safe until she'd gotten involved with Sophie. Deni had been safe. She shook her head and went to the window, gazing out at the road, half-expecting to see the wardens waiting for them once more. What was it the warden had said about the spy? They had a spy.

A black cat jumped up onto the wall beside the gate and proceeded to wash its paws. Allery stared at it. The spy could be anywhere, be anything. She chewed her lip.

"I'm going to bed," Deni said, turning and heading from the room. "You do whatever the fuck you like. I've had enough."

Allery drew the curtains and fingered the phone in her pocket.

*

Max snorted himself awake and sat up in bed, going over the events of the night before. He'd gone clubbing, got very drunk, and ended up pulling some bird and going back to her flat for a shag. He scratched his head and squinted towards where the ratty curtains let in the daylight. The bloody kids would come looking for him soon, badgering him to get back to work. Well, he was bloody working—Jacob wanted a demon baby and that meant shagging mortals.

His date lay face down on the pillow beside him, her bleached-blonde hair splayed around her head like an insipid bird's nest. She'd probably sleep for the rest of the day after he'd come inside her. At least she wasn't dead. He pressed his fingers against her neck, just in case, and found that, no, she was definitely not dead. Briefly, he pondered fucking her again but decided he couldn't be arsed, so he got up, scratched his bollocks, and wandered through the flat looking for the toilet to take a piss.

He froze in the hallway at the jangle of keys and the front door opened a moment later. A buxom redhead did a double take before scowling at him. "You still here?" she asked, closing the door behind her and hanging her keys on the hook. "Jana?" she called. "I'm on my lunch break. You up, hun?"

She didn't seem at all put out that Max was naked, so he placed his hands on his hips and treated her to a full frontal. "Do I know you?" he asked.

"You tried to hit on me last night when you were shit-faced," she said, passing him in the hall and heading into the lounge. Max wandered after her. "You're not my type."

"Oh yeah?" He perched himself delicately on the arm of the faux leather sofa, watching as the woman went to the fridge and took out a cartoon of juice. He remembered her, now he thought about it. The kid, what's his face, Dillon, had pointed her out in the street and they'd followed her and her mate at a distance until they'd ended up at the club and he'd shooed the kid away.

It's my mum, Dillon said. Max couldn't work out the brat's feelings on the matter but decided he was gonna fuck her and have her carry his child just for the craic.

"Susie, innit?" he said.

"Sophie." She grabbed a bowl of something from the fridge and stuck a fork in it. "Oi, get your sweaty bollocks off the sofa."

Max stood up, his skin peeling away from the fabric with a slurp. He held up his hands in apology. "Sophie. Look, you mind if I have a shower? Your mate's not gonna wake up any time soon—silly bitch had too much to drink—but I want to be around when she does, you know? Make sure she's all right."

"You're a gent. Knock yourself out."

Max didn't fail to notice the sarcasm in her voice. He liked her already. All he had to do was get her to like him back, then getting her up the duff should be a piece of cake. He gave her a wink, ignored her eye roll, and turned to make his way to the bathroom.

He spotted the photographs on the side table beside the sofa as he went. Photographs of Dillon.

*

Allery had almost dozed off to sleep on the sofa when she heard Deni rush from her bedroom upstairs and into the bathroom where she started vomiting. She frowned and sat up, wondering if she should go and offer some comfort. Her phone beeped and she took it from her pocket to read the text.

> *Nick STILL not back. D getting angry. Says he'll drag u home himself if u don't come back soon.*

"Shit." Allery called Esme's number and held the phone to her ear. It had barely begun ringing before Esme was shouting at her.

"Where are you? Nick's *gone*, Al, he's vanished! It's those bloody wardens. They've taken him, I know they have. Are you still in Australia? Driscoll's threatened to go and fetch you. He's not happy you ran out on us. What are you even *doing*?"

"Calm down. I'm sure the wardens won't have Nick. Why would they? I'm not in Australia any more, I'm..." She rubbed her forehead and listened as the toilet flushed upstairs. "I'm looking after Deni. She needs me."

"Where are you?"

Allery sighed. She couldn't do this on her own any longer. She needed Driscoll's level head and Esme's light heart. The gang had to get back together, find Nick, and kick Jacob's arse.

"I'm at Deni's cottage," she said. "Back in Cricket St. Nicholas."

"Right, we're coming."

Esme cut the call before Allery could say anything else. Allery left the phone on the arm of the sofa and headed upstairs. She tapped softly on Deni's bedroom door and let herself in. Deni lay on the bed, pale and shivering, and Allery sat on the corner, tucking her hands between her knees.

"Esme and Driscoll are on their way over."

"Why?"

"Because we need to work together, find out where we can find this Jacob, and kick his arse so that he'll never bother you again."

Deni lay trembling and silent, until she curled up in a little ball and began sobbing. Allery, taken aback, sat and stared for a moment. Then she shifted herself down the bed and rubbed Deni's back gently. "Hey, it's all right! Den?"

Deni sat up and wrapped her arms around Allery, sobbing into her chest. "You'd do that for me?"

"Kick Jacob's arse? Too right! I'd take on Satan if it kept you safe. Course, it might be a different story if I were mortal."

Deni laughed a little. "Must be nice not being afraid of anything."

"I'm not unafraid," Allery admitted, rocking Deni. She breathed in the scent of her, smiling that she smelled of toothpaste and not sick. "The thought of living forever is terrifying. Watching everybody I love die. Watching the world change. I won't age beyond how I look now—imagine having to look at this face every day for all eternity!"

Deni pulled back and swiped at her tear-stained cheeks before gazing into Allery's eyes. "I wouldn't mind that, you know."

Allery was sure her face must've turned red. "Well, thanks." She brushed Deni's hair aside and kissed her forehead.

They held each other again and curled up on the bed together, their limbs entangled. Allery ran her fingers through Deni's hair until her shivering ceased. They lay quietly for a while.

Deni lifted her finger to Allery's lips. "You know, you might've compromised my safety but I'm not lonely any more."

Allery chuckled. "Thanks. I think." She took hold of Deni's hand and kissed it. Then kissed her on the lips, hesitant until Deni responded. Their kiss was soft and dry until Deni opened her mouth and Allery tasted mint on her tongue. She shifted on the bed, moving on top of Deni, breaking the kiss to press her lips across Deni's jawline instead, tasting salt tears. She moved down her neck, her kisses featherlight.

Deni's hands found their way beneath Allery's T-shirt, cold hands that Allery wanted to warm up. "Wait," she said, and she sat up to remove her T-shirt.

Deni lay beneath her, an odd half-smile on her face. She traced a finger from Allery's navel up to a scar just beneath her breastbone. "How did you get this?"

"Stab wound," Allery replied. "An angry bokor thought he could kill me."

"A what?"

"Bokor. Voodoo priest. You know, zombies and the like."

"Probably wasn't surprised when you came back to life then."

Allery laughed. "You'd think so, wouldn't you? No, he shit himself." She leaned down again and kissed Deni's throat as Deni chuckled. Deni's hands traced multiple scars on her back before she unhooked Allery's bra. Allery moved to throw the item to the floor.

"Allery," Deni said. "I'm usually a bit self-conscious. And I think the last time I did this I did it in the dark. With a man."

"The last time you did this was with me. We were both drunk."

"Poedan," Deni said, softly. She wriggled out from beneath Allery, pulled off her top, and chucked it to the carpet with Allery's bra. She held out her arms to show Allery the track lines.

Allery ran her hands up Deni's arms to show her that she

didn't *care* about any of that. Then she took her face between her hands and kissed her again, hungry, letting out a soft moan when Deni brushed her hands over her breasts—even though her hands were bloody cold—encouraging her, letting her know it was okay. They lay together again, kissing and touching, exploring every inch of each other's bodies, kissing, licking and nibbling, slowly removing the rest of their clothes to reveal yet more scars. They moved against each other, and Allery held Deni as close as she could, wanting to protect her and—"Yes, there," she murmured in Deni's ear. "Harder"—and maybe get her to forget about everything but this moment, just like she wanted to.

When they were done, they lay back on the bed side by side and Allery, her chest heaving and her skin with a sheen of sweat, let out a slow breath to combat the buzzing in her ears. She raised her eyebrows at Deni as Deni propped herself up on an elbow and traced a finger down her chest.

"That was fucking amazing," Deni said.

Allery couldn't help but grin, pleased with herself. She shifted comfortably. "Yeah," she agreed. She watched as Deni touched a long scar on her right thigh.

"Werewolf," Allery explained. "That one didn't kill me, but it did almost take my bloody leg off."

"How come," Deni said, settling back down beside her, "you're not a werewolf then?"

"I'm a supernatural. Werewolves can only turn humans into werewolves."

"Oh right." Deni clasped her hands across her chest and stared at the ceiling. "So, Esme wasn't born a werewolf?"

Allery smiled a little. The familiar bittersweet pang of regret whenever she thought of Esme bubbled up in her chest and dissipated. Esme would never be hers. Their love was platonic only and as she gazed at Deni she realised that was okay. It was okay. "No," she said, softly. "She wasn't."

"You know a lot about all that stuff."

"Well, it's my job. Or it was." She frowned. "No, it still is. Or it will be. I just have to sort a few things out first."

"Like me."

"Like you," Allery agreed, leaning over to kiss Deni's cheek. "And Dillon. That's my ex's son—he's one of Jacob's now but I'll find a way to free him. There must be a way."

"I guess." Deni looked over at Allery and smiled. "I feel okay now."

"I'm glad," Allery said gently. "Let's keep it that way."

Deni nodded, and Allery gazed at her until she fell asleep.

Chapter Twenty

Max hung around the flat all day, waiting for Sophie to come home. Jana didn't wake—he knew she wouldn't—and he didn't hear from the wardens at all; little delinquents were probably too busy causing havoc somewhere. He poked around the flat and found a box under Sophie's bed containing newspaper clippings and police reports concerning Dillon's disappearance. He guessed Sophie would be home just after five, so he cooked up a meal for the pair of them using a couple of fillets of salmon he found in the fridge. He briefly debated laying the table and lighting some candles but didn't want to come over as trying too hard.

He was just taking the fish out of the oven, singing along to the radio, when the front door opened and Sophie called, "Something smells nice, Jan!"

He flashed Sophie a grin as she walked into the kitchen. "Thanks."

"Oh, it's you." Sophie scowled. "Well, if you two are planning a romantic evening I'll head out."

"No, wait, this is for you. Uh, us." Max turned to lift his home-made chips from the oil and plonked them onto some kitchen towel to mop up the excess fat.

"Where's Jana?"

"In bed still. She woke up earlier, but she's not feeling too great so has zonked out again. Hungover to buggery."

Sophie plonked her handbag on the kitchen worktop beside Max. "Don't you have a home to go to?"

Max nodded. If he wanted Sophie to fall pregnant, he couldn't use his incubus charms on her—he'd have to get her to like him the human way. "Yeah. It's just...it's quiet there. Ever since my daughter ran away, I don't like spending much time there."

Sophie folded her arms across her ample bosom. "Ran away?"

"Yeah." Max cleared his throat and plated up the food. "After her mum died, well...I was a bit of a shit dad to be honest, too busy grieving myself to see she also needed help. I guess she thought she'd be better off elsewhere."

He noticed Sophie's expression soften slightly and he passed over a plate. She took it from him. "Thanks. That's terrible. You don't know where she is?"

Max shrugged. He took his own plate of food to the lounge and sat on the sofa, looking to Sophie to join him. She sat by his side. "Police have looked. Reckon they're still looking. But I dunno. Bunch of useless bastards. She's probably joined a cult, they reckon. There's a lot of that happening."

Sophie nodded. She ate a couple of mouthfuls of salmon before she spoke again. "My son, Dillon, he ran off and joined a cult. I've tried looking for him myself, but..." She shook her head.

"Hey, you mustn't give up," Max said, pointing his fork at her.

"I won't. I've hired a private investigator. That's the only reason I'm still working. The man costs a fortune, but Dillon's worth it, you know?"

"I get that." He watched Sophie eat, struck by how full her lips were.

"What's your daughter called?"

"What?"

Sophie looked at him. "Your daughter. What's her name?"

"Oh!" Max thought about it. What was that girl's name? The one Dillon mentioned. "Tia. Her name's Tia."

"Pretty name."

"Yeah? I thought it was slutty at first; took her mum a while to convince me."

Sophie laughed and Max smiled at how her face lit up. "Slutty? You can't say that!"

"What?" Max grinned. "I just did."

"What are you like?" Sophie nudged him and turned her attention back to her food. "You sure Jana's okay?"

"She'll be fine once she's over the hangover."

"You really like her?"

"Jana? Nice enough lass and everything but she was really just meant to be a one-nighter."

"At least you're honest." Sophie stuck her hand down the sofa cushion and pulled out the remote control for the TV. "Surprised you hung around this long. All just to make sure she's okay?"

"Hey, I'm a nice guy."

"Sure you are." She turned the television on.

Max, pleased she hadn't told him to bugger off, enjoyed his food in companionable silence. He definitely liked her, and it was more than the tightening in his pants, too. Once they'd both finished eating, he took the plates without having to be asked and headed into the kitchen to wash up. When he glanced back to the sofa, he caught Sophie watching him with a bemused smile on her face, though she looked away quickly when he gave her a wink. He vaguely wondered if Jacob would release Dillon if he asked nicely enough. He snuck another look at Sophie and smiled.

*

Nick poked at the bandage the girl had wrapped around his arm and offered her an awkward smile when she placed a plate of food on the table in front of him—a jacket potato and baked beans, steaming hot from the microwave. The wardens had taken him "home", an abandoned run-down school in Bristol. The building, crumbling and covered in ivy and other vines which pushed through the brickwork to the inside, was conveniently hidden be-tween office buildings and a multi-storey car park. If it wasn't for nature trying to reclaim the building, Nick would've felt stifled and out of sorts. The place was full of children—wardens—though they were silent and morose and didn't seem at all interested in him. It was their base, the driver had told him, the place that sheltered them while they waited for instructions from Jacob. It had elec-tricity, as a couple of the older lads were pretty good at siphoning power from the office block, though Nick had no idea how they did it. He supposed it wasn't all that bad, considering, and it was cer-tainly a hell of a lot better than Merrybell.

He picked up his knife and fork and tucked into the food when his stomach growled at him. The girl sat opposite him at the table and watched with a blank expression. He'd asked for her name, but she couldn't remember it, so he mentally referred to her as Jane.

Jane Doe.

"Why do you work for Jacob?" he asked, pretending to be more interested in pushing beans onto his fork in case he scared her off answering.

"We want to help," Jane said. "We know what an honour it is to be chosen by him. The power he gives us, the opportunities…it's more than any of us had when we were human."

Nick frowned a little. "You're not human at all, any more?"

Jane shrugged, so he ate more of his food.

"Jacob really just wants doors opened so the supernaturals can come and go as they please?" he asked. "Preferably go. I'm really not sure them coming here is a good idea. I mean, there's so many *people*."

"Would you like to meet Jacob?" Jane asked.

Nick pushed his plate away and wiped his mouth. "You know what, I do." It was about time somebody actually found out something constructive about the whole situation, Allery's guesswork, the old wardens' evasiveness… If he, Nicholas Lode, could sit down and talk with this Jacob and find out what he was planning, then maybe it'd transpire there was no problem after all and they were fighting against each other for no reason. That'd make him a bloody hero in his book. He got to his feet and when Jane offered him her hand, he took it.

Lode & Co. It had a much better ring to it.

*

Nick's eyes took a moment to adjust to the new light as the flash from Jane's door left after-images burned into his retinas. He blinked and stared at the trees surrounding him, reaching above him in the half-light. He had no idea where they were, but the forest was ancient; every twisted root and gnarled branch swathed in history, calling out to him to touch—

Jane snatched at his hand. "Don't get lost," she warned.

He put his hands under his armpits and followed her as she

set off through the trees, dry leaves crunching beneath her feet. "Where are we?"

"This is where Jacob lives."

"Yes, but *where*? Are we still in our own dimension, even?"

Jane glanced back at him but didn't answer his question. He looked back over his shoulder, his skin crawling at the feeling someone was watching him. Beech leaves rustled as he walked through them and a breeze made the trees creak and sway but there was no other sound to be heard.

He could make out a large sessile oak—ridiculously large, its girth had to be twelve metres at least—through the trees. It was ancient, a thousand years or more, and he gaped at it as they approached. It didn't call to him, didn't speak, didn't beckon him to touch it and join with his ancestors and he staggered back when he realised why. The tree had been silenced, a thick metal band wrapped around its trunk.

"I don't...I don't want to be here," Nick muttered, his heart pounding as he stared at the oak.

Jane stopped just before the tree and looked back at him, unperturbed by his change in mood. "Jacob is here," she said.

Nick swallowed hard and pulled his attention from the tree as a figure stepped in front of him. It was a warden, an old warden, his skin papery and pale, his eyes black as coal.

"Mr Lode," he said. "An honour to meet you."

Nick stared at him, then at the oak once more. "Did you do that?" he demanded, waving a hand at the metal.

Jacob raised his eyebrows and glanced back at the tree. "No." He smiled at Nick. "Humans do not understand that these things hurt us."

"Humans." So, he was still in their realm. Good. He faced Jacob. "What do you want? Why are you doing all this? Taking children?" He flapped a hand at Jane. "We're pretty convinced you're the bad guy at the moment."

Jacob held out his hand for Jane and she took it and came to stand by his side. "I love my children," he said. "I love them when no one else will. They are from broken homes, or they have run away. They are lost, or sick, or sad. They have been abandoned by their humans."

Nick frowned. "And opening doors, you think this is a good idea?"

"We need balance," Jacob said, his voice calming. "We need... freedom. My warden brothers are the ones who want control. I want only the natural order of things, whereas they want restrictions. They seek to blinker the humans, to cut them off from the other worlds. I want only equality."

It sounded good. Nick couldn't work out if it was *too* good to be true. His head pounded and his heart became a dull ache in his chest. His eyes flicked to the oak once again.

"I understand your concern, Mr Lode," Jacob said. "Please, let me do something for you to convince you of my good will."

"Do something for me?"

Jacob let go of Jane's hand and spread his arms wide. "I can offer you a gift. A glimpse of your mother, your *real* mother, or—"

"No!"

"Or something else. I sense a great pain in your past. Let me take it from you."

Hands held him down.

"No." Nick folded his arms. "I don't want you to do anything for me. I..." *Esme. The wolf.* "Wait. My girlfriend...she's a werewolf. Could you, I don't know, could you make her human again?"

Jacob smiled. "Of course."

"Really?"

"You must bring her to me."

"That easy? You won't hurt her or anything?"

"Mr Lode, I have offered you a gift. It's up to you whether you accept it."

Nick nodded. He looked at Jane, ready to head back, and she, understanding what he wanted, ripped open a door. It shimmered softly in the air between them, and Nick caught a look at Jacob's face—lips parted, eyes closed—before the warden straightened his expression and gestured at the door. "I hope to see you soon, Mr Lode."

"Yeah," Nick said. "Likewise." He turned to Jane and together they walked through the door.

Chapter Twenty-One

The only thing remotely approaching a meal at Deni's cottage was a bag of chips and chicken nuggets in the freezer, so Allery cooked it all up while Deni dozed upstairs. She had just pulled the chips from the oven when a knock at the door made her heart pound.

Shit. She'd left the gun in Australia, neatly stowed away in the dressing table drawer in their room. It'd give the housckeeping staff a fright, that was for sure. She removed the oven gloves, went into the lounge, and picked up the guitar propped beside the bookcase. She went to the door, brandishing it like a weapon.

The knocking came louder, more insistent. Allery took a breath to steady her nerves and opened the door a crack. Esme barged in.

"At last! Can we *do* something about Nick now, please?"

Allery turned instead to Driscoll. He looked drawn and haggard, but he offered her a grin and clapped her on the shoulder as he passed. "What are you planning to do with that, serenade us to death?"

Allery put the guitar down and closed the door. "Sorry."

"It's good to see you again, Al," Driscoll said. "Sure, something smells grand. Are you cooking?"

"Chips in the kitchen." Allery reached for Esme's hand as Driscoll headed off, following his nose. "We'll find Nick. What happened?"

Esme pulled away, heaved a dramatic sigh, and flopped down on the sofa. "He went to see his mother at the hospital, and he never came back. I've tried ringing and ringing and he's not picking up. Driscoll's looked for him and can't find him. He's gone; he's just disappeared off the face of the Earth!"

"I'm sure—"

"No, you're not sure! They've taken him. Those bastards have taken him!"

Allery sat by Esme's side. "Have you tried ringing his brother?"

"Of course I have. He was no help."

"And the hospital?"

"Nobody knows where he is, Allery!" Esme's voice became shrill, and Allery held up her hands to calm her down.

"It's all right."

"No, it's *not* all right!"

Deni opened the lounge door and glared at them both, her hair dishevelled and clothes crumpled. "What the fuck's all the shouting for?" she hissed. She pressed a hand to her temple and squinted into the room.

"Nick's still missing," Allery explained.

Driscoll emerged from the kitchen carrying two plates. He set them both on the coffee table in front of Allery and Esme. "We'll look for him again in the morning," he said. "Who wants ketchup?"

Allery shook her head. She gave Esme's hand a squeeze. "Driscoll's right. We'll look for him in the morning and we'll find him, I promise." She'd ring Angel; she'd find him. Now, though, she just wanted to eat and sleep and not worry about Nick.

Driscoll came back with two more plates, handed one to Deni, and perched on the arm of the sofa to eat his own.

Allery watched as Deni picked up a chip and popped it in her mouth, pleased to see her eat. She took her own plate onto her lap and stuck the fork into a chicken nugget. By her side, Esme stared at her plate unmoving, until eventually, beaten, she reached for a chip and blew on it daintily.

"Things are going to get better now," Allery said. "I can tell."

*

Allery slept beside Deni and dreamed of her father. He sat upon a cloud playing a lyre and he winked at her when he noticed her clambering up a ladder to reach him. Allery, vaguely aware she was dreaming, knew her dad had somehow manipulated the scene into something he found amusing. She eyed the cloud dubiously and didn't attempt to stand on it in case she fell through. Instead, she clung to the ladder and reached out to touch his hand. Behind him, a black cat jumped up onto a wall, hissed, and leaped into a bush.

The cloud turned grey.

"Somebody got the door," her father said.

Allery opened her eyes to the gloom of the bedroom, blinked, and glanced over at Deni. All was quiet in the cottage—Esme slept in the room next door and Driscoll had taken the sofa. Her feet were cold, and she debated getting out of bed to put some socks on.

A creaky floorboard made her freeze. *It's an old house. They creak.* Still, her heart thumped. She sat up and when the floorboard creaked again, she nudged Deni to wake her up.

"What?" Deni murmured.

"I think there's somebody outside the room," Allery whispered, getting out of bed now.

"Probably Esme going to the loo." Deni squinted at her in the gloom.

It probably *was* Esme going to the loo, now she thought about it. She wandered to the door and opened it a crack. Somebody stood in the hallway, somebody male, his back to her. She drew in a sharp breath, and he spun around, teeth flashing in the dark as he grinned at her. Thinking quickly, she hurried out into the hallway and closed the door behind her, shutting Deni in.

"Who the hell are you?" she demanded, loud enough to wake Esme.

He approached her, and she realised he was a demon and that he was trying to charm her. Waves of seduction emanated off him, making her lightheaded. "Won't work, incubus," she said. "You're not my type." Then over his shoulder she called, "Es!"

The incubus chuckled. "Lads?"

There was a scuffle of feet and a muffled voice before two wardens dragged Esme out of the second bedroom, one with his hand clamped over her mouth. The other had a gun against her temple.

"Silver bullet," the incubus explained.

Allery stared. It had taken her a moment to recognise him in the half-light of the hallway, but it was definitely him. That shock of white-blond hair unmistakable. "Dillon?"

The boy didn't even blink. His hand didn't falter on the gun. The incubus looked from him and back to Allery again. "You two know each other, eh? Bugger me if that isn't interesting."

Allery backed up until she was against Deni's bedroom door. "Driscoll!" she cried.

The incubus smirked. A girl ran up the stairs and halted at the top. "Hurry up and fetch the key," she said.

"Keep your knickers on," the incubus snapped back at her. He offered Allery a smile. "Look, how about we make this nice and easy? You ask your little friend to come out here, and I'll ask my mates not to blow the werewolf's pretty head off?"

Esme squirmed and let out a muffled squeal as Dillon gripped her arm tighter. Her blue eyes were blown wide as she stared at Allery. Nerves fluttered in Allery's stomach. "Dillon," she said, "listen to me. You don't want to do this. I'm a friend of your mother's. Put the gun away and I'll take you back to her, okay? You remember your mum?"

Dillon looked at the incubus, as if for guidance.

The incubus rolled his eyes. "Just shoot her. I haven't got all day."

"Wait, wait!" Allery cried, raising her hands as Esme screwed her eyes shut. Behind her, the bedroom door opened, and Deni touched the small of her back as she joined her in the hallway.

"It's me you want, right?" she said. "Leave my friends alone."

"Skinnier than I'd imagined," the incubus commented. He waved her away from Allery and she went to stand by his side.

"Don't do this," Allery begged her, holding her hands out imploringly towards Deni. "Please."

"Let Esme go," Deni said, "and I'll go with you."

"Nah, that's not how this works," the incubus said. "You come with me, *then* my pals will let the girl go. Tia, shift your arse out the way."

The warden moved from the top of the stairs and went to grab Allery. She pulled her away from Deni.

"Wait," Deni said. "How about...you come with me instead?" She winked at Allery, then tore open a doorway. She pulled the incubus through it with her and slammed it shut before anybody had time to react.

Tia, cursing, let Allery go and opened a door herself before diving into it after Deni. The boys, clearly not knowing what to do without instruction, released Esme and ran after Tia. They disappeared through the door seconds before it closed.

Esme dropped to her knees, her hands trembling as she lifted them to her mouth to cover a shaky sob. Allery hurried to her side and put an arm around her shoulders. "You're okay," she said. "You're okay."

Where the hell is Driscoll? What have they done to him? She stared at the empty space in the hallway where the door had closed.

Then there was a tearing sound, and the hallway lit up as a doorway opened in the ceiling. Deni dropped down, landed heavily, then rolled over onto her back and half-laughed, half-groaned, as the door closed again. Allery checked Esme was okay, then rushed to Deni's side.

"What happened? Are you all right?"

"We need to get out of here before they follow me," Deni said, struggling to sit up. "Feel so fucking weak."

Allery hooked Deni's arm around her shoulders and pulled her to her feet; Esme, recovered sufficiently to help, did the same. They made their way awkwardly down the stairs and Allery hit the lights in the lounge.

"Driscoll?" she called. She could hear him vomiting into the sink in the kitchen and she frowned. Esme helped her get Deni onto the sofa, then she left them and peered into the kitchen. Driscoll moved away from the sink, wiping a hand across his mouth.

He waved a hand at Allery.

"I'm all right. Had too much to drink. Let's get out of here."

"How did they get in?" Allery asked, going back to help Deni up again.

"No fecking idea," Driscoll said, staggering to the front door to open it. "I was drunk, I'm sorry. They snuck past me, the bastards."

Allery snatched up the car keys from where they hung beside the door and passed over the care of Deni to Driscoll, who led her down the garden path with Esme's help. Allery locked the front door, briefly inspecting it for any signs of a break-in, then hurried after the others. She pressed the button on the car keys and spotted which car was theirs when the indicator lights flashed on a silver Ford across the road. She opened the back door and made sure Deni was settled before getting into the driver's seat. Esme joined her in the front.

"What do we do now, Al?" Esme asked.

"Uh." Allery gripped the steering wheel and stared at the empty road. The streetlights had gone off now that the sun was coming up, and birds twittered in a tree on the village green.

"You might as well take us back to Merrybell," Driscoll said. "We can recuperate there for a bit until we can work out a plan of action."

"Right." Allery turned the key in the ignition and started the engine. "Yes. Good idea."

Her mind buzzed as she glanced over her shoulder before pulling out into the road. The wardens were closing in. Nick was missing. And she'd found Dillon only to lose him again. She cursed under her breath and drove out of the village.

Chapter Twenty-Two

"Shit!" Max marched through the door, kicked a lamp post, and turned back to glare at the wardens as they joined him back in Cricket St. Nicholas. "Shit. Shit. Shit. We were this close! That stupid bloody cow." He kicked the post again and sat angrily on the wall bordering the park. He hated the village now, hated the place, hated staring at the church over the road where Bill died—where Bill was *murdered* by those horrible bloody brats. He grabbed Dillon and pulled him close. "Locke knows you," he said. "How?"

"Mum's ex," Dillon said.

Max shoved him away. He could use that. After he'd seduced Sophie and got her pregnant, he could use her to lure the immortal and her key to him, then he'd hand them all over to Jacob and be done with the whole sorry affair. He was sick of being a skivvy now; if Jacob wasn't so damn terrifying, he'd tell him to bugger off.

He scratched his thigh, then waved a hand at Tia. "Opening those doors hasn't upset anything, has it?"

"No."

"Open a door to the sixth, eh? Let some imps out."

"What for?"

"Because I'm pissed off, that's what for," Max snapped. "Let the imps out. Let them destroy this place, then those bastards won't be coming back here again."

He jumped up off the wall and folded his arms. Tia, rolling her eyes, turned from him and with Dillon's help, opened a door. It had barely opened fully before an imp was clawing its way out. The creature had brown-red skin, sharp teeth, pointed ears, and a mean little face. It looked like a hideous bald monkey. With rabies. Max fetched a kick at it as it jumped at him, and it growled and darted off into the village. More imps quickly followed and either disappeared or hung around to destroy parked cars, setting off alarms. The door snapped shut, catching an imp half-in half-out, and its severed body dropped to the pavement and crawled on its arms a little way, gibbering, until it expired.

Max sniffed and set off down the road, glancing back at the kids to follow. *Bloody place.* He was looking forward to seeing Sophie again. He wondered if he should get her some flowers.

*

Allery almost groaned when she opened the door to Merrybell Cottage and caught the smell of damp and rats. Instead, she turned to help Deni inside and took her to the sofa. Deni's skin was cool and clammy, and she trembled and muttered as if she wasn't quite conscious. Driscoll also looked pale, though he offered Allery a smile when she met his gaze.

"Just need to sleep it off," he said, and he wandered off

through the cottage, the sound of his footsteps disappearing up the stairs.

Esme stood in the middle of the lounge as if she were frozen with her arms hugging her waist. "We need Nick," she said.

Allery didn't think Nick would've been much help given the situation, but she nodded anyway. "Get some rest, just for a little while, then we'll find him, I promise."

Esme rolled her eyes and headed off after Driscoll, muttering complaints about the smell of mould and mouse droppings as she went.

Sunlight streamed through the broken lounge window and Allery left Deni long enough to cover it over with a blanket. Then she returned to her side, sitting on the floor by the sofa, and stroking Deni's hair. She heaved a sigh. "It's okay," she murmured. "Just rest. I'll watch over you. Get your strength back. You're okay, everything's okay." She gazed at Deni until she settled and lapsed into a calmer sleep.

Methadone. I'll get Driscoll to find some methadone. She checked Deni once more, then got up to fetch a bucket to fill with water, deciding she might as well keep busy otherwise she was in danger of falling asleep herself. Once her friends were recovered, she'd give Angel a call. Nick would have to manage without them for a few hours more yet. *He'll be fine*, she told herself. *If the wardens have him… If they've done something to him…* She shook her head at herself and headed off to get the water.

*

Allery didn't know how long she'd spent cleaning and tidying Merrybell's living room, but it couldn't have been much more than an hour before Esme joined her in the kitchen. She'd pulled her blonde hair back in a business-like ponytail and she'd changed into a pair of jeans which told Allery that whatever it was she was planning, she was serious.

Allery put down her cloth and raised her hands as Esme opened her mouth to speak. "Let me stop you right there," she said. "You cannot go out and find Nick on your own."

"So, *help* me! Please!"

Allery took her phone from her back pocket. "I'll call Angel. She'll be able to connect with you to locate him. It just means she'll have to..." She frowned, a twinge of jealousy poking at her chest.

"To?"

"Kiss you."

Esme shrugged. "Angel's the demon you were dating before Sophie, right? Just after we moved into the offices. Yeah, I remember her. She lectured me on my lipstick; said it was tested on bunnies." She pouted at Allery. "I didn't mean to hurt any bunnies."

"No," Allery agreed, listening to the phone ring. It was taking a while to pick up and Allery hoped she wasn't imposing on Angel's work time again.

Eventually, the demon answered. "Babe, you still in the village? Are you seeing what I'm seeing?"

"What? No, what's happening?"

"Place is crawling with imps. You might want to get your crew together and get over here."

"Shit." Allery looked at Esme, who frowned at her expression. "Yeah. We'll be right there."

"Al? This doesn't look like an anomaly. Somebody's purposely let these things out."

"Bloody wardens." Allery scratched the back of her head and paced the kitchen. "Are the old wardens on the scene? If anybody's called the police, or the fire service, or, shit, the press—"

"There's an old guy in the park," Angel said. "Got his eyes shut.

He must be doing something because where I'm at nobody's moving at all. It's like they're all frozen."

"Manipulating space-time," Allery said, more to herself than Angel. She mouthed *"get the weapons"* to Esme and watched her hurry away. "I'm not sure how long he'll be able to hold them. Where are you? Can you get here, like, right now?"

"Course, babe. I'm in the pub—the White Hart, is it? The landlord had been putting down poison for the rats, I was going to show him the error—"

"Can you get here?"

"Put the phone down."

Allery placed the phone on the kitchen worktop and stepped back as it let out a plume of thick black smoke before Angel appeared, sitting on the newly cleaned surface with her legs crossed. She folded her arms. "Now, why do you need me here?"

"Sorry. Can you watch over Deni? Just while we deal with the imps."

Angel jumped down off the worktop. "You owe me, Allery Locke," she said, moving into the lounge. "Big time."

"I know." Allery followed Angel, noticed Deni had woken and was curled up on the sofa with a what-the-hell-is-going-on look on her face, and quickly explained the situation just as Esme and Driscoll joined them. Driscoll had a cricket bat in hand; Esme had a pair of escrima sticks which she passed over to Allery.

"This is all we have?" Allery asked, loosening a notch on her belt so that she could shove the sticks through.

"That's it," Esme said. "I guess we're not getting Nick yet, then?"

Allery winced. "Not yet. Sorry." She sighed inwardly, realising she apologised far too much lately. "Driscoll, car keys, let's go."

"Why don't I stay here and watch over the girl?" Driscoll

suggested. "I'm sure Angel would rather kick imp-arse than baby-sit."

"No, Angel's staying here. I need you with me—no arguing."

Allery headed to the door just as Deni called out, "Don't I get a say in this? I can't come?"

"There are wardens around," Allery explained, turning back briefly. "So no, you can't come. Behave yourself, okay?" She gave Deni what she hoped was a confident smile, though was sure it came across as shaky, before opening the door and heading out into the sun.

"If we found Nick he could've helped," Esme said, jogging to catch up with Allery down the path. "We could've got Nick first."

"We have no idea where he is," Allery explained, as Driscoll unlocked the car. "If he's in trouble, we don't know how long it'll take for us to help him. We need to deal with this *first*."

Esme sighed loudly but she didn't argue her case further and instead got into the back of the car as Allery got into the passenger seat. She looked over at Driscoll. "You okay to drive?"

"Fine," Driscoll said, though he sounded bad-tempered.

Allery said nothing else. She glanced at Merrybell, then watched the cottage disappear in the car's wing mirror. *Deni will be safe with Angel*, she told herself. She drummed her fingers on her knees, deciding she'd enjoy beating some imps.

*

As they drove up the hill back into the village, Allery spotted an imp hanging off a lamp post. She was so distracted watching it that when another jumped onto the bonnet of their car, she gasped. Driscoll slammed on the brakes and the imp fell to the ground. He floored the accelerator and the car bumped over the creature, crushing it beneath the tyres.

"Urgh, I hate imps," Esme commented from the back. "They're seriously gross."

"I'm just glad I've not got alloys," Driscoll said. "Imp guts would be an absolute nightmare to clean off."

"Pull over here," Allery said, as they neared the village green. She unclipped her seat belt and jumped out before Driscoll had even stopped the engine, pulling free her escrima sticks as soon as her feet touched the road.

She ignored the warden on the green, not wanting to distract him while he was busy keeping the area stable, and instead drew back one of the sticks to strike an imp jumping up and down on a litter bin. Glass shattered behind and she stopped mid-strike, turning to see five imps spilling out of the local shop's window, each one gibbering and clutching some sort of stolen item. One ripped open a bag of popcorn and when the kernels sprayed everywhere, the others descended upon the first, screeching and clawing.

"Al!" Driscoll shouted.

Allery turned from the scene. Driscoll pointed to something across the road, and she looked, grimacing when she spotted an imp dragging a severed arm—a human's arm, blood staining the pavement red. She nodded and Driscoll vanished, only to appear behind the imp where he smashed the creature's head in with the cricket bat.

Esme leaped over her, in wolf-form, and tore into the group of five. Allery, clutching her sticks, lashed out at the bin-imp just as it jumped at her, its teeth flashing before she smashed them out of its mouth. Now that they were being fought, imps rallied around, appearing from all quarters to fight back.

Allery ducked as an imp launched itself at her. She turned and caught it in the neck with a hard *thunk*, the blow sending reverberations up her arm. The creature scuttled away, head bent, before she could finish it off. Something sharp bit into her calf, sending hot needles of pain into her flesh, and she jabbed at the imp with the end of the stick until it let go.

Driscoll appeared by her side just as her stick pierced the creature's eye and exploded out the back of its head. "Thatta girl," he commented. "A fair few of 'em, eh?"

"I hate imps." Allery grimaced at the blood splattered over her jeans; she trod on the imp's body to pull her stick from its skull. When she looked up, the wolf had a creature between its jaws and shook the thing like a ragdoll before tossing it away.

"Can you check for any stragglers?" Allery asked Driscoll. "We don't want to miss any."

The leprechaun ran his fingers over his moustache, gave her a nod, and disappeared. Allery rested her sticks on her shoulders, watched Esme briefly, then scanned the area for more imps. Satisfied she couldn't see any, she approached the warden on the green.

He opened his eyes as she drew near. "Miss Locke."

"You've got some cleaning up to do. What'll the story be, rabid monkeys escaped from the zoo?"

The warden didn't blink. "You have the key?"

"Not yet." Allery bent to wipe her sticks clean on the grass, hoping he wouldn't pick up on her lie. "Who's Jacob?"

"You are in debt, Miss Locke. If you do not give us the key, we will take your immortality."

Allery raised her eyebrows. She pushed her sticks through her belt and folded her arms. "Who is Jacob?" she asked again. "If you want the key, you need to help me."

The warden looked over her shoulder and she followed his gaze. Esme, blood soaking her chin and T-shirt, tottered towards them across the grass, muttering "ew" under her breath. "This is *so* gross," she said, as she joined them. "Can't you do anything about the young wardens? This is getting out of hand. This should be your problem, not ours!"

"They are controlled by Jacob," the warden said. "We have no—"

"And *who* is Jacob?" Allery asked again. "We need to know more about him so we can stop him. We can stop all this!"

The warden turned his dark gaze upon Allery. "Jacob will stop once we have destroyed the key. Without the key, he will have no reason to continue this madness."

Allery chanced a look at Esme, who gave the barest shake of her head. Allery could've hugged her. "Tell us about Jacob," she said. "Who is he? How can we find him?"

The warden said nothing for a moment, and neither did Allery, as he looked from her to Esme and back again. Then, he closed his eyes, and his eyelids flickered as he communicated with his fellows. Allery wondered if he was looking for permission to tell the truth or help in concocting a lie.

"He was one of us," the warden said, opening his eyes. "But...a twisted version. Whereas we expend energy opening doors, he feeds off it. Like a leech. He became *heavy* with leeched power and so fed it into his acolytes. With the key, he will be able to open permanent gateways to the other dimensions, and he will feed off the power. He cannot stop himself."

"Like a junkie," Esme said.

The warden blinked at her. "We believe he would gorge himself unto death."

"We should let him do that."

"No," the warden told Esme. "We should not. There is a reason we control the opening and closing of the doors. A reason we create safe rooms. You have seen the chaos supernaturals can cause—we protect humanity from this. We protect them not only from becoming prey, but from multi-dimensional wars. Beyond this, all doors permanently open would lead to a catastrophic event, not only the destruction of this dimension, but of them all. A black hole would consume everything."

"Where can we find him?" Allery asked.

"You cannot."

Allery almost rolled her eyes. She rubbed the bridge of her nose and took a deep breath. "Can *you* find him?"

"No. He has completely separated from us. If we cannot find him, you will not be able to."

"With all due respect," Allery said, "you expected us to be able to find the key when you couldn't. And we *have* found the key."

Esme sucked in a breath. "Allery!"

"It's all right." She looked at the warden. His eyes were closed as he spoke to the others once more. She waited.

"You must hand it over to us."

"*It* is a *she*," Allery said. "And I will *not*." She raised a hand to stop the warden as he took a step towards her, and he stopped abruptly. "Leave us alone. Let us find Jacob. If we can't stop him, if we can't find him, I'll give you the girl."

"You do not have long, Allery Locke," the warden said. He stepped back, closer to the tree. "Leave me. I have work to do."

Allery reached for Esme's hand and turned away with her, walking quickly across the green, her heart pounding.

"Do you have a plan?" Esme asked, struggling to keep up with Allery's longer strides. "Al?"

"Catch a young warden. Force them to take us to Jacob. Kill Jacob." Allery gave Esme a grim smile as she stopped beside the car. "Simple."

Esme didn't look totally convinced. Driscoll, who'd been waiting in the car, rolled down the window and leaned out. "We're clear of imps," he said. "Two dead humans."

"Shit." Allery glanced back at the warden before getting into the passenger side. "Time to go."

Esme got into the back of the car and buckled her seat belt. "Hey," she said. "I've got missed calls from an unknown number. Oh wait, they've sent a text, too."

Allery watched the village pass by. A young man, frozen halfway down his garden path, moved again as if nothing had happened. She turned away and gave Esme her attention instead.

"It's Nick," Esme said. She looked up from the phone to grin at Allery. "He's all right. I've told him to meet us at Merrybell."

And where the hell has he been? "Good," she said. "That's good."

Chapter Twenty-Three

Nick sat on the cracked doorstep of the cottage and watched a ladybird flick its wings until it took off and disappeared out of sight. He tried to picture how Esme would react when he told her she didn't have to be the wolf any more. *Crying.* He smiled a little. *There'll be crying. Maybe she'll pounce on me right here on the doorstep.* He grinned to himself, then got to his feet as he spotted the car coming down the track and waved to greet it.

Allery and Driscoll looked grim-faced when the car pulled up, but he ignored them and winked at Esme sitting in the back. He noticed her unclip her belt before the engine had even stopped. She practically tumbled out of the car and ran up to him, smacking him on the chest before he could react.

"Where the hell have you been?" she asked, before throwing her arms around his shoulders. "I was so worried! You couldn't call?"

Nick hugged her gratefully, breathing in the coconut scent of her hair. "Sorry. I dropped my phone and broke it. Had to get another one. Are you okay? The blood…"

"It's not my blood," Esme said. "I'm okay. Are you?"

"I have some news. Big news."

He released his grip on her as Allery and Driscoll passed by on their way into the cottage. Allery stopped on the doorstep. "It better be good, Nick," she said.

Nick pursed his lips and said nothing. He took Esme's hand and headed inside with her. They gathered in the lounge—Driscoll sitting on the sofa while Allery perched on the arm with a scowl on her face. Esme stayed clinging to his hand as if she were afraid to let him go again. He squeezed her hand.

"I've been with the wardens."

Allery let out a derisive snort. Nick ignored her. "I think we've got them wrong. They're not as bad as all that! This girl, I've been calling her Jane, she's been so nice to me, looking after me. They even do the same job as us! I went with them on a call-out and we had to fight this beast—what did they call it? A hodag. We fought it together—"

"A hodag, Nick?" Allery got to her feet and glared at him. "You are fucking kidding me?"

Driscoll groaned. Nick looked from him to Allery again, wondering what their problem was. He folded his arms. "Yeah. So?"

Allery gave a humourless laugh. "Get your head out the trees. If you knew *anything* you'd know a hodag wasn't a real crypto! It's a hoax. Some shit story made up a long time ago and the wardens have used it to play you."

It was Nick's turn to laugh. He shook his head and rolled up his sleeve. "Yeah, you know everything, don't you, Allery? If it wasn't real, then how did I get this?" He unwrapped the bandage from around his arm and stared at his unmarked skin, a heavy feeling settling in the pit of his stomach. "I don't...understand."

"Course you don't. Do you know what happened today while you were playing with your new warden pals? They opened a door in Cricket St. Nicholas and let out a load of imps. People died. So don't you *dare* tell me they're not that bad." Allery dragged a hand through her hair. "Please don't tell me you've forgotten what happened to our parents. My mum? Your dad? Have a fucking word, Nick!"

"Allery," Esme said, her voice soft.

Nick stared at his girlfriend, numb. Had they lied about that, too? He couldn't tell her now, couldn't get her hopes up only to have them crushed. He couldn't bring himself to speak. Allery barged past him, her shoulder knocking into his. Her footsteps clunked up the stairs, and he finally lifted his gaze to look into Esme's eyes. "Mum died," he said.

"Oh, Nick."

Driscoll got up, gave Nick's arm a pat as he passed, and quietly left the room to give them some space. Nick broke down as soon as Esme put her arms around him.

*

Angel left as soon as she could—work again—and Allery joined Deni in the bedroom. "I've asked Driscoll to pick you up some methadone," she said, when she noticed Deni's hands trembling.

Deni nodded. She picked at a tatty thread sticking from the corner of the grubby mattress. "How'd it go?"

"I found out a bit about Jacob," Allery said, sitting on the bed. "And why he wants you."

Deni looked up, a grim smile on her face. "Do I want to know?"

"He wants you to open all doors, permanently, so he can feed off the power."

"Right." Deni laughed and lay back. She covered her face with her hands, briefly, then scrubbed at her skin as if to wake herself up. "I can barely open *one* door, let alone all of them. Look at the state of me!"

Allery sighed. "You'll get better soon. We'll stop Jacob before he can do anything!"

Deni gazed at Allery for a moment, then sat up and moved close to her, taking hold of her hand and twisting their fingers together. "I heard raised voices. You and Nick."

"Yeah." Allery shrugged and shifted her attention to their clasped hands. "We'll get over it."

"You mentioned your mum."

Allery smoothed her thumb over Deni's hand, noting how warm her skin was. She didn't say anything, wondering if Deni expected a response or whether she could pretend she hadn't heard her.

"She died," she said, eventually. Her voice was so quiet she wasn't sure Deni had even heard. She chanced a look into Deni's eye and her concerned expression told her she had. "Death is...confusing. I understand the concept. I understand the feeling. But the purpose... What's the purpose?"

"You don't have to talk about this," Deni said.

"No. No, I'm okay." She smiled a little. "My mum died, and I'll never see her again. I think sometimes it's a blessing that I didn't know her for long because the pain of knowing her, or loving her for years, of seeing her age... I don't think I could cope with that. This way, I'll forget her sooner."

"You won't forget her!"

Again she smiled. "I'm going to be hanging around for a long, long time. I'll forget her eventually." *Just as I'll forget you.*

Deni raised Allery's hand to her lips and kissed it. Allery

closed her eyes. "She's been gone six years."

"How...?"

"We were at a shopping centre and there was this...shriek. There were phantoms everywhere. Just everywhere. They...they got her. They killed several people; it wasn't just my mum. Nick's dad, too. We didn't know each other at the time, me and Nick. It's how we met."

"Wow." Deni had hold of Allery's hand between both of hers now. It was comforting.

"Me and Nick, we knew we were both supernaturals as soon as we laid eyes on each other. We vowed to find out what had happened. That's when we discovered the anomalies with the doors—that sometimes things get stuck here. We set up Locke & Co to fix these things."

"You are fucking amazing," Deni said, and when Allery laughed, she added, "I mean it! Completely fucking amazing."

"Mm. Well, I don't know about that." She lifted her hand to Deni's cheek and kissed her. "Thank you," she said.

Deni shrugged, and they lay down together on the bed.

Catch a warden. Allery stared at a patch of black mould on the ceiling. *Dillon. Find Dillon.*

Already she could feel Deni trembling next to her and she moved closer and wrapped her arms around her.

*

Max rolled out of bed when he felt like it, peered out of the hotel window, and rolled his eyes when he spotted Dillon waiting outside. The kid sat on the low wall surrounding the car park on the other side of the road, kicking his heels into the brickwork. Max scratched his chin, scratched his arse, then wandered into the bathroom to have a shower. He'd visit Sophie today, woo her a bit more. The kids could cope on their own. Fuck them.

When he was ready, he grabbed his jacket and headed outside, ignoring Dillon even when the boy ran across the road to intercept him.

"Well?" Dillon asked, after he'd trailed after Max for a good ten minutes.

"Well, what?"

"How mad was Jacob?"

"Jacob wasn't mad."

"We failed to get the key. Again."

Max sighed. "Not my fault. I blame you." He turned into the shopping precinct, shoulder-barged a woman who shouted "hey" after him, and continued on, looking for the shop where Sophie worked. He'd have to lose the kid. "Look, Jacob seems to think Nick Lode'll take him the werewolf, then he'll use the pair of them as bait."

"What do you think?"

Max stopped walking and turned to Dillon. "The fairy's broken, up here." He tapped the side of his head. "Trust me. He might just do it."

"Where are you going?" Dillon asked.

"To visit your old mum, so you need to scarper."

"Can't I see her?"

Max muttered curses under his breath. "No, you can't bloody see her. Why do you want to, anyway? You're soulless now. You don't do feelings and shit."

Dillon shrugged.

"You can't see her. Look at the bloody state of your eyes, all creepy and dead like that. You'll give her a heart attack. She'll ask too many questions. Go and fetch Tia and that other one and find out where Locke & Co are hiding now. Make yourself useful."

Dillon scowled at him until Max shooed him away. He shook his head at the audacity of the kid and snatched an orange flower from one of the large planters in the middle of the pedestrian area. He headed over to the clothes shop where Sophie worked and sauntered inside.

The shop was dark and dingy with crappy music playing—presumably to distract people from the ugly clothes on offer—and smelt a little too strongly of Shake n' Vac. He spotted Sophie at the back of the shop, chatting to one of her colleagues, so he painted on his smile and joined her, presenting the flower with a flourish.

"Pretty bloom for a pretty lady," he said.

She wrinkled her nose. "Cheesy as fuck, Max."

"Ah come on," said her colleague, "it's sweet!"

"There, see," Max agreed. "Sweet."

Sophie took the flower off him and eyed it as if it were covered in spider babies. "What do you want?" she asked. "You shouldn't be bothering me at work."

"Yeah, cos you're so busy." Max leaned against the counter. "I want to take you out to dinner. Tonight. Lady's choice."

Sophie and her workmate exchanged a look. The workmate nodded enthusiastically. Max waited.

"All right." Sophie folded her arms across her bosom and smiled at him in such a way that he already knew he wouldn't like the answer. "I've always fancied Aqua Bistro."

"What the bloody hell's that?"

"Posh place on the harbour, overlooking the river. Dead romantic."

"Dead expensive too, eh?" Max straightened up. "It's a deal. I'll book a table, and I'll see you there at eight. Wear something fancy."

He winked at Sophie, and she and her companion giggled together as Max made his way out of the shop, feeling pleased with himself. It was about time he had a bit of good luck.

Chapter Twenty-Four

Allery watched Deni improve on the methadone while Driscoll appeared to go downhill—aging before her eyes, vomiting in the night. When she asked what was wrong, he brushed aside her concerns, saying it was nothing. Just a bug. Nick avoided her as much as he was able in the little cottage; he and Esme disappeared for two days to God knows where. Esme said they "needed a break."

She didn't know how to find Dillon. She wasn't close enough to the boy for Angel to help her and there was no way she could ask for her dad's help without having to approach the wardens. She stewed in the cottage, cleaning things she'd already cleaned, and thought about Sophie. Should she tell Sophie she'd seen Dillon with a demon?

She wouldn't believe me.

She was staring at a crack in the wall in the lounge area of the cottage, wondering if mould spores had already entered her lungs, when Nick cleared his throat. She hadn't heard him come in and he apologised when she startled.

"It's all right," she said, sitting up. "You okay?"

"I need to tell you something."

"Okay." She spoke carefully in case he decided to retreat into himself again.

"When I was with the wardens... I think they took me to their base. I mean, the place was full of them..."

Allery's heart pounded. *You're only just telling me this now?* She said nothing, so that she wouldn't shout.

"It was an old school in Bristol. I can find it again."

"Yeah?" Allery got to her feet, a grin spreading across her face. "That's brilliant! We'll be able to grab one of them and make them tell us where Jacob is—"

"I met Jacob."

"Well, why didn't you tell me?" She held up her hands, to stop herself. "It's okay. Sorry. You're telling me now. This is great, Nick. We might actually be getting somewhere."

"I couldn't tell you where Jacob was," Nick said. "He was in a forest somewhere—it could've been anywhere, and I don't know if he's still there."

"No. That's okay. We can get one of the kids." She turned to go and fetch Deni and the others when Nick grabbed her arm.

"He said he could cure Esme. Is that true?"

Allery looked at his hand on her arm and he let her go. "I don't know. I know we don't know the full extent of their abilities, but I don't know if anybody can cure a werewolf. I've not heard of it happening before. Have you told her?"

"No! I'm not crazy. It'd get her hopes up, and she'd want me to take her to them, and I just... I can't put her in danger. Look, I know if I had her with me, I could just walk straight back in there and I'd get an audience with Jacob right away, but—"

"No, I agree. Too dangerous." She gave Nick a smile. "We're on the same side, remember? I know we have our moments, but I'd die for you guys."

Nick laughed a little. "Yeah. Again, right?"

"Right." She smiled. "Wait there, I'll get the team together. Oh, Nick?" She turned back. "We're good?"

"All good, Al."

Allery relaxed. She left Nick in the lounge and headed upstairs to fetch the others.

*

After seeing how haggard Driscoll looked, Allery ignored his protestations that he was fine and told him to rest up while the rest of them went on without him. The leprechaun gave his car keys to Nick, and Allery left him alone at Merrybell. She sat in the back of the car with Deni and stared out of the window as they bombed up the motorway.

"Penny for them?" Deni asked, her voice soft.

"Hmm? Oh." Allery pulled her attention away from the grass verges and smiled at Deni. "I'm trying not to think of anything. If I think I'll only worry."

"I'll make sure nobody sees me."

"Yeah. I know. And we'll just grab one of them and go. In and out as quick and quiet as we can." *Something usually goes wrong, though.*

Deni reached over and gave Allery's hand a squeeze. Her grip was firm and warm and her expression as untroubled as Allery had ever seen on her. The methadone clearly worked, but that meant if the wardens got hold of her now, she'd have no trouble opening doors if they forced her to.

Deni let go and sat back in her seat, fidgeting uncomfortably. "I could do with a piss," she commented. "Do we get a bathroom stop before we get there?"

"I need a wee, too," Esme said.

"Actually, yeah, Nick, can we stop?" Allery tugged at her belt, wondering if it were just the nerves making her need the loo or if she shouldn't have had that third cup of coffee earlier.

Nick indicated, and they pulled off the motorway and into a service station, where the women practically tumbled out of the car before it had even stopped and headed off to the toilets together.

Allery had never taken much notice of other people before, or rather she'd not taken any more notice of them than most people usually do, but as they bustled about in the service station, buying crisps and sandwiches, chasing after errant kids, or queueing for the loos or cash machines, she was struck by just how *human* they all were. The thought that she'd watch these people change and evolve and die struck her so suddenly that she paused, and Esme had to tug her arm to get her to move again.

"Come on," Esme said, disappearing into the ladies as the queue shortened.

"You okay?" Deni asked.

"I'm fine." She followed Esme into the ladies and chose an empty cubicle. If they couldn't stop Jacob and he managed to destroy everything, then what would happen to her and her fellow immortals?

A deep feeling of loneliness settled in the pit of her stomach and left her staring at the back of the cubicle door long after she'd finished peeing.

"Al, have you finished in there?" Esme called.

"Yeah. Sorry." She sorted herself out and left the cubicle. Esme was reapplying her lipstick and laughing with Deni. Allery watched their faces in the mirror, alight with life. *I will not fail either of you. Jacob's done for.*

She smiled, washed her hands, and the three of them headed back to Nick and the car. She felt better now she'd been to the toilet—it wasn't nerves after all; it was just the coffee.

Just the coffee.

*

They parked across the road from the old school and peered at it through the window. Allery wondered if Nick had been fooled again, if the place was as empty as it looked, until she caught the barest of shadows passing across one of the lower windows which still had its glass.

She unclipped her seat belt. "Nick, stay here with Deni and be ready for us to scarper. Es, you're with me."

"Can't I come?" Deni asked. "I thought I was here to *do* something."

"If they see you—"

"Do they even know who I am?"

"Wardens share information; the ones who've already seen you would've passed your image to every single one of their friends. So yeah, they know."

Deni muttered something inaudible and folded her arms like a sulky teenager. Allery gave Nick a "watch her" look and he nodded in return. Then she left the car with Esme and the two of them walked back along the pavement before crossing over, coming at the school from the direction of the car park. Graffiti covered boarded-up windows, and the space in front of the building had become a dumping ground of waste—broken pallets and bottles, black bin bags, a rotting armchair. Esme wrinkled her nose and mumbled an "ew" as Allery inched closer to the building, looking for a way in. She pointed to an open window up on the second floor.

"How are we meant to get up there?" Esme asked.

"Climb," Allery replied, heading to the wall alongside the building and grabbing a handful of ivy to help herself get a good purchase.

"In these heels?"

"Well, we can't let ourselves in the front door."

She'd just taken her first step up when the wolf jumped up the wall, kicked bits of plant and brickwork out with its claws, and squeezed into the open window before Esme appeared and looked down at her.

"Hope nobody saw you," Allery commented, climbing up until she was close enough to grab Esme's outstretched hand.

"No other way, Al." Esme pulled Allery in through the window and the two of them turned to take in their surroundings.

Dust motes twinkled in the shaft of light coming in the windows along the hallway. Broken plaster and bits of wall and ceiling covered the ground in a way that suggested nobody went there. Muffled voices sounded through the floorboards from downstairs.

"Grab the first one we can," Allery said quietly. "Careful where you step."

She tiptoed along the hallway, picking her way through the debris, wincing when Esme's heels crunched plaster. A wide stairway came off the hallway, its steps dusty and chipped, and Allery peered down to the corridor below, holding up her hand to stop Esme bumping into her.

"I hear voices," Esme murmured.

"Shh."

She took a few tentative steps down the stairs, her heart in her throat and her breath held. At the bottom of the stairs, more doors led off into what she presumed had been old classrooms—one directly ahead of the staircase, wooden slats hanging off the bottom of it, led outdoors, judging by the cool breeze blowing in. A shadow fell across the dirty floor from the broken slats and Allery's eyes widened as the handle turned. Before she could turn and scramble back up the stairs, a teenage girl entered, and their gazes locked. Allery recognised her as the girl from Deni's cottage, the one the incubus had called Tia.

She hurried down the stairs, grabbed Tia, and pressed her back against the wall with her hand over the girl's mouth, as quickly as she could. Heart thumping, she chanced a look back at Esme, who was following her down the stairs.

Tia squealed and squirmed, so Allery gave her a shake to quiet her. "You're going to tell us everything you know about Jacob," she said.

The corners of Tia's black eyes crinkled as she smirked beneath Allery's hand and Allery, annoyed, pulled the girl away from the wall and pushed her instead towards the door.

Esme moved in front of them and opened the door as Allery had her hands full and they stepped out into a fairly undamaged courtyard. Allery ignored Tia's nails digging into her arms and forced the girl onwards, wanting her in the car and out of the way before they bumped into anybody else.

"Allery!"

Esme's urgent whisper made her stop, and she cursed when a boy emerged from the shadows at the other end of the courtyard, a black hood pulled up over his head.

She didn't quite know what to do, so she stood and waited as he approached. As he dropped his hood and revealed his blond hair, she gasped.

"What do we do?" Esme asked. "Shall I...?"

"No, that's Dillon!" She thrust Tia at Esme, then held up her hands to show Dillon she meant no harm. "Do you know who I am?" she asked.

"Mum's ex," Dillon said.

He remembers. "That's right. Do you want to come with us, Dillon? I can take you back to your mum. She's been so worried about you. I can see you're not like the others. You...you still have a soul, don't you?"

Dillon folded his arms across his skinny chest and lifted his chin. "If you could die and stay dead, I'd kill you."

Allery frowned. "Right. Dillon, please. Come with us and we can help you."

"Ask him about Jacob," Esme prompted. Allery glanced at her. She held Tia tight, but the girl was as big as her and could probably break free if she wanted to.

She turned back to Dillon. "Do you know how to find Jacob?"

"I won't tell you," Dillon said. "You can't win; you might as well give up." His gaze flicked to Tia, then back to Allery. "Will you keep Mum away from Max?"

"Max?"

Behind her, Esme cried out. Tia ran past Allery and joined Dillon, where she punched the younger warden on the arm and hissed "shut it" at him.

Esme changed into the wolf and snarled at Allery's side. Allery grabbed a fistful of the animal's fur as it took a lunge towards the wardens and pulled hard to get it to stop.

"Don't!"

The wolf turned and flashed its teeth at her. Allery ignored it. Tia was yelling, *"Help! Help! Help!"*

And behind them, the school door opened.

*

Deni drummed her fingers on the car door, over and over again. She could sense from Nick's posture in the driver's seat that she was beginning to annoy him, but she didn't particularly care. What was taking Allery so damn long? They only had to grab one of the brats and scarper.

"Will you stop that?" Nick asked. "You're giving me a headache."

"What's taking them so long?"

"They've been ten minutes. Chill out, you're worse than Es."

Deni stared at the school. The fact it was full of wardens sent a tingle of fear down her spine, and part of her wanted to run away. The stupid, cowardly, weak part. The part that made her take—

She sucked in a breath. Don't even think about *that.*

She crossed her arms to stop from tapping, then immediately unfolded them and drummed her fingers on her knees instead. She caught Nick's gaze in the rear-view mirror.

"I'm going in," she said, unclipping her belt.

"No, you're not."

"Watch me." She opened the car door, ignoring Nick's curses, and stepped out onto the road. Her stomach flipped and she startled when Nick grabbed her arm.

"You can't go in there. Are you crazy?"

"Little bit." She grinned at Nick. She certainly felt crazy. "I have to do something. This waiting's driving me nuts. Something could've happened to them. Aren't you worried about Esme?"

Nick scoffed. "I'd be more worried about the wardens if Es decides to turn in there."

"I'm going in. I'm sick of being a fucking damsel." She took a step towards the school, but Nick pulled her back again. He let go as a car drove past.

"If I let you in there, they'll get hold of you and then what'll happen?"

"I don't know. I don't care! What was the point in me being here if I'm not allowed to *do* anything?"

"Don't ask me. I'd have left you home."

Deni scratched her arms, distracted. She had to go and save Allery. Why had Allery brought her along if it wasn't for back-up? She couldn't have wanted to hand her over. Swap her for her ex's kid. Wait. Could she? She frowned to herself. Nick was staring at her.

"I'm going in," she said, and she crossed the road before Nick could grab her again.

She got a leg up onto the wall she'd seen Allery climb before Nick caught her up. He pulled her back down and, instinctively, she turned and slapped him across the face.

"Don't do that again," he warned. "I'm trying to keep you safe."

"Sorry." She pushed her hair back from her face. "It's just... I need—"

Somebody screamed, the sound carrying from behind the school. Deni turned back to the wall and this time Nick took off around the side of the building, calling to her to stay where she was.

"Fuck that," she muttered, and she followed him.

Across an area littered with other people's crap, there was a stone stairway leading up to a courtyard where the scuff of feet and raised voices told Deni that she probably needed to be running in the opposite direction. Nick bounded up the steps and she hurried behind.

In the courtyard, wardens circled Allery and Esme, the wolf snapping at any who dared too close. "Don't kill them," Allery shouted, her fingers twisted in the wolf's fur. "Don't hurt them!"

Deni saw the moment Allery realised she was there—the look of horror on her face when she spotted her made a finger of guilt stab at her guts. Nick turned, realising she'd followed him, and snapped at her to stay behind him. He knelt on the ground and pressed his palm into the grit.

As the ground trembled and split and age-old roots from God knows where began pushing up to the surface, the wardens turned. The wolf pounced, swatting aside teenagers as if they were nothing. Allery punched a lad who made a grab at her arm, and yelled again, "Don't kill any!"

Deni took a step back. Roots burst forth from the ground, wrapping around ankles and pushing wardens away. Allery was surrounded now, desperately fighting off more than she could handle.

"I can do this," Deni muttered. All she had to do was open the right door, the one that didn't let out monsters or demons but served as some sort of distraction so they could make their escape. "Shit."

Her fingers tingled, needle points of energy sparking beneath her skin as she reached for a doorway. *Concentrate*, she told herself. *Think.*

She glanced at Allery, then looked again when a warden at least a head taller grabbed hold of her. He stood behind Allery, one arm around her waist, the other clutching her chin. Allery fought his grip to no avail and Deni opened her mouth to shout...what? *No? Stop?* The warden twisted Allery's head in one quick movement and dropped her as soon as her neck snapped.

Deni screamed, the door forgotten. Her whole body shook. She sucked in a breath to scream again, her eyes wide, staring at Allery's fallen body even as the wardens advanced, when Nick took hold of her and forced her to look at him.

"She's immortal," he snapped. "We're not. Get us out of here!"

"What?"

"Open a door!"

Esme swept wardens aside with a heavily clawed paw and scooped up Allery's body. Nick turned from Deni and brought forth more roots, cutting off the wardens' advance. Deni was numb inside though her skin prickled with energy as she found the edge of a door and pulled. Light blinded her, burning an after-image into her retinas as she stepped through the door and trusted the others to follow.

Drained, she sank to her knees on the dusty ground as soon as the door closed. The wolf laid Allery down and transformed back into Esme, who crouched beside Deni and put a comforting hand to her shoulder.

"She'll come back," she said.

"Can they follow us?" Nick asked. "Where are we?"

Deni shook her head. "Not through that one. It's closed for good." She stared at Allery's body and frowned at how still she was. "We're in Poedan's world." She raised her gaze and looked at Nick. "You'll like Poedan. She's big into trees." Her head swam and Esme caught her in her arms as she fell forward. "Tired," she murmured. "Take me to Poedan."

"We don't know wh—" Esme started.

Deni pointed down the cobbled street to where a sign creaked in the breeze above a wooden door. "There," she said. "Just there."

*

Nick decided he wasn't a fan of being in another dimension as he awkwardly scooped Allery's body up into his arms and struggled with her down the street to the building Deni had pointed out. There was something too otherworldly yet too familiar about the denizens of the place as they walked on by and carried about their business as if he and Esme weren't there at all. He glanced at Esme as she supported Deni.

"I don't like it here," he told her.

"Wouldn't think you'd need grounding here, baby," she replied.

He frowned. Truth was, he *didn't*. He felt more connected to the place than anywhere he'd ever stepped foot before and he didn't bloody like it. As much as he was all too aware he wasn't human, this place made him feel like the fact was rammed home to him—he felt it in his soul. It made him realise, with a prickly sensation up his spine, that his beloved parents weren't his parents. They were nothing to do with him at all.

Esme opened the door to the tavern, and he carried Allery inside. He felt as if he should be surprised the room was empty, but he wasn't. Allery was heavy and his arms ached, so he put her down on the floor. "What now?" he asked Deni.

"Poedan's usually out back," Deni said, straightening up from Esme. "Is Allery okay? How long will it be before she...you know?"

"I don't know, a couple of hours maybe." He looked at Allery's lifeless body. "I guess she's healing internally or...something."

A creak made him turn his attention towards the back of the room where a door opened and a very tall blonde lady stepped out. She steepled her fingers in front of her chest and walked towards them. "I am Poedan," she said. "Welcome."

Deni took a step forward. "Poedan, hey. I need some of that sap."

"Two memories," Poedan said, and she stretched her finger towards Esme's forehead.

Nick slapped her hand away. "Hey!"

"It does not hurt." Poedan turned her gaze on him and smiled.

"A drus. I am most honoured."

"Right. Thanks." Nick scowled at her. "What's this sap? Is this something we really need, or can we just get out of here now?"

"I need it," Deni said. "So yeah, we can't leave until I've got it."

"Fine." Nick folded his arms and gave Poedan a nod to let him know to take whatever it was she wanted from him and not Esme. He moved back a little as Poedan's cool fingertip touched his skin.

A weird sensation entered his mind and memories stirred and faded before he could grasp them. He blinked as Poedan withdrew.

"You have met Jacob," she said.

"Yeah."

"You must stop him."

"We're trying, but we don't even know where to find him."

Poedan gave him a puzzled smile. "But you have met him. And you are drus."

"He doesn't know where he was," Esme explained. "It's not somewhere we've been before."

The room trembled as Poedan laughed and Nick reached out to take Esme's hand. A thick branch pushed out of the floor in the centre of the room and snaked across the floorboards where it climbed the wall and crossed the ceiling before returning to the floor again.

"All you have to do is connect," Poedan said. "Listen, and let your ancestors guide you. You have seen where he lives. You can find it again."

She turned as the tree finished wrapping the room and snapped off one of the smaller branches. After she produced a glass from the pocket of her apron, she filled it with golden sap. Esme wrinkled her nose as Deni reached past her to take the connection.

"Stinks," Esme commented.

Nick nodded vaguely. He could find Jacob again. He supposed a part of him already knew that; all he had to do was join with the trees and share their awareness until he recognised the forest Jacob hid in. But then, what if he lost himself? What if he fell too deep?

He looked at Esme, who smiled in return.

"We can go now," Deni said. "Thank you."

The room filled with creaking as the tree slid back to wherever it had come from. Nick muttered thanks to Poedan and turned to collect Allery. She stirred in his arms as he carried her outside.

"Nick?"

"Welcome back." He put her down and she rubbed her neck with a grimace.

"Where are we?"

Deni reached for Allery's hand, a look of relief on her face. "I never wanna see you die again," she said. "Fucking terrified me."

"Deni brought us here," Nick said. "We should never have confronted the wardens like that. It could've got us all killed."

"I know," Allery said. "It was a stupid plan. But at least we know now that they can be helped."

Nick frowned. "What?"

"The wardens. They still have souls. Or parts of them, I'm sure of it."

Esme slipped an arm around his waist and Nick held her close, knowing the guilt would hit her hard. "They're not human any more," he said. "They *have* no souls. Even your father said that."

"I know," Allery said. "But he was wrong."

Nick shook his head a little and hugged Esme tighter. "It's all right," he told her, turning his face away as Deni opened a door. "Everything we've done, we've done for a reason."

"I've killed so many of them." Tears glistened in her eyes, reflecting the light as she gazed at him.

"Allery is *wrong*," he said, ushering her towards the door. "Please don't worry about this. We're at war, and they're the other side."

"They're children."

"They're demons. Es, please. We have to go." He took her hand and encouraged her to walk with him, pushing down the thought that he had hurt them, too.

Chapter Twenty-Five

A fox screamed into the night outside, but Allery wasn't asleep anyway. She pulled back the threadbare curtain to peer out of the window but couldn't spot the animal. The rest of the cottage slept. Esme and Nick next door, Deni behind her on the bed curled up beneath the blanket. Allery grabbed a denim jacket from the pile of clothes on the floor and put it on before heading downstairs as quietly as she could.

She stopped in the lounge. Driscoll slept on the sofa, his arm dangling over the side and a couple of empty cans of lager on the floor by his fingers. He was never going to get over his hangover if he kept drinking. Frowning, she crept past him and reached for the car keys on the coffee table, wincing at the jangle.

Once in the car, she put the radio on and headed for Bristol, humming along to the music. She'd be back before anybody had realised she'd gone missing, and this was something that just couldn't wait. What Dillon had said played on her mind.

Keep Mum away from Max.
She had to see Sophie.

*

In the morning's half-light, Allery stood outside the block of flats where Sophie used to live, hoping that Sophie did indeed still live there. A car drove down the road, muffled music thumping, and Allery let it distract her for a moment before turning and pressing the buzzer.

As she expected, there was no reply at first. She waited, then pressed it again, holding it down until, finally, Sophie's sleepy voice said, "Who is it?"

"Allery. I need to talk to you."

"What the hell? It's half past three in the fucking morning."

"I know. It's important." She paused. "It's about Dillon."

There was a click as the door unlocked, and Allery opened it up and headed upstairs to Sophie's apartment. Sophie was standing in the doorway when she got there, her arms wrapped tightly around her pink nightie and a scowl on her face.

"It's good to see you," Allery said.

"What about Dillon?"

"The guy you're seeing... Max? You need to stay away from him—"

"What's that got to do with Dillon? Or you? How do you know about Max, anyway? Are you stalking me?"

"What? No!"

"I told you not to answer the door, babe." The incubus's smirking face appeared over Sophie's shoulder, and he winked at her before putting an arm around Sophie's waist.

Allery bristled. "What is he doing here? You need to get away from him, Soph, now. He's dangerous."

Max flapped a hand at her. "Who is this nutjob?"

"Nobody." Sophie made to close the door, but Allery grabbed hold of her hand.

"Please, listen to me. I've seen Dillon. He asked me to keep you away from Max. Ask him where Dillon is. He knows!"

Sophie tugged her hand free. A look of uncertainty settled on her pretty face. "Max?" She turned to the incubus.

Max gave an incredulous laugh. "I don't even know this woman! No idea how she knows who I am. Jealous ex, is she?" He sighed and took hold of both Sophie's hands. "Listen. You know that if I knew *anything* about Dillon's whereabouts, I'd tell you straight away. You know how much I worry about Tia. I'd never leave you hanging if I knew something!"

"Dillon is with Tia," Allery said. "Max *knows* where they are. He's fooling you, Soph, to get you into bed. He's an incubus!"

"Fuck sake," Sophie snapped. "You know, I was just starting to believe you then until you brought up that bullshit. Piss off, Allery, I can't believe you'd stoop so low."

"No, listen to me. This is important." She snatched Sophie's arm and pulled her away from Max, ignoring her squeal of protest and Max's attempt to pull her back. "Tia and Dillon and all the other kids are at the old school in Clifton. Let me take you there. I can take you there right now."

"I'm calling the police," Max said. "She's off her nut."

"No." Sophie raised her hand. "I'll go with her; it won't take long. Just...wait here and keep your phone on."

Allery didn't even bother giving Max a second look. She turned and headed downstairs quickly, pleased that Sophie was following her.

"Are you all right?" she asked when they got outside, realising Sophie didn't even have anything on her feet.

Sophie waved her away, so Allery opened the car door for her instead and ran round to the driver's side. "This won't take long," she promised. "You'll see Dillon, but he's not how you remember, okay? But he will be again, I promise."

"Just don't, Allery." Sophie turned her face aside and stared out of the window instead.

Allery decided to stay quiet and let Sophie see for herself when she got there. The journey to the old school took only half an hour, but Allery's guts twisted with nerves the whole way there. Once she'd stopped the car, she hadn't even chance to turn off the engine before Sophie unclipped her seat belt and headed outside, heedless of her bare feet against the gritty ground.

Allery joined her and silently directed her to the courtyard around the back, watching where Sophie put her feet as she paid no mind.

"You should've called the police if you knew they were here," Sophie hissed. "Dillon!"

"Keep your voice down. We need to go quietly!"

"Dillon!"

Sophie pulled open the back door and ran inside the building calling for Dillon before Allery, cursing her stupid idea, could stop her. Allery followed her inside and grabbed her by the arm to stop her from blindly running in any farther. She put her fingers to her lips to shush Sophie, then carefully opened one of the internal doors.

The room—a large hall, perhaps an assembly room—was deserted. It didn't look like anybody had ever been there, judging by the thin layer of dust coating all the surfaces.

"He's not here," Sophie said. "You lying bitch."

She turned and stormed back outside, and Allery hurried after her. "He was here, I swear it. They must've got spooked and abandoned the place—"

"Leave me alone." Sophie took out her phone, stabbed in a number, and held it to her ear. She glared at Allery.

"Sophie, please. Come with me, don't go back to Max!"

"This is what it's all about, isn't it?" Sophie snapped. "Me and Max. I am *not* your girlfriend any more—you were the biggest mistake of my life."

"Max is an incubus. He'll hurt you!"

Sophie rolled her eyes. She turned from Allery and spoke into the phone. "Come and get me. No, she was lying. Come and get me, please."

"Sophie." She reached for Sophie's arm but was smacked away. Cursing, she backed up and dragged a hand through her hair. "I can help you get Dillon back. I will—"

"Don't you *ever* say his name again," Sophie said, rounding on her with her eyes blazing. "Get the hell away from me, Allery, before I do something I regret. *Get away from me!*"

Allery turned quickly, blinking away tears before they blinded her, and crossed the road back to the car. She sat in the driver's seat, gripping the wheel, and watched Sophie over the road. Her ex paced the pavement, hugging her arms around her waist.

"Shit." She smacked the steering wheel. "Shit. Shit." She rubbed her forehead, debated getting out of the car and forcing Sophie to join her, anything to keep her safe from that incubus. She could...she could...what? Keep her tied up at Merrybell? She cursed quietly again and turned the key in the ignition. There was only one thing she could do.

Stop Jacob.

Chapter Twenty-Six

A weight pressed against his back, forcing him down. Panic made his heart pound.

Nick woke with a start and stared at the ceiling, his heart thumping. He sighed and rubbed his eyes before sitting up in bed and fussing with his hair. Esme slept soundly by his side, so he left her quietly and headed off to get dressed. As he brushed his teeth, he thought again about what Poedan said. Nerves made him hurry back to the bedroom, where Esme sat looking dishevelled and lovely in an old blue T-shirt of his. She offered him a sleepy smile.

"Morning, baby."

"Hey." He perched on the side of the bed. "Can I talk to you?"

"Sure!" Esme shuffled over and draped her arms around him. "What's up?"

"I've been thinking about what Poedan said. You know, about being able to find Jacob."

"I think it's great that you can do that. Have you told Allery?"

Nick ran his thumb over the back of Esme's warm hand, feeling how soft her skin was. "No. I'm not *entirely* sure I can do what Poedan said. I could get lost—I'd have to go deep. If I can't come back—"

"I'd get you back."

Nick smiled. "I know you'd try."

Esme got off the bed and crouched in front of him, taking both his hands in hers. "I would get you back," she said. "I would do everything in my power. I'd ask all the angels... I wouldn't lose you."

Nick leaned in and kissed Esme gently on the lips. "I love you," he said.

"Love you, too."

A knock at the door made him look up. Driscoll's voice sounded on the other side. "Cup of tea for you both. I'll leave it out here, don't want to interrupt anything."

Nick rolled his eyes and Esme grinned at him. He got up and went to open the door. "We're not doing anything," he told Driscoll. He frowned at how pale the leprechaun looked. "You okay?"

"Just grand. Nothing a black coffee won't fix." He held out the mugs and Nick took them from him.

"Cheers. Since when did you play tea maid?"

"Hey, can't a guy make tea for his mates? I needed my morning coffee—figured I'd make drinks for the household seeing as I haven't exactly been pulling my weight recently."

Esme came and slipped her arm around Nick's waist. She took a mug from his hand. "You can't help it if you've not been feeling well," she said. "Are you sure you're okay?"

Driscoll smiled. "Don't you worry about me." He backed up, then turned and headed off down the corridor as Nick closed the door.

"Must be feeling guilty," Nick commented. He took a sip of tea and returned to the bed with Esme. "Might as well enjoy it."

Esme leaned against him, and they drank their tea in bed together like an old married couple. Nick wondered vaguely if Esme would marry him, if he asked. He sighed and closed his eyes. God, he was tired.

He pulled his eyes open again and blinked blearily at the wall opposite, the plaster cracked and crumbling. "Es?" he murmured.

She didn't reply.

"Es?" His whole body was heavy and he couldn't keep his eyes open. He slumped against Esme and fell fast asleep.

*

Allery mumbled a protest as Deni prodded her awake. Yawning, she shifted over in bed and sat up.

"Morning." Deni passed her a mug of tea. "Where were you last night?"

"Oh." Allery took a sip of tea to give herself breathing space to gather her thoughts. "Sorry. Tried not to wake you."

"You didn't. Woke up and you were gone."

"I just popped to the bathroom." She put the mug down on the bedside table. "Thanks for the tea."

"Driscoll made it, and don't change the subject. Bathroom, my arse."

Allery rubbed her face. "I went to see Sophie." She glanced at Deni, noticed she was washed and dressed, and wondered how long she'd been up for.

Deni crossed her arms. "What for?"

"I had to warn her about Max. She's in trouble." Was Deni jealous? She couldn't help but smile a little.

"Silly cow's own fault if she hooks up with an incubus," Deni said, flapping a hand. She perched on the edge of the bed. "You still in love with her or something?"

Allery shrugged. "Don't think so. No. I mean, I still care about her. I'd warn anybody I thought was in trouble."

Deni held a hand to her head and for a moment looked as if she'd pitch off the bed.

"All right?" Allery asked. She wondered if Deni had taken her methadone yet, if withdrawals were kicking in already. "Den?"

"I'm fine." Deni lifted her legs up onto the bed and shook her head. "Woozy."

"Yeah? Hey!" She lurched forward and caught Deni as she collapsed in her arms. "Deni? Den?" Cursing, she tapped Deni's cheek. When that didn't get any response, she got up and left the bedroom. "Driscoll?" she called.

"Allery." He was heading up the stairs, a look of surprise on his face. "I made you a cup—"

"Something's happened to Deni. She's collapsed. I think we need to take her to hospital. We need—"

Wardens gathered at the bottom of the stairs, four, five, six of them, staring up at her. One said, "Thought you'd taken care of them?"

"Just stay back," Driscoll snapped. He turned to Allery and held up his hands. "Al, I need you to know, I had no choice—"

"What the hell have you done?" Allery backed up towards the bedroom, her head spinning. She knew there'd be no point alerting Nick and Esme—Driscoll had drugged them, had tried to drug all of them. "*You* were the spy? All along... Every time they found us, every time they were one step ahead...it was you! I trusted you! *We* trusted you!"

"When you were in prison," Driscoll said, "they got a hold of me, wouldn't let me go. I'm a leprechaun, Allery. The only way for me to get free was to grant them a wish. They wished for the key!"

"You didn't have to give her to them!"

"Look at me!" He was at the top of the stairs now, his pale eyes wide, a sheen of sweat on his skin. "This is happening to me because I've delayed for so long. I can't fight it any more. I *have no choice!*"

Wardens pushed past Driscoll, pulled Allery out of the way, and hurried into the bedroom to grab Deni. Allery yelled and struggled and twisted free enough to punch a young lad in the face before she was caught hold of again. She glared at Driscoll as two of the wardens carried Deni out of the room and down the stairs. "You are scum," she hissed at him.

Driscoll pulled himself up a little and took a step towards her. "Get over yourself," he said. "No wonder Nick can't stand you. You know, I never saw it before."

Taken aback, Allery could only blink. Tia came and stood beside Driscoll. "You two, do something about her so she doesn't follow," she said, waving a hand at the wardens holding Allery. "And you, you're free."

Driscoll sighed and the colour returned to his skin before Allery's eyes. She shook her head slightly and tried to catch his gaze, but he muttered his thanks to Tia and disappeared, just like that.

"Don't do this," Allery begged as Tia turned to the stairs. "Whatever humanity you have left, you—"

Something heavy struck her from behind and she fell forward on the landing. As everything darkened around her, she had time to catch sight of one of the warden's trainers as he strode past her face.

Chapter Twenty-Seven

"Nick?"

Nick opened his eyes and looked up at Esme peering over him. "What happened?" he asked, touching his head.

"I don't know. I fell asleep."

Nick swung his legs over the side of the bed, waited for his head to stop spinning, then stood up. He squeezed Esme's hand and left the room with her. He froze when he saw Allery face down on the landing.

"Allery!" Esme rushed over to her friend and rolled her over. "She's alive," she said. "Al?"

Nick helped Allery sit up as she groaned and started to come round. "What happened?" he asked. "That's a nasty bump on the head you've got."

"Driscoll," Allery muttered.

"I haven't seen him," Nick said, wincing at the blood matted into Allery's hair.

"No." She squinted bleary-eyed at him. "He's a traitor. He drugged us, called the wardens… Deni's gone. They've got her."

"What do you—"

Allery pushed him aside and struggled to her feet. "Driscoll's fucked us over. He was working with them all along."

Nick shook his head. Allery had obviously taken too hard a knock. "I don't believe it."

"Believe it." Allery grabbed the banister and made her way gingerly down the stairs. Esme headed after her.

"Where are you going?" Nick asked. "You can't just accuse Driscoll and expect us to—"

Allery halted at the bottom of the stairs and looked back up at him, her expression bleak. "He drugged us, and let the wardens in." She spoke slowly, as if he was stupid. "How do you think the wardens always knew where we were? They were always one step ahead. Driscoll betrayed us."

Anger stirred in Nick's gut and replaced any sense of wooziness. Driscoll? After they'd worked together for so long, after everything they'd been through…. He clenched his fists. "We have to find Deni, baby," Esme said, looking back up at him briefly. "Are you coming?"

"We don't even know where to look!" Nick threw his arms in the air in exasperation before turning back into the bedroom to get his phone, and as Esme seemed quite determined to head out wearing only his old blue T-shirt, he grabbed a pair of shorts for her, too, before hurrying down the stairs after the girls.

He stopped when he saw them in the lounge, Allery with her phone pressed against her ear.

"Ringing Angel," Esme explained.

Nick nodded. He thought about Driscoll. The leprechaun had disappeared on several occasions moments before the wardens arrived. And he had gone missing for quite some time while Allery was in prison. Why hadn't he quizzed him more on where he'd been? They were friends. He could've talked Driscoll out of doing anything stupid. He should've known what was going on. Should've seen it.

He jumped out of his skin when his phone rang in his hand and stared at the unknown number on the screen with a frown. Esme raised her eyebrows at him, so he accepted the call and lifted the phone to his ear.

"Hello?"

"How did you do it, eh? How?" Jack spat at him as soon as he answered.

Nick sighed. "No idea what you're talking about. How did you get my number?"

"No idea?" Jack scoffed. "Pull the other one. I bet you're there now, aren't you? Mum's house. I've got no idea what possessed her to leave it to you."

"What?" He mouthed "Jack" to Esme in answer to her quizzical look. "Mum left me the house? I had no idea. I've been busy. I haven't had chance to contact the solicitors about the will or anything."

Jack gave a bitter laugh. "You're so full of bullshit. Why did she leave it to you, eh? I'm her only real son!"

"Maybe because she knew I'm practically bloody homeless," Nick said, scowling. He turned his back when he realised Allery had finished her phone call and was also watching him along with Esme. "Look, you're just going to have to get over the fact that Mum *loved me* and stop being such a jealous dick. Don't call me again, Jack." He cut the call and turned around again.

"She left you the house?" Esme said. "That's brilliant! We can get out of this dump soon as."

Nick sighed. "Think we've got more important things to worry about at the moment." He looked at Allery. "What did Angel say?"

"She can't find Deni," Allery said. "Doesn't think she's in this dimension." She sat on the arm of the sofa and flicked through her phone. "I don't know what to do. I think we need to get out of here, in case the wardens come back for us."

"And go where?" Esme asked.

"I don't know. I don't know what to do any more. I can't think. I should've seen all this. I should've known. Driscoll..."

Nick almost smiled. They weren't so different after all. "There's no way you could've known," he said, as much to convince himself. There was no time for self-flagellation. "We all trusted him. It's done. Look, I'll take a trip to the solicitors—we'll be safe at my mum's. Then, Al..." He sighed. "Maybe we need to let the old wardens know what's happened. We need all the help we can get."

Esme looked from him to Allery and back again. "What about Driscoll?" she asked. "We just let him get away with this?"

Nick looked at Allery to answer that one. She'd known the leprechaun longer than he had, after all.

"Forget him," Allery said. "Nick's right. I think we need the wardens' help."

Nick raised his eyebrows a little, surprised she had agreed to his suggestion so easily. He blocked Jack's number from his phone and pushed it into his pocket. "Back to Bristol then. Let's go get ourselves a house."

Esme let out a squeal of delight and clapped her hands. Nick smiled despite himself. They'd all be safe at his mum's house at least, and it'd be nice to have proper running hot water and electricity while they sought out the wardens. Nobody would know they were there, except Jack, and despite being a total dickhead, he was still Nick's brother. He wouldn't do anything to them. Or to his mother's house.

Nick caught the car keys when Allery tossed them over to him and headed out of the door.

Chapter Twenty-Eight

Deni woke with a gasp and the instant she tried to move her hands, she realised she was cuffed to a pipe in an empty room...somewhere. Her feet scuffed through dust and grit as she scrabbled onto her knees, and she tugged uselessly at the cuffs.

It was gloomy. There was a window, but it was boarded up and the only light coming into the room filtered through cracks in the wood and under the door.

"Hello?" she called. She cursed and yanked at the chain until her wrists hurt. "You can't keep me in here, you freaks!"

A dull ache persisted behind her eyes, and the dust made her sneeze. She sat back down and wondered how the hell she was going to get out of there. It was no good opening a door if she couldn't actually get through it.

Granddad, if you're still watching over me, now would be a great time to start acting all guardian angel-y.

She sighed, gave a final tug at the cuffs, and cursed again.

Somebody opened the door and Deni sneezed as disturbed dust floated in the air. She squinted at the wardens who entered: a tall lad with a shaved head, probably in his late teens, and the girl she recognised as Tia. She shifted back against the pipe and jerked the chains.

"This is pointless," she said. "I'm not gonna open any doors for you, so you might as well do one."

"Jacob can make you," Tia said, crouching down in front of Deni and peering into her eyes.

Deni shuddered. "Fuck off," she said, laughing. "Allery will find me before you can do anything anyway. You might as well give up now."

Tia sighed and straightened up. "Let's just get her straight to Jacob. All this false hope makes me feel sick. Unlock her cuffs and we'll get her through the door."

Deni kicked out at the lad as he came closer, but, unperturbed, he yanked her to her feet and stuck a key in the cuff's lock. Her heart pounded. She could feel the energy from a door and as Tia reached to open it, she raised her palm and sent a blast of her own energy towards it, needles prickling her skin as the doorway shimmered and disappeared.

The lad took the key from the lock and looked at Tia for an explanation. Deni laughed a little and sagged back against the wall. "Good luck getting that one open, bitch."

"You try it," Tia demanded, waving a hand at the other warden. "Open it."

Silently, he stepped forward and lifted his hands. A frown settled across his brow.

"I've locked it, you dozy cow." Deni laughed again and sank down to her backside in the dust. Her head pulsed with pain. "Only the key can unlock it. And before you even think of taking me elsewhere, or knocking me out, I've locked all the doors in the vicinity. So...piss off."

That last part wasn't true, but Deni bet on Tia not knowing that, judging by how red her face was. Tia lashed out and backhanded Deni across the face with a look of fury. Deni's ears rang with the force of the blow, and she tasted blood in her mouth. She ran her tongue along her teeth and offered Tia a bloodied grin. "Go fuck yourself," she said.

"She can rot in here," Tia said, pulling the other warden away with her. When the door closed, Deni leaned her head back against the wall and sighed.

She was in another dimension; she knew that now. The door had felt different, but she couldn't place where it originated. How on Earth was Allery supposed to find her here?

You'll just have to get yourself out of this.

She had to stay alert, stay awake. Fight off any bloody withdrawals and *think*. The wardens would try to take her to Jacob again and she had to get away before they did.

*

Max gripped Sophie's hips tighter, his palms sweaty, as he thrust into her. She was on all fours before him, making all the appropriate noises as his mouth ran dry from lust. Bed springs creaked.

"Max," she gasped, reaching back to push him into her. "Harder."

"Right." He shifted position and thrust again. If this didn't make a fucking baby...

The doorbell buzzed. Max ignored it. Sophie hopefully hadn't heard it. He kept pounding into her, trying to ignore the image of Jacob that popped into his head. "That good for you, love?" he asked.

The doorbell buzzed again.

"Go and see who it is," Sophie said.

Max didn't stop what he was doing. "What?"

She turned to look at him, flicking her hair out of her eyes. "Go and see. It might be important."

"I'm a bit fucking busy!"

Sophie pushed him away and he growled in irritation and snatched up his shorts. "Fuck's sake. You stay right there—don't put any clothes on!" He gave her a warning look, smirked when she stuck her tongue out at him, then went to peer out of the window. He frowned when he caught sight of Tia stepping back onto the pavement and looking up at him.

Cursing, he left the room and headed downstairs and outside. He shoved his hands under his armpits and glared at the warden. "Well?"

"We have the key in a secure location."

Max blinked. "Really?"

"Yes."

Max raised his eyebrows in surprise, then glanced back up at the bedroom window, wondering if Jacob would still need that baby. He could leave Sophie alone and get on with his life. He shifted uncomfortably, his bare feet cold on the ground. He didn't want to leave Sophie.

"Bollocks. Well…that's great. Good news. Get on and take her to Jacob, eh?"

"She's locked the doors. We can't move her."

Max rolled his eyes. "You've heard of a fucking car? Stick her in the boot and drive her to Jacob. Bloody hell."

"She's not in this dimension."

Max threw his arms in the air in despair. "Kids! Fucking hell. Right, give me an hour to sort myself out, then I'll come and help you. Okay? Shouldn't have to do everything my damn self."

He turned away from Tia and stomped back inside, thoroughly pissed off. When he got back to the bedroom, Sophie was sitting on the edge of the bed with her legs crossed, though she was still naked.

"Who was it?"

"Some bloody Jehovah or something, I don't know. Someone selling something." He dropped his shorts and waved a hand at his flaccid cock. "Put me right off."

Sophie chuckled. "Aw," she said. "Come here and let me sort that out for you."

Sulkily, Max approached the bed and stood in front of Sophie. He sighed when she put his cock in her mouth. "You're a good girl," he told her.

Sophie pulled back and gave him a wicked grin that made his heart race. "Would you rather I be a bad girl?"

"Yeah," Max said, grinning as he crawled onto the bed with her. She giggled as he pushed her down. *Fucking love this girl.* He pulled her legs around his waist.

*

Allery had waited in the car, anxiously chewing her fingernails as Nick and Esme spoke to the solicitor and picked up the house keys. They didn't really have time for all this, she knew that. She needed to find Deni right away, needed to get her home and safe before Jacob could get anywhere near her. But she felt numb inside. Betrayed by Driscoll and terrified for Deni, the feelings had boiled over until she'd smothered them deep inside. She'd let Nick take charge, let him fetch the keys and take them to his mother's house. It might give her time to *think,* to come up with a plan, to work out a way to find Deni that didn't involve going anywhere near the old wardens.

"Shit," she cursed softly and rubbed her face before sitting up when she spotted Nick and Esme heading back to the car.

"Got them," Esme said, jangling a set of keys at her as she climbed into the passenger side. "It's not far from here, Al. Then we can get our heads together and come up with a plan."

Allery just nodded. She lifted her gaze and it met with Nick's in the rear-view mirror as he sat in the driver's seat. "We'll get her back," he said. "Even if it means calling in favours. We've still got a few tricks left up our sleeves."

Allery wasn't so sure. She looked away out of the window and watched as Bristol passed by.

It didn't take long before they were out of the city centre and driving alongside the river Avon. If Allery turned in her seat she could see the famous Clifton Suspension Bridge in the back window. Given the river, and the trees, the cliffs, and all the greenery of the area, she figured they wouldn't have to look far before they found one of the old wardens. Nick turned away from the river eventually and up a little suburban road filled with 1930s semi-detached houses. He pulled into the driveway of one of the white-fronted ones, its neat front lawn and tidy shrubs suggesting it had been a well-loved house. Allery unbuckled her seat belt and got out of the car before Nick had even stopped the engine, but he stayed inside for a moment, staring at the front door with Esme reaching over to give his arm a comforting squeeze.

Allery wondered if it would be too hard for him. If being in his mother's house would be too raw. She needed him and Esme to have their heads together; she needed them to help her get Deni back. She waited. Several minutes passed before Nick killed the engine and got out of the car with Esme. Allery let him pass as he walked up the path to the front door.

"Do you guys need me to wait out here?" she asked.

Nick shook his head a little. He looked down at the door key in his hand. "I'm not going to break down."

"No." Allery sighed. "I'm going to sound like a bitch," she said, "but getting Deni back before Jacob gets hold of her is more important than anything else right now. If he gets her, it'll be the end for all of us, all the humans—"

"I'm not going to break down," Nick said again. He looked at her briefly, then unlocked the door and went inside.

Allery mouthed "sorry" to Esme when she received a brief glare from her friend before she followed after Nick.

A hallway with pink carpet led them to a lounge with more pink carpet and magnolia walls. There was a flowery sofa and a fluffy white rug. A mantelpiece over an electric fire housed a collection of family photos: baby pictures of Nick and his brother Jack, pictures of Nick's father, a wedding photo of both Nick's parents and one of an older couple Allery presumed must be his grandparents. She tore her gaze away and looked at Nick. He threw the car keys down on the coffee table and sat on the sofa, looking up at her and Esme.

"I'm fine," he said, opening his palms. "What's the plan?"

"Speak to the wardens," Allery said. "I don't know what else to do, unless either of you...?"

Esme shook her head.

Nick sighed. "I know it sucks," he said, "but I really think it's our only option. There's no way we can find Deni without their help. Even with their help, we might not be able to find her..." He stared into the middle distance with his mouth slightly open.

"What?" Allery asked. "What? Have you thought of something?" She perched herself on the arm of the sofa and watched him intently.

Nick glanced up at her and past her to Esme. "We need to find

Jacob. I can find Jacob."

"Are you sure, baby?" Esme asked.

Allery's heart thumped and she looked from Nick to Esme and back again, hoping he was right, hoping it would be easy, although Esme's concerned expression suggested otherwise.

"I'm sure." Nick got up from the sofa. He crossed the room to the patio doors at the back, unlocked them, and stepped outside.

Allery let Esme go ahead and followed the pair of them into the garden. The garden was mainly laid to lawn, with borders either side filled with shrubs and bedding plants, but there, right in the middle of the lawn, a small wooden bench beneath it, was a gnarly old oak tree.

"Mum lived here her whole life," Nick said, stepping closer to the tree. "I... This tree...she loved this tree. Cared for it. Spoke to it. It was the gateway for me, my way into this world."

Allery raised her eyebrows. She had her suspicions that Nick was a changeling, but they'd never spoken about it, and she guessed this was as much confirmation as they were going to get. She didn't say anything. Esme reached for Nick's hand and gave it a squeeze.

Nick cleared his throat. "He wasn't...taken," he said. "The *other* Nicholas Lode. I'm not a... He doesn't exist elsewhere. He died. I was gifted to Mum by my...by the dryads. I am Nick Lode."

"It's all right," Allery said. "We understand."

Nick's gaze met hers. "Do you? Because if I do this, here, I might not come back."

As much as Allery didn't want anything to happen to Nick, she didn't want to dissuade him either. She nodded and said nothing, leaving Esme as the one to lend him support. Ultimately it didn't matter what happened to any of them; stopping Jacob from using Deni was more important.

For the whole universe. Although a tiny voice told her even the universe could go jump if it meant Deni would be okay.

*

Nick held on to Esme tightly, not wanting to let her go. "You come back to me," she told him, her voice soft against his ear. "You come back, Nick. I know you can do this, okay? You can do it." She pulled back and gave him such an earnest look that his heart melted. He kissed her on the lips, committing the feel of her, the taste of her, to his memory.

Then he stepped away and approached the tree. A sense of unease made his stomach turn, but he forced the feeling away and reached out to the trunk, quietly pleased his hand was so steady.

Whispers tickled at the back of his mind before he'd even touched it, and he hesitated, his fingertips poised over the bark. Then he pressed his palm against the tree and closed his eyes.

Nick. Nick. Nicholas. Son of Balanos. Come home. Nick.

Nick lifted both hands to the tree, his brow furrowed in concentration as the whispers intensified, calling to him, their voices merging and repeating and tumbling over one another. *No,* he told them.

Come home. Son of Balanos. —nosNickhome, sonNick, Balahomenos Nick, Son—

No, he told them again.

The tree showed him his mother, his human mother, crying in the garden, her body racked with grief, her shoulders shaking as she covered her face with trembling hands. *My baby. My baby.* She rocked back and forth. He wanted to touch her, to hold her in his arms.

I gifted you, my child. Time to come home.

The voice chilled him. With a wrench he forced his awareness past and beyond, down into the tree's roots and into the ground, stretching and connecting with the soil, with other roots, spreading outwards, touching other trees, sharing their memories, on and on and deeper and deeper.

Animals snuffled and crunched, badgers and squirrels and voles. Forests burned and fire filled his soul, bubbling in his veins until blackened roots twitched their last and broke up to become part of the earth. Humans came with their saws, ripping and tearing into the trunks, the trees silently screaming while the dryads wept. Chainsaws ate into him, breaking him apart.

He became lost, for a time, lost a sense of his self as he lived centuries past, seasons came and went, dryads came and went, wardens...wardens...

He could see them. Old wardens, patrolling the forests and the riversides, checking the places where dimension seams thinned and frayed, doors opened and closed. The wardens grew younger. All but one. Jacob. He stood in the forest, his black eyes staring at nothing. Waiting.

Wind rustled leaves on the branches and trees groaned. Jacob moved his head.

Nick pulled back sharply. He tried to feel for his body, but his family called him home.

Nick. Nicholas. Come home. Son of Balanos. Nick.

Something touched him.

Come home. Son.

It would be easy to let them take him. All he had to do was let go and he'd sink into their embrace. Into her embrace.

Come home, my son. He wanted to. It would be so much easier to give up the earthly realm and go back to his roots. He turned towards her when another presence merged with his, neither drus nor dryad.

A deep, feminine voice, soft and strong, filled his mind. *You must go. They need you. You have found Jacob and now you must end this. She needs you.* Poedan? A hazy image of the goddess flashed before him. *She needs you.*

Nick! Nick! Baby, please! Please don't leave me! I love you. Please, come back now!

"Nick!"

Nick gasped and pulled back from the tree as if he'd had an electric shock. His hands trembled and he tried hard to focus on Esme as she took his face between her hands. The world spun unpleasantly around him, and his knees buckled. Esme caught him up in her arms.

"Savernake Forest," he told her, shaking. He felt light-headed, as if he hadn't quite returned. His limbs were heavy and strange. "Es."

"I'm here, I'm here," she said, cradling him in her lap. "Don't leave me again, don't ever leave me again!"

Nick looked past her to Allery, who frowned in concern over her shoulder. "S-Savernake Forest," he told her. "I found him."

Chapter Twenty-Nine

Deni sang quietly to herself about how much she hated the wardens and wanted them all to fuck off and leave her alone. It seemed to be doing a pretty decent job of distracting her from her headache and the itch in her palms which, if she thought about them too much, made her think of heroin and how much she needed—

No. "They can fuck off all the way to fuck," she sang. "I'll open a door and send them there…" She sat up, her chains rattling against the pipe. "Open a door."

She eyed the cuffs thoughtfully. All she had to do was open a door big enough to get the whole damn building through and…and what good would that do? She'd still be chained up, she'd just be in another dimension, although it'd confuse the shit out of the wardens. She wondered if any of them had stayed behind in the building in case she did manage to escape somehow. How long would it take them to work out all they had to do was sedate her and they could move her wherever the hell they liked?

She let out a desperate sob and screamed in frustration. She felt so fucking *useless*! She had all that power and—even when she did have enough energy to use it properly—she was too bloody stupid to work out how to do anything remotely helpful.

That was it. She'd have to kill herself then. When they came to take her to Jacob, she'd kill herself to save the world. She laughed a little.

How the hell are you gonna do that?

She had nothing sharp on her. Nothing to strangle herself with—her trainers were bloody Velcro so she didn't even have any shoelaces. Maybe she could smash her head against the wall until her skull cracked. She grimaced at that idea.

"Fuck," she whispered. Her soles itched. She stared at the cuffs again in case a flash of inspiration were to strike. Then she lifted her gaze and looked at the pipe. Up at the top, where it connected to the ceiling, it was rusty.

She stood and gaped upwards. The metal looked fairly worn there, thin... If she could reach up there, she was sure she could break it. Only...how the fuck was she meant to get up there?

"Balls," she muttered. If only the wardens had taken her to a dimension with low gravity, she could've jumped up there or floated.

She laughed suddenly. Float! Shit. Shit. She had to get the right dimension, had to find the right door. Shit. Okay. She closed her eyes and took a deep breath. Raising her hands, she shifted around as much as she could until she felt a seam, then she tugged it carefully, concentrating on where she wanted to go. Pressure built behind her eyes and warm, wet blood dribbled from her nose. She sniffed.

Then she felt it. Water pushed against her fingers as she

wiggled them into the crevice, forcing the door to open slowly.

God, if I drown...

The water ran down the seams and into the room and as she pulled further it came faster. She made sure to open only a small door, one that wouldn't stay open forever. Water gushed out into the room now, as if she'd opened a porthole in a submarine.

Deni laughed and stepped back out the way. The room was rapidly filling up; already the water lapped around her ankles. She watched it pour from the hole, vaguely hoping nothing but water would come through. It wasn't cold, at least.

It filled to her waist, her chest, her shoulders, then she lifted her chin as it rose further still. Her heart thumped hard, and she took a deep breath and allowed the water to rise over her head before she lifted her feet and floated to the surface. She rode the water upwards, pushing herself hand over hand up the pipe, and as soon as she neared the top, she braced her feet against the wall and pulled hard with the chains against the rusted metal.

Come on!

She tugged desperately, using all her strength. The metal of the cuffs cut into her wrists but she ignored it, ignored the water lapping round her ears, and with a guttural yell, pulled as hard as she could. She felt the metal give a little, but she was very close to the ceiling now with only an inch of breathing space, and she knew that if she couldn't get free soon, she'd die.

At least that solves that problem. Come on, you bastard!

More desperate tugging and at last the chain pulled through the pipe and she fell back into the water. She spluttered and choked and pushed upwards for a final gasp of air, her lips brushing the ceiling, then she dived down, kicking hard, and reached for the door.

It was unlocked—no point locking a door if she was secured—

but she fumbled with it for a moment until she managed to get it open, the force of the water ripping it from her hands.

Her eyes widened as the water spat her out into the corridor and she hit the wall hard. As the water rushed away, she lay on the floor, coughing and shaking.

Get up, she told herself. She pushed herself to her feet and staggered down the corridor towards a bent metal door, which she yanked open, letting the water seep out into the sand. She looked up. Sand surrounded the building for as far as she could see, and a heat haze shimmered over the horizon.

"Weird," she muttered, stepping back to peer up at the building. It was an odd, conical structure made entirely out of metal, and didn't appear to have any windows. Her head spun and her energy flagged, and she dropped to her knees. It was no good just getting out of that room. She had to get out of that dimension before the wardens came back for her.

"You've got this." She lifted her hands, though even that felt like a monumental effort, and felt for an edge. *Concentrate.* She took a breath, let it out shakily, and opened a door. She staggered through it, then fell.

Chapter Thirty

Max sat on a low wall outside a McDonald's, eating a burger from a tray, and eyeing Dillon, Tia, and that other kid whose name he didn't know and couldn't be arsed to learn. He licked meat juices from his fingers. "So...when you say gone?"

"Vanished," Tia said. "Everything was wet."

Max grunted. He stuffed a chip in his mouth and watched a young family leaving McDonald's, the two little girls skipping ahead with their happy meals. Nobody would notice the wardens, of course, not unless they drew attention to themselves, so he decided he'd better not start shouting at them, even though he wanted to kick their arses all the way into the next dimension.

"You obviously didn't secure her properly. You didn't think of leaving somebody as guard, eh? No?" The wardens looked at one another and said nothing. Max picked up his burger and took another bite. "Useless," he muttered. "So, who's telling Jacob?"

"We thought—"

Max raised his hand to stop Dillon saying anything else. "No way. You think I'm going to tell him? Fuck off. You'll just have to find her again, that's all. Look, if you get all your little mates to keep their eyes and ears open, I'm sure you'll find her soon enough. Hold up."

His phone rang out from his back pocket, and he pulled it out and stared at the screen. *Sophie.* He was tempted to ignore it, but he'd rather speak to her than the wardens, so he answered it. "I'm at work, babe, better make it quick."

"I'm pregnant."

Max almost choked on his chips. He put the tray down on the wall and got to his feet. "Hell's bells, you couldn't have eased me in?"

"We've been at it like bunnies, Max. This is a surprise to you?"

Jacob would be pleased. He ran a hand through his hair. "Well...that's great news! Yeah. This is great. We should celebrate."

"I don't know if I'm going to keep it yet."

Max frowned. He turned his back on the wardens. "What do you mean? We'll be great parents. I love babies."

Sophie sighed. "It's just...with Dillon missing and everything, I really feel I should be concentrating on him. I feel like... I dunno, like I'm replacing him or something."

Max glanced back at Dillon briefly. The kid was frowning at him. "Soph, you're not giving up on Dillon, yeah? The new little one won't be replacing him—Dillon'd love a little baby brother or sister! Listen, it'll be good for you. Good for us. It'll give us something positive to think about."

Sophie stayed silent on the other end of the line, so Max chewed his thumbnail. If she decided to get rid of the baby, then he'd have to look for another woman and he liked Sophie too much to give her up.

"You really want this baby?" she asked quietly.

"I really do," he said. "Fuck me. I really do."

Silence again. Then, "Okay. If we do this, Max, you'd better not fuck it up. I'll need you with me. Dillon's dad was a waste of space—"

"I won't fuck it up!" Max laughed a little, though a tiny stirring of guilt turned the burger in his stomach. "Listen, Soph, I've gotta go. I'll catch you later, babe." He ended the call and snatched up his remaining chips. "Well. Guess who's gonna be a daddy?"

Dillon scowled at him. "I don't want a little brother or sister."

"You don't get to have an opinion on the subject, mate," Max said, grinning at him. "You're soulless, remember? Dead inside. Just think yourself lucky—this bit of good news'll cheer Jacob right up. Maybe he won't kick any arses after all, eh? Come on."

He lobbed his tray into the bin and headed off across the car park, glancing back briefly to make sure the wardens were following him.

*

"Weapons," Allery said, sitting on Nick's mum's sofa. "We'll need weapons before we go there. We don't know how many wardens will be hanging round, but I'm hoping we can just catch Jacob unawares and kill him before anybody else realises we're there."

"And if they do realise we're there?" Nick asked. "What then? There's three of us."

Allery frowned. "Shit."

Nick groaned and held his head in his hands. "We're all going to die," he said. "Well. *We're* going to die." He rubbed his forehead and looked at Allery again. "We need a real plan."

"Right." Allery couldn't think of anything other than finding

Jacob and killing him before he got hold of Deni. "Maybe I should go alone. Or I could create a diversion to lure Jacob out and then one of you guys could shoot him in the head?"

"I think we need help," Esme said. "Ooh, I could ask my friend Stacy?"

Allery had no idea who Stacy was.

"Stacy the werewolf," Esme clarified. "We were turned together. Wait a minute, I think I still have her number."

Allery smiled a little as Esme flicked through her phone. "I think we'll need more than Stacy the werewolf," she said. "But it's a good idea. We have contacts from Locke & Co, and we have favours to call in. I'm sure Angel will help us. And, oh, remember Hirotoshi the kitsune? He definitely owes us."

"If we can get hold of him," Nick said. "What about your dad?"

"I'd have to contact the wardens to reach him, and I'm not keen on that idea." Allery got to her feet. "I need to head back to Merrybell and pick up a few bits—weapons, names... You two stay here and see what else you can come up with. Nick, any information you have about Savernake would be great, too."

Nick nodded. "Keys are hung up by the door," he said. "Go careful, Al. You don't know if Driscoll might've returned there."

"The thought crossed my mind," she admitted. "If I see him, I'll kick his arse. I'll be back before it gets dark, and if I'm not...don't come looking for me. Getting Deni away from Jacob is more important."

"Got it."

Allery left Nick and Esme in the lounge and grabbed the car keys on the way out. It took a little while to get back to Merrybell, and she listened to music all the way there, hoping to distract herself from thinking, well, anything. It didn't really work, though, and when she finally reached the cottage, she had a headache from frowning so much. She scanned the area as she got out of the car and, satisfied Driscoll wasn't around, jogged down the path to the door and let herself in. The place was eerie when it was empty, and a mouse skittered across the kitchen floor before disappearing under one of the units. She hurried upstairs and snatched up the cricket bat and escrima sticks from where she'd left them under her bed, wishing she had something *sharper*. Or a gun. Next, she opened a drawer on the chest beside the bed and pulled out a pile of old Locke & Co paperwork. She rummaged through it for the diary.

She was frowning over some of Nick's squiggles on an invoice when a bright flash of light in the room made her gasp and screw her eyes shut. She reached for the cricket bat and gripped it tight before jumping to her feet.

She blinked when she could see properly again and dropped the bat. Deni lay on the bed, soaked through and shivering. Allery's heart leaped into her mouth.

"Shit! Den?" She rounded the bed and took Deni's hand, frowning at how cold her skin was. "Deni, can you hear me?"

Deni opened her eyes weakly. "M—" she said, grasping Allery's hand tight. "Meth—"

"Right, stay there." Allery turned away and opened another drawer. She fumbled with Deni's methadone supply, pouring out the liquid into the dose-measuring cup which she then held to Deni's lips. "It's okay. You're safe now. You're safe." She kissed Deni's forehead and moved the cup away. "Let me get those cuffs off."

She used a hair grip to pick the lock and tossed the cuffs aside, then she went into the bathroom, grabbed a towel, and shook dust off it as she returned to Deni. She rubbed the girl's arms, trying to bring a little warmth back to her skin.

Deni pushed her away and sat up a little shakily. She pulled her top off over her head. "Can you get me some dry clothes, please? I'm okay."

"Your wrists are red raw," Allery said, collecting up an old jumper and a pair of jeans for Deni to change into. "I'm so glad you're safe. What happened?"

"They took me to another dimension," Deni said, her voice briefly muffled by the jumper as she pulled it on. "I don't know which. Had to flood the room to get out."

"Driscoll drugged us." Allery sat beside Deni on the bed and gazed down at her hands in her lap. "I should never have trusted him."

"You never had any reason not to trust him," Deni said, her voice soft. "Did you?"

Allery shook her head. Then she shrugged. "I feel like I should know everything that's going on with my team. I had no idea Nick felt the way he does either, not really. I've been too wrapped up in myself."

"That's not true! You look after me."

"I guess." Allery sighed. "I've made a massive cock-up of a lot of things. The only way to put things right is to kill Jacob. I'm going to kill Jacob. Then we'll all be safe."

"Until the next thing comes along," Deni said, draping her arms around Allery's shoulders.

"Oh God. I've got an eternity of this. I should quit and go work in a supermarket. It's probably safer for the rest of humanity."

"Hey." Deni let Allery go and sat by her side to take hold of her hands instead. "Bullshit. It's because you're gonna live forever that you've got to do all this! You're our protector. Imagine all the shit you'll learn in the next couple hundred years. You'll be amazing!" She squeezed Allery's hands. "Besides, do you really think supermarkets will be around forever? I'm sure when we're all riding round in our flying cars we won't be stopping off at Asda."

Allery smiled. "I'm feeling sorry for myself, aren't I?"

"Yeah. Pull yourself together. We've got a freak to kill."

"Right. Sorry. Are you okay to move on? We're staying at Nick's mother's house now. I just came back here to tool up."

"Is that all you've got?" Deni asked, waving a hand at the cricket bat on the floor. She flashed Allery a grin. "We can do a *lot* better than that."

"Yeah?"

Deni nodded, took Allery's face between her hands, and placed a kiss on her lips. "Come with me. This is going to be *fun*."

Allery couldn't help but grin. "It's about time I had a little fun."

Chapter Thirty-One

As the door closed behind her, it took a moment for Allery's eyes to adjust to the new light. All sorts of sounds and smells assaulted her senses, and she blinked a couple of times before gaping at the scene before her.

"Cool as fuck, right?" Deni said.

A market scene spread before her eyes, hundreds upon hundreds of stalls, illuminated under a black sky, manned by people flicking in and out of existence, and browsed by all manner of bizarre creatures. Languages she couldn't understand, snatches of English, laughter, shouting. The smell of meat and something burning, incense and bread, and something sharp like ammonia. Allery didn't know where to look first.

"Where the hell...?"

"This is kind of an in between," Deni said. "Hard to find, really. I only found it the first time by accident." She took hold of Allery's hand and led her to the nearest stall where the stallholder, a man dressed like an old-fashioned American sheriff, appeared and disappeared and fuzzed with static as if he was beamed from an old TV set.

Allery's skin crawled. "What do you mean, an in between?" She eyed the horseshoes the man was selling.

"It's not a proper dimension; this is all there is of it. It's like a...a slip in time or something."

"I don't think we should be here." Allery kept hold of Deni's hand as they squeezed through the crowds between the stalls. "Where are we going?"

"To look for weapons. Relax!"

This is exactly why the wardens make us wait in rooms. What if the place was full of people who'd become lost? Who'd slipped between the seams of their own realities and become stuck in some strange dreamworld. What if they were all ghosts? She shuddered.

Deni stopped and pulled her hand free from Allery's, giving her a grin. "You're going to cut off my blood supply if you squeeze me that tight." Her eyes glittered in the dark, reflecting stars of light from the market stalls. "Chill out. I get it. It feels odd here, but it's fine! Nobody will hurt you."

Allery rolled her eyes, though she was smiling. "I'm chilled. I'm just not as used to all this flitting between dimensions as you are."

"Well, if there's ever a time we get a break from running, hiding, or trying to kill something, I'll take you to more places," Deni said, wrapping her arms around Allery. "God, you're beautiful."

The compliment took Allery by surprise and her cheeks burned. "Really?" She laughed a little. "Nobody's ever said that before."

"That's sad."

Deni kissed Allery, her lips soft and warm, and Allery responded, feeling strangely isolated despite everything going on around them. Eventually she pulled away. "Weapons," she said. "We can't forget. How are you feeling?"

Deni held out her hand. It was steady. "I'm good," she said. "Let's look for weapons."

They wandered off through the market, past stalls and the other entities. Allery realised little puffs of black soot bubbled up round her feet as she walked, but as it didn't appear to bother Deni, she didn't question it.

Light glinting from something metallic caught her eye and she tugged Deni's hand to pull her down another aisle towards what she'd seen. The stallholder was an elderly gentleman with a bald head and spectacles. He smiled pointed teeth at them when they stopped in front of his goods. Allery raised her eyebrows at what was on offer: maces, hardwood staffs, an assortment of blades, throwing stars, a halberd. "This looks perfect," she said.

"I am pleased you like what you see," said the old man, inclining his head. His image fizzed and buzzed and became opaque again. "Please, take your time."

Deni picked up a musket. "How much for this?" she asked.

"You don't want that," Allery said. "Too heavy and too awkward to load."

"But it looks cool." Deni sighed and pointed out a smaller gun. "How about that one?"

"Looks like a Glock." She nodded. "That'll do you."

Her eyes were drawn to a straight-bladed sword displayed in its scabbard on a plinth made of black marble. A navy-blue tassel hung from the hilt, and she looked to the stallholder for permission to touch it before she took it up and admired the stitching on the casing. She drew the sword and studied the blade. It was thin and deadly sharp and looked to be made of silver.

"An excellent all-round demon slayer," the old man said. "Or of course, it will also slay non-demons, if that's more your taste."

Allery kept hold of it and inspected a couple of broadswords to see if they'd be any good for Nick. Once she'd found one she thought he'd like, she waved a hand at all three weapons. "How much for these?"

The stallholder showed his teeth again. "I ask no payment," he said. "I ask only that you prove you can use the weapons you have chosen."

Allery frowned, sure there was going to be a catch somewhere. By her side, Deni raised the Glock and pointed it at the old man's head. "And how do we prove that?" she asked.

"My dear, I'm glad you asked." He stepped back, took off his spectacles, and placed them on his stall, then spread his arms wide. He laughed and began to change, his skin bubbling and stretching and splitting, until there was another of him, and another, and they were the shape of hideous bald boars with sharp tusks and glinting eyes.

One squealed and leaped over the stall, while another dived beneath it. Allery cursed, discarded Nick's broadsword, and clutched her weapon tight. Deni fired off a couple of shots.

"There's too many of them! Run!"

They dashed through the crowd, pushing people out the way in their haste. Allery chanced a look back over her shoulder and saw three angry-looking pigs charging after them.

She caught a blur of movement from the corner of her eye just in time to dive to one side as a pig hurdled another stall and bowled into someone else. Deni fired off a shot and the pig disappeared in an explosion of black dust. Cursing, Allery pushed herself to her feet and slashed out wildly as another of the creatures came at her. The thing vanished as her sword sliced through it.

"This is all kinds of fucked up!" Deni cried, pointing her weapon into the air and firing as a pig jumped at her. Black dust showered down around them.

"Don't shoot anyone!" Allery cried back, darting forward to skewer another pig.

They fought on, ducking down behind stalls and dashing through the crowd until, crouched down together behind a pile of wooden crates and breathing heavily to catch their breath, Deni said, "I think that's all of them."

"Bloody hope so." Allery chanced a peek out from behind the crates, the movement sending little motes of soot dancing up around her again. She grimaced as she realised her hands and clothes were covered in the stuff.

"Al." Deni tugged on her arm.

When Allery looked up, she realised they hid opposite pig-man's weapon stall, and that he stood there smiling at them in his human form as if nothing was wrong.

Allery got to her feet and approached the stall, annoyed. "What the hell are you playing at? We could've killed someone!"

"But you didn't." He picked up his spectacles, cleaned them on his sleeve, and put them back on. "You may take your weapons."

Allery scowled at him, so Deni took up the broadsword and pushed it through her belt. "I need more bullets," she said.

"What do you get out of this?" Allery asked, as the stallholder bent down beneath his table to fetch a box of bullets for Deni.

"I feed off chaos," he said. "I've had a good feed. Thank you." He presented Deni with the bullets and smiled his pointed teeth at them again.

Allery returned her blade to its scabbard and turned away. "Let's get out of here."

"Right," Deni agreed. "Hey, it's all good, right? I'm bloody knackered, though. There better be a comfy bed at Nick's."

Allery nodded. She attempted to brush soot from her clothes, failed, and hurried after Deni.

Chapter Thirty-Two

Nick pulled back the net curtain and peered outside for what felt like the hundredth time that morning. The sun shone and the neighbours over the road were outside pottering in the front garden. The man waved when he noticed Nick looking.

"Baby, I really think we should go looking for her." Esme sat on the sofa, one of her feet up on the coffee table as she painted her toenails baby pink. "She's been gone too long."

"We'll give her until the end of the day," Nick said, stepping back from the window. He joined Esme on the sofa and watched her for a little while.

"You don't think Driscoll's taken her?"

"I honestly don't believe Driscoll's that much of an arsehole. He's scarpered. I doubt we'll see him again."

Esme screwed the lid back on her nail varnish, leaned forward to blow on her toes, then sat back and looked at Nick. "When this is all over," she said, "can we live here?"

"Course we can!"

"Properly. Just me and you. I could get a job as a beautician or something, and you could...you could be a gardener! Nick, this house is just so perfect, and I know it's full of memories of your mum, but she wanted you here and I don't think she'd mind me living here—"

"Of course she wouldn't!"

"And we could have a proper life. Ooh, we could get a cat!"

Nick smiled. "I love you, Esme Roberts."

Esme leaned over and kissed him. "I love you too, Nicholas Lode," she said.

"Marry me." He said it before he'd even had a chance to mull over the thought. He grimaced a little, but he wanted it suddenly, all of it. The house and the cat and the bloody ridiculous gardening job and most of all Esme, as his wife.

She gasped. "What?"

Nick got up off the sofa. He didn't have a ring, but he'd be damned if that was going to stop him from at least trying to do it properly. He got down on one knee before her and took hold of her hands. "Will you marry me?"

Esme squealed and pulled him into a hug, holding him tight. "Yes, yes!" She kissed his cheek, then kissed him on the lips, and he laughed and kissed her back.

He looked up when the living room door opened and Allery—with Deni close behind—walked in. "That looked like a proposal to me," Allery said, taking off her backpack and placing it by the sofa.

Esme jumped to her feet. "It was! Nick proposed! Oh, Al..." She turned back to Nick suddenly. "I don't have a ring!"

"I'll get you one," Nick promised. "The biggest, brightest, best one."

He watched as Esme turned away and hugged Allery and Deni.

His gaze met Allery's, but he couldn't exactly tell what she felt about the whole thing, though she at least offered him a smile.

"Good to see you back," he said to Deni, getting to his feet. "And you, Al, we were about to go looking for you."

"Time seems to have raced ahead of us here," Allery said. "We're exhausted, but…" She opened her backpack and took out a load of paperwork. "We have contacts. And supplies. And even better, weapons."

"Oh yeah? Anything for me?"

Deni pulled a scabbard from her belt and passed it over. "A bloody heavy sword," she said. "Probably medieval or something. Looks it."

Nick took the sword and pulled it from the scabbard a little. It was a two-handed broadsword. The metal made him uncomfortable, so he sheathed it quickly and nodded his thanks.

"We need to sleep before we drop," Allery said. "Nick, could you go through the contacts and see who you can get to help us?"

"I will. Go and get some kip. Second door down the hall is the spare room. It's made up."

"Thanks. Hey, Nick?"

"Yeah?"

Allery reached out her hand. "Congratulations. I'm happy for you both. You're made for each other."

Nick smiled. He took Allery's hand gratefully and laughed in surprise when she pulled him into a hug. She pushed him away, her cheeks flushed with embarrassment, and turned to head upstairs with Deni who winked at him before leaving the room.

He sighed in contentment and joined Esme on the sofa again. "Right. Let's see what we've got here." He picked up the pile of paperwork and looked through the list of names.

*

Max stood behind the wardens with his arms folded across his chest while he attempted to look as disapproving of their explanations at losing the key as Jacob surely expected him to be. They were in the creepy white dimension again and Jacob sat upon his throne on the dais with his long fingers splayed on the arms. He raised a hand to silence Tia and stood up.

"You have good news for me, incubus," he said.

Max uncrossed his arms. "Course. You can rely on old Max not to disappoint the boss man, eh?" He scratched the back of his head, not entirely willing to tell Jacob about Sophie but resigned to the fact he didn't really have a choice. "I'm gonna be a dad."

Jacob stepped down from the platform and touched Max's face as if he were a proud father. His features, as well as his hand, remained cold, and Max tried not to flinch. "Bring me the woman."

"Yeah. Look, about that. I'm really fond of Soph, I can't just drag her—"

Bring her to me.

Jacob's voice sounded all around them. His lips didn't move.

Max cleared his throat. "Course."

"Your child will help us secure the key," Jacob said. "It is an honour."

"I get that." Sophie wouldn't, though. Max decided he'd just have to get it over and done with as soon as possible. He relaxed a little as Jacob stepped back up onto the dais and took a seat once again.

Leave me.

"Come on, kids. Let's get out of here, eh?" Max waited for Dillon to open a door and then made sure he was the first one through it, not wanting to end up trapped with Jacob in case it closed too soon.

"Don't hurt my mum," Dillon said, almost as soon as the door closed behind them and they stepped out into the dark playground. Drizzle and mist hung in the air and the nearby swings creaked in the breeze.

"It really freaks me out that you're worried about her," Max said, annoyed. "I'm not gonna hurt her. This is just to give Jacob a bit of a boost so he can concentrate on finding the key. You want that, don't you?"

Dillon nodded. Condensation had gathered in his blond eyelashes, almost making it look as if he were crying. If Max wasn't a demon the scene might've damn near broken his heart. Instead, he clapped his hands. "Right, piss off, the lot of you. Don't bother me again tonight. Tia, make sure you're outside Sophie's flat first thing. Got it?"

The teen scowled at him but didn't argue. Max waited for them to disperse before he thrust his hands into his pockets and headed out of the playground to walk back to Sophie's. He sighed when he thought about how his life had been before Jacob—he'd be out doing what he did best right about this time of night, fucking as many pretty girls as he could. He'd have to make do with taking energy from Sophie instead, just enough to make her sleep. He knew he wouldn't be able to take her to Jacob any other way; he couldn't face the look he knew he'd see in her eyes once she realised what he was.

He stopped walking with a frown as pain stabbed low in his stomach and he wondered if he'd eaten something dodgy. When it happened again, he doubled over with a groan and reached out a hand to steady himself against a litter bin. His hand was smoking and he realised with a curse what was happening to him. His vision doubled and the world began to fade away around him.

"Someone dares summon me?" he roared, before black smoke engulfed him entirely.

The smoke cleared and Max stood as tall and imposing as he could muster. The sulphuric smell of magic lingered in the air, and he wrinkled his nose. He was in somebody's grotty little bedroom, trapped inside a bloody pentacle, and surrounded by candles and empty beer cans. He faced threadbare curtains, and he turned around to see an unmade bed and—

"Fuck's sake. What do *you* want?" Max eyed the man sitting on the edge of the bed, not liking the smirk on his face.

"I want you to fuck my brother. To death this time."

Max rolled his eyes. "You couldn't summon a succubus, Jack? You really need to let this whole thing with your brother go."

Jack got to his feet and stood as close to Max as the pentacle would allow. It was close enough that Max could smell the alcohol on him. "Fuck that *fairy* to death," he snarled. "I order you!"

"Shagging men doesn't really do it for me. Didn't it fuck him up enough last time?" He glanced down at the pentacle, but all the lines seemed to be in order.

"This time I want him dead." Jack dragged a heavy book across the bed and flicked through it. "If you don't do as I command, Max, I'll have to banish you somewhere. Or kill you. There was a good spell in here somewhere..."

"All right, calm your fucking tits," Max snapped. "I'll do it. Got a few other errands to sort out first, though. There's not a time frame on this, is there?"

Jack closed the book. "Just make sure I'm there to see it."

"Kinky."

Jack waved a hand and Max doubled over and clutched at his stomach again. "Go," Jack said, and Max glowered at him until smoke clouded his vision once more.

Chapter Thirty-Three

After being summoned, Max hadn't the energy or heart to take on Sophie, so he returned to his hotel room and spent the night alone. Morning came and went. At lunchtime, he sat in a McDonald's and stuffed his face with a burger and chips. He bought Sophie a bunch of flowers and waited for her to finish work, sitting opposite her shop and kicking his feet like a moody teenager. When he caught sight of her leaving, he jumped up to go and join her.

"Soph!"

She stopped when she saw him, and she smiled. "You stalking me?"

"Yeah, I'm stalking you. Here." He handed over the flowers.

"What's this for?" Sophie asked. She sniffed one of the roses and pulled a suitably impressed face. "You getting soft, Max, or are you after something?"

"Getting soft," Max muttered, walking with her. "Listen,

should you be working in your condition?"

"What condition?" She laughed. "I'm pregnant, not fucking dying. Little'n's still a bean at the minute."

Not for much longer. Max nodded. He scratched the back of his head, then took hold of Sophie's hand as they walked. She smiled but didn't protest, and they walked back to her flat together in companionable silence.

It wasn't until Sophie had unlocked her front door that she said, "Is all this because of Tia?"

Max screwed up his nose as he followed her inside. "What?"

"This. The flowers. The hand-holding." She turned to give him a smile before depositing her bag in her room, slipping off her shoes, and taking the flowers into the kitchen. "Is it some sort of guilt thing? I'm pregnant and you're thinking about Tia, wherever she is, worrying that you're replacing her. Like me with Dillon."

Max wished he'd never mentioned Tia in the first place. The fact that he'd lied to her made him uncomfortable now in a way he'd never felt before, and he didn't bloody like it. "I suppose it is guilt," he said. "Yeah."

"Half of me wants to take advantage of that." Sophie put the flowers in a vase of water and took them into the lounge where she faffed about with them on the coffee table. She straightened up and put her arms around Max. "You know, get you to cook me dinner and all that, too. The other half of me wants to comfort you. I know what you're going through. We'll find our kids, and all five of us are gonna live happily ever after. I fucking deserve that much."

"You do."

She kissed him and when he responded, kissing her back, she slipped a hand inside his pants.

This is for demon-kind everywhere, Max told himself. He

pushed her down onto the sofa gently and unbuttoned her blouse. "You're the best, Soph. The absolute dog's bollocks."

She laughed, and he laughed, too, and they kissed again.

*

Max heaved a sigh and sat on the arm of the sofa, feeling dejected. Sophie slept soundly, naked as a baby—she'd toed off her socks while they'd been at it, though he wasn't sure why she'd bothered. He smiled a little as he watched her sleep. A bomb could go off and she wouldn't wake. It was an unnatural sleep; he'd drained just enough energy to keep her and the baby alive. He picked at a suspect stain on the arm of the sofa, eyed the hole in his right sock, clicked his teeth, and tried to work out what an abstract piece of art on the wall above the fake fireplace actually *was*. Then he figured he'd dithered enough and he should just pull on his big boy pants and get it over with, so he got up, got dressed, and gathered up Sophie's clothes before dressing her, too.

He lifted her in his arms and met Tia and the other warden— not Dillon, he'd forbidden him from helping out in case he got any funny ideas—at the door.

"You ready?" Tia asked.

"What do you fucking think?" Max asked. Sophie was pretty heavy and the whole situation was making him annoyed. He glowered to himself as the two wardens opened a door to wherever the hell Jacob had decided to hole up.

The light blinded him temporarily and when his eyes finally adjusted, he realised they were in a forest, and that it was the middle of the night. The sky was clear and bright above the canopy, stars twinkling through the branches. The moonlight made Sophie's pale skin beautiful, and a shot of pain right in Max's heart made him wince.

Guilt. Fucking guilt.

He carried Sophie through the trees, flanked on either side by the wardens, feeling like he was attending some sort of bizarre funeral. Or wedding. A cool wind made the hair rise on his arms. Somewhere in the distance, one fox screeched to another.

If he wasn't a demon, he'd have felt pretty fucking freaked out by now. A shadowy figure lurked by a fat-bodied tree ahead. It stepped out into the moonlight as they drew nearer.

"Put her down," Jacob said, and Max laid Sophie at his feet.

"Don't hurt her, eh?" he asked, his voice gruff. He smoothed Sophie's red hair away from her face before straightening up.

Jacob's face remained impassive, and he held out his palms above Sophie's stomach. "I must bring the baby to term. Step away."

Reluctantly, Max took a step backwards. He folded his arms across his chest and watched. For a moment, nothing seemed to be happening, then Sophie's stomach began to swell. She took a great breath and opened her eyes, her face contorted in pain, and she clasped at her belly.

Jacob's hands trembled, though his expression never changed, and when Tia opened a door by his side, he seemed to draw energy from it and his hands stilled.

Sophie gasped. Her gaze met with Max's and she reached out a hand for him. "What's...happening?"

Max grimaced. "I'm sorry," he said. "It'll be over soon."

Sophie sobbed and curled up at Jacob's feet. Max looked away, half-tempted to run through Tia's door and escape. When he braved another look at Sophie, she was quite clearly nine months gone and ready to pop. Cursing, he ignored Jacob and the wardens and knelt by her side, gathering her up into his arms. "It's all right," he said. "I had to do it. I had to."

"Baby's coming now," Sophie said, gazing up at him. Her skin was slick with sweat. "Help me! Please!"

Jacob stood back, his arms once more by his side. "Deliver the child," he said.

"Go fuck yourself!" Sophie screamed at him. She grasped Max, her eyes wide, and he rocked her in his arms.

"Tia, help me here! You'll be okay, Soph."

"Why is the baby coming?" Sophie sobbed and shoved Max away before letting out a scream. She moved onto all fours and groaned.

"Tia, help her!" Max demanded again, stepping back and dragging a hand through his hair. He glared at Jacob.

"Once it is done, give the child to me," Jacob said.

Max sorely wanted to tell Jacob to fuck off. Instead, he knelt by Sophie again and rubbed her back while Tia helped her deliver the baby. He had no idea how much time had passed before he heard the first cries. They echoed through the forest.

He glanced back. "It's a girl, Soph," he said, his voice breaking. "A baby girl."

Sophie was in tears. She pushed Max away with her remaining strength and reached out to take the baby from Tia. Instead, Tia got to her feet and turned towards Jacob.

"No!" Max cried.

"Yes." Jacob took the baby, naked and bloodied—her face scrunched up as she wailed—and held her in his arms.

Max lunged forward, but the other warden grabbed hold of him and held him tight. He roared out his frustration as Sophie screamed in loss at his feet.

"She is strong," Jacob said, his eyes alight as he gazed at the baby. He shifted the child in his arms and held a palm over her as he drew out her energy. "Very strong!"

Max watched, fists clenched. He was barely aware of Tia and Sophie, only his child and Jacob, and the warden's grip on his arm.

The baby's wails grew quieter. Sophie's became clearer. *"You're killing her! You're killing her!"*

"Fuck this." Max turned and punched the warden in the face. Then he snatched Sophie by her arm and heaved her to her feet before shoving her through Tia's barely there door. Jacob paid him no mind, engrossed only in draining the baby. Max pulled the baby from his arms, and before he had time to think, he dived after Sophie. The door closed behind him.

Chapter Thirty-Four

Allery and the others sat at the dining table in Nick's mother's lounge surrounded by discarded Chinese food tubs and paperwork from the old office. All the chatter was beginning to give Allery a headache and she glanced over at Deni to see how she was coping. Deni was busy fishing the last few prawn crackers out of the bag.

"What if we get there and Jacob's somewhere else?" Esme asked.

"Then we wait," Allery said.

"He'll go back there eventually," Nick agreed. "Savernake is so old it's almost fizzing with power. He'll not be able to keep away."

"Yeah, and he's gonna be terrified when we show up with our army of…" Deni turned a piece of paper so she could read it and said, "Six people."

"We'll get more people to help us than Angel and Stacy the werewolf," Allery said. "What about Poedan?"

"Seeing as I'm the only one of us here who can travel between dimensions, I guess that means I'm the one who has to ask her?" Deni said. She screwed up the prawn cracker bag and sucked her fingers. "Are we just inviting all these people here and then...what? Are we needing to hire a bus or something? Won't a bus load of supernaturals look a bit odd heading up the M5?"

"They'll have to make their own way to Savernake," Allery said. "Meet us there or something."

"When?"

Allery shrugged. "The day after tomorrow?"

Deni laughed. "This is the worst fucking plan. I say we go there now, just the four of us, and I stick a bullet in Jacob's brain."

"I think we're missing a trick," Nick said, leaning across the table. "You two are descended from angels. Don't we have them on our side?"

"The only way I can contact my dad is through the wardens," Allery said. "Unless..." She looked at Deni expectantly.

Deni looked at Allery, then round at Nick and Esme before her gaze met Allery's again. "I haven't got a clue how to find the angels. Never stumbled across their dimension. Never even seen one besides my granddad and that doesn't really count because he just looked like your average granddad."

"You must be able to feel him or something," Nick said. "Whenever I connect with the trees, if I was to listen hard enough, I'd find my family. I can always feel them there even if I'm not totally aware of it. Don't you get any sense of something more when you open doors?"

Deni shrugged. "Opening a door is knackering. I don't really get chance to feel for anything other than how to get the bloody thing open in the first place."

"Maybe you could try?" Allery suggested gently. Deni folded

her arms and scowled around the table, so Allery reached over and gave her hand a squeeze. "I believe you could do this. If it helps, maybe we could go back to your place in Cricket St. Nicholas? He was protecting the cottage; he must be keeping an eye on it."

"I don't want to go back there," Deni said. "The wardens are probably crawling all over the place waiting for me to go back."

Allery didn't want an argument. She squeezed Deni's hand before sitting back in her chair. "We can think of another way."

"Wait, I didn't say I wouldn't *try*. Just...nobody watch me."

"Okay." Allery realised she felt at a loss with what to do, or suggest, and the fact that Deni hadn't asked for her help stirred up something in her guts. A sense of not being needed. "Whatever you want to do."

Deni pushed back her chair and got to her feet. "I'll go upstairs."

"Good luck." Allery sighed as Deni left the room. "If this doesn't work, I'll go to the wardens on my own and ask for their help."

"You don't need to go alone, Al," Esme said. "We're all with you."

"I know, I just... I want everybody to be safe."

"Let's see what Deni can do," Nick suggested.

Allery nodded. She looked around at the mess they'd made on the table—the dirty plates and discarded packaging and the spots of greasy sauce on the wood—and realised she really needed to clean up. She stood up and grabbed a couple of the empty packets, and she was only at it a couple of seconds before both Nick and Esme joined in.

*

Deni sat on the small double bed and gazed around the bedroom. The walls were covered in floral wallpaper and a large painting of a meadow hung above the headboard. The duvet cover was a faded pink, and she picked at a loose cotton thread. She had no idea how to contact the angels but knew everybody downstairs was depending on her and she was damned if she was going to let them down. She sighed, tentatively lifted her hand, and felt for the edge of a door.

Think of Granddad, she told herself.

She remembered him taking her to the park when she was small. Her mother was doing God knows what God knows where and she would've been completely alone had it not been for him. He had wispy grey hair, thinning on top, a chin covered in patchy stubble, and liver spots covering his arms and hands. He smelled like peanut butter. She remembered holding his hand as he walked them slowly towards the duck pond. He'd knelt by her side so she could take bread from the bag, and they'd laughed together as the ducks squabbled.

The door opened a crack beneath her fingertips and light seeped through. A familiar tug almost made her pull the door open completely, but she closed it instead with a curse, knowing it only went to the third.

"I can't do this," she muttered. How the hell was she supposed to find angels? Weren't they in heaven? Not that she was in any way religious, but a fucking cloud seemed the most likely place to look.

A thought occurred to her, and she touched the Glock in its holster against her thigh. Death was the fastest way to heaven. Wasn't it? If she shot herself, she was sure to find her granddad, and if not… If she just died for no reason then…then Jacob would give up anyway, wouldn't he? Either way, Allery and the others would be safe, and she would be free.

She placed the gun on the bed and stared at it for a long time, her heart racing until a strange feeling of calm settled over her. She'd die a hero, she thought, picking up the gun, and that was more than she could ever hope for. With a deep breath, she opened a door a crack with her right hand, and with her left she lifted the gun to her temple.

"Granddad," she said. "I'm coming to see you."

She squeezed the trigger.

Somebody burst through the door, widening the crack, and snatched the gun from Deni's hand. "Don't ever do that!" the man exclaimed. He tossed the gun onto the bed and pulled Deni into a hug. "I'm here now. I'm here."

Deni frowned, though she hugged the man in return. He pulled back to look at her. His face was young and handsome, his hair jet black, and his eyes a golden brown. "It's me, sweetheart," he said, touching her face. "Granddad."

"You don't look like you."

He gave her a sheepish grin before straightening up. He changed before her eyes, becoming the grandfather she remembered, and she gasped.

"A glamour," he explained, changing back again. "I wanted you to have some sense of normality growing up. I'm so, so sorry about your mother."

"You wanted me to have *normality*? Then why the hell did you leave me alone with her? Look at me, Granddad, look at what she did to me!"

He reached for her hands, but she backed up and shook her head. "I'm sorry," he said. "Really, I am! Us angels, we have children with mortals, but grandchildren? It's unheard of! I didn't know what I was supposed to *do*."

Deni laughed. "I was a child; you were supposed to look after me."

A pained expression lined his perfect face and had he actually looked like the granddad she remembered, she might've felt sorry for him. Instead, she folded her arms and waited for more excuses.

"I'm sorry. I can't change the past, but I'm here now. You were going to kill yourself, Deni. Have things got that bad?" He sighed and sat on the edge of the bed. "I should've kept a closer eye on you."

"I wasn't going to kill myself. I mean, I wasn't intending to kill myself. I was trying to find you. Worked, didn't it?"

"It was a very dangerous thing to do, don't ever do that again." He looked at her. "How can I help?"

"I'm going to kill Jacob." She snatched up the gun when her grandfather raised his eyebrows. "With this. Blow a hole right in his head."

"Sounds dangerous."

"This is why you have to help me. I've got friends downstairs— a werewolf, an immortal and...well, I'm not quite sure what Nick is. Some sort of tree fairy. Anyway. I've got friends and they're going to help me save the whole bloody world."

"What do you want me to do?"

Deni holstered the gun. "We're going to need more people behind us. Jacob's pretty powerful and he has God knows how many wardens working for him. I need you to gather as many angels as you can, and whoever else you can get hold of, and come help us kick some arse. Allery said it'd be the day after tomorrow, but if you can keep an ear out in case we need you sooner, that'd be great."

Her granddad hesitated, then he nodded. "Jacob's unsettled a lot of things. We can feel the ripples of it across dimensions. I agree he needs to be stopped, but...Deni, does it have to be you?"

Deni shrugged. "It doesn't matter who kills him, I guess. But I need to be there, and I need to do my bloody best to stop him. I'm sick of being a worthless junkie, Granddad. And I need some fucking closure."

"Language." He got to his feet and held out his hand. Deni eyed it for a moment before taking it and allowing him to pull her into a hug. "I'll be there. I'll get whoever I can, and we'll all be there."

Deni nodded, relaxing a little in his arms. "Savernake," she said. "It's all gonna kick off at Savernake Forest. Please be there."

"I won't let you down again." He pulled back and offered her a smile and she realised his eyes hadn't changed at all.

Chapter Thirty-Five

Max sat on the cold pavement under the yellow glow of the streetlight and stared at the door to Sophie's block of flats. A fox rooted through the bins put out for the morning and its eyes flashed as it turned and spooked at something before disappearing off down an alleyway.

It was done now and that was that. Sophie hated him—understandably, he supposed—but at least she and the baby were still alive. His baby girl. He'd held her and she'd squinted up at him from her wrinkly little prune face, then he'd given her back to her mother. The kid would grow up a boring arse human anyway after Jacob had sucked all the power out of her so he told himself he wouldn't be missing anything. He scratched the back of his neck and stared at his feet instead.

"Getting soft, Max," he told himself. "Fuck this."

He got to his feet and thrust his hands into his pockets. He'd go and find a passed-out-drunk bird to shag; that'd make him feel better. Where was the nearest pub?

A stab of pain in his guts made him double over and he groaned. His heart rate increased when he wondered if Jacob was summoning him. Would he kill him? He couldn't think of an excuse quick enough before the smoke engulfed him.

When the smoke cleared, he realised he was back in Jack's bedroom and he roared out in frustration and kicked at the edge of the pentacle, cursing when flames licked at his feet.

"Don't you ever fucking *sleep*?" he hissed, turning to glare at Jack sitting on the bed. "What do you want?"

Jack lobbed an empty beer can at him, but it missed, hit the edge of the pentacle, and bounced out. Max eyed a droplet of beer as it smudged one of the chalk lines. "You know what I want," Jack slurred. "I've told you where he is. Why haven't you done it yet?"

"You've not told me anything," Max snapped back. "I dunno where the bloody hell he is. You need therapy, you know? A bloody shrink would have a field day with you."

Jack got up off the bed and lurched drunkenly towards him. He stopped short of the pentacle, much to Max's annoyance. "He has my mother's house—55 Church Street, Clifton. Now go and do what I fucking ordered you to do!"

He clapped his hands, and Max felt a twinge in his kidneys and heat beneath his skin before the room vanished and he was back in the street outside Sophie's.

He frowned. Had Jack just told him where to find the key? If Nick Lode was there, then Miss Locke was bound to be nearby and if not, then the fairy would surely know where to find her...and she was looking after the girl. He laughed into the empty street. If that didn't get him back into Jacob's good books, then nothing would. He shoved his hands in his pockets once more and set off down the road in a good mood.

*

Max barely acknowledged Dillon as the kid closed the door behind them. The forest was so dark it took his eyes a moment to adjust, but he knew something was going on as soon as his feet sank into the soft earth. The air practically fizzed with supernatural energy, making the hairs rise on his arms.

"What's going on?" He nudged Dillon with his elbow. "Hey, I said what's going on?"

Dillon shrugged.

Max rolled his eyes and headed off through the forest. He glanced back briefly to make sure the warden was following him, vaguely aware Sophie would be upset if the kid was to get lost and die out in the cold in the middle of nowhere.

He caught snatches of dark shapes moving through the trees alongside him, though when he turned his full attention on them, they whisked away and vanished. He was fairly confident he could hear sinister laughter and whispered voices that made even his skin crawl.

There were demons, then there were *demons*. Flies buzzed and crawled over the tree trunks, their black bodies glistening unpleasantly as they clambered over one another. A stench of cat shit, fox shit...the worst kind of shit imaginable filled his nostrils.

Dillon walked so close alongside him that Max actually felt a little sorry for the kid and he grabbed hold of his sleeve just to make sure he wasn't taken away.

"Piss off!" he snapped, glaring into the forest at the whispering entities.

Light in the distance caught his eye and he practically dragged Dillon towards it, aware of more and more demons weaving in and out of the trees as he approached.

"Jacob?" he called.

Max. The parasites whispered his name back to him, all their voices as one. *Max.*

He could see Jacob now, standing perfectly still and serene next to a glowing door spilling abomination after abomination into the clearing. He scratched the back of his head with one hand and kept a tight hold of Dillon with the other as he moved forward. Jacob turned his gaze upon him.

"So, uh, this is what you've done with my daughter's energy, yeah?" He laughed nervously. "Nice one."

"My army," Jacob said. "They will bring me the key."

"Right. Yeah, about that. I know where she is."

Jacob took a step towards him and Max almost took a step back. Instead, he gripped Dillon a little tighter, ignoring the kid's "ow" of protest.

"Tell me."

"Okay. Firstly, you've got to promise me you're not gonna go batshit insane and kill me, and secondly, you've got to promise me you'll not drag me into anything that's gonna result in my death. If you're opening doors to let supernaturals come and go when they please, then I'm all for that, but if something fucks up this dimension, then I'm off. And I want to take Sophie with me. And the baby. And maybe this one, but I'm not sold on that." He jabbed a finger at Dillon.

"Tell me, where is the key?"

"Bristol. Clifton, to be more precise." He grimaced as a dark shape breezed close to him, turning his skin to ice. "Look, I'll give you the exact address but—"

"I will not kill you," Jacob said.

Jacob agreed a little too quickly for Max's liking but as he didn't have a lot of choice left, he nodded. "It's 55 Church Street.

You'll probably find Locke & Co there, too, so, you know, a nice little bonus."

Jacob stepped closer to him and raised a hand to gently touch Max's cheek. Max winced. "They will bring them here," he said. "You have pleased me, Max."

"Good," Max said, moving away. "That's good. Right. Well. It's past Dillon's bedtime so…"

Jacob turned away and gave his attention back to the doorway so Max took the opportunity to indicate to Dillon that they should get the hell out of there while they had the chance. As soon as Dillon ripped open a door, they both jumped through it.

*

Allery woke up with her heart racing and a feeling of someone watching her. She sat up, gripped the duvet, and stared into the corners of the dark bedroom until her eyes adjusted. The movement of a fly flicking its wings on the bedside table caught her eye. Deni slept soundly by her side, but she nudged her awake anyway.

"Did you hear anything?" she whispered, when Deni moved.

"No."

"Whispers."

"You're whispering."

A creeping sense of unease made her reach over and turn on the bedside light, and as soon as she did, a black entity hissed and shot back into the wall. She threw off the duvet and snatched up her sword from where she'd left it propped against the cabinet.

"Go," she told Deni, who'd now also hurried out of bed. "Get out of here. Nick! Es—"

The demon came at her again, all teeth and claws, with a body of black tar and red eyes. She swung the sword at it, catching it across the chest, and drew the blade right through and out the other side. The demon gathered itself back together and retreated once more into the wall. Allery's sword dripped sludge onto the carpet.

She glanced back at Deni, whose mouth hung open. "Get out of here! Now!"

"What the hell is going on?"

"Just—"

More demons came out of the walls all around them, black and nebulous and bringing the stench of shit. Deni screamed. Allery struck out with her sword until four of them grabbed hold of her and pulled her backwards. She stared wide-eyed at Deni, also fighting off demons, willing her to get away.

"I'm sorry!" Deni cried, kicking a demon backwards before tearing open a door. "I'll come back for you!"

Then she was gone. Allery struggled against the demons, their touch ichorous and icy cold against her skin. She fought wildly, kicking and flailing, until they overwhelmed her. Their stench filled her nostrils, making her gag, and a buzzing filled her ears. She struggled to breathe. Hands slammed her head against the wall. Pain exploded through her skull, and she blacked out.

Chapter Thirty-Six

Allery woke only briefly. In the blackness she could make out red eyes and dark shapes, and two lighter shapes—the white of Esme's pyjama bottoms and the pale blue of Nick's T-shirt—let her recognise her two friends moved with her. And they *were* moving. She registered that much. A jolt made her head spin, and she passed out again.

*

When Allery did wake, her heart beat so hard it drowned out the pain in her skull and with a groan, she pulled herself up into a sitting position. Her wrists were chained, the chain secured to a thick-bodied tree, and she squinted in the daylight. The forest was unnaturally still and empty. The sky above was just the right shade of grey that she knew something was off.

"Esme?" she called. "Nick?" Her voice hung flat in the air, as if she spoke in a dream. Something rumbled and moved behind her, and she turned with a gasp to see nothing there.

Demons. The air felt almost thick with their presence. They were watching her; she knew that much. Fat-bodied beetles crawled out of the ground around her. "Es?" she called again. She wanted to call for Deni, wanted her to open a door before her and take her away to safety. She wanted her dad. And her mum.

I don't know what to do. She stared at the chains around her wrists—if they'd left her there to starve would she eventually lose enough weight to slip free? No, no, she had to think logically. She was in a forest—Savernake probably. Nick would be there, too, and there was no way they could keep a drus confined in such a place, and Esme was strong enough as the wolf to rip up a tree if she put her mind to it. The angels would come, too. They were coming.

She just wished she could shake the feeling of being watched.

"Miss Locke."

The warden's voice made her jump, and she cursed and looked up at him as he walked towards her. His feet made no sound, though they left prints in the earth. He stopped and turned his palms to her as if in greeting, though he didn't smile. "I am Jacob."

"Whatever you're doing, you need to stop," Allery said, glaring at him. "Give up now."

"When I am so close? You have given me challenges, Miss Locke, but ultimately you have failed. The key will come for you and when she does, I will take her and use her."

"She won't come."

"I am going to hurt you," Jacob said. "Your screams will bring her to me." He closed his eyes, and a creepy half-smile touched his lips.

Allery took the opportunity to give the chain a yank, but it didn't budge. "If you open too many doors you'll create havoc, you'll destroy this dimension and God knows what it'll do to the others! What will you do when everything's gone? You fucking id-iot."

"What will *you* do when everything's gone?" Jacob asked. "Will you die at last?"

A cold stab of fear made Allery double over and she stared wide-eyed at the ground in front of her. What would happen to her? If the entire planet was swallowed up in a black hole and she was left in the vastness of space only to die over and over and over...

She took a deep breath and looked up at Jacob again. "You won't get Deni, no matter what you do to me."

Jacob sighed. "If you mean nothing to her and she won't come for you, or the other two, then you must tell me where to find her."

Allery laughed then. "You are completely fucking mad! No! I don't know where she is anyway. Jesus, you are something else." She chuckled again, though it was quieter, and shook her head.

Jacob took hold of her chin and held her tight, forcing her to look him in the eye. She lifted her hands and grabbed his arm to push him off but couldn't get him to move at all. He brought forth a small, needle-sharp blade which he pointed at her eye, and he moved it slowly closer until she screwed her eyes shut.

"Scream for me," he said.

And though she tried not to, she did.

*

Allery had experienced pain before. Painful deaths. Pain was usu-ally sudden and brief and death a relief. When she woke, she was healed anyway. She heard a story—it might have been her father who'd told her—of an immortal who'd been torn limb from limb back in the thirteenth century for...she couldn't remember the rea-son. But the remains had been gathered up and burned, and the man—was it a man? He'd risen from the flames like the phoenix. Whole again.

Allery didn't know if she'd regain her eye if she died and came back again. Perhaps someone would need to push the eye back into her skull so her body could reattach it during the healing process. She almost wanted to laugh.

Blood ran down her cheek, hot and sluggish. Her body trembled and her skin burned. Jacob pushed the blade into the soft part just beneath her shoulder and twisted slowly. Blood and saliva made her choke, but she managed to turn it into a savage laugh before she spat in his face.

She slumped forward as Jacob stepped back in disgust. "If she will not come, you must tell me where she is."

"Go. Fuck. Yourself."

"Miss Locke, I wonder how long you can hold out before you die? I can repeat this process for as long as I need." He crouched down in front of her and grasped her chin again, making her look up. "You still have one eye."

"*No!*" She screamed at him and pushed him back with as much force as she could muster before she managed to stagger to her feet and retreat to the full length of the chain.

Dizziness made her stumble, and she clung to the tree for support. Jacob approached her and she screamed again.

A flash of light forced her to screw her eye shut and she huddled against the tree, her heart thumping so fast she wondered if it'd give up on her. When she opened her eye, she saw Deni step through the doorway, her gun pointed at Jacob.

"Shoot him!" she cried.

Deni looked at her and her eyes widened, and the gun lowered in her grip. "Allery, what the hell...?"

"Shoot him, shoot him, shoot *him!*" She screamed it so

desperately that spittle and blood flew from her lips, and she collapsed to her knees afterwards.

Deni raised the gun again, but the demons came, whipping past the trees like black smoke, and held her tight.

"Jacob, don't do this," Allery cried, as the warden stepped towards Deni. "You'll destroy us all!"

"Allery, it'll be all right," Deni said, as she struggled briefly against the demons. "I won't open any doors for the cunt. I'll get you free and we'll be okay, yeah? We'll be okay!"

Allery gazed at Deni, her heart torn in two. She smiled and though she didn't believe it, she said, "We'll be okay."

Chapter Thirty-Seven

"Let Allery go," Deni demanded as she squirmed in the demons' grasp. They held her tightly, her feet not even touching the ground. "Let Allery go!"

She hoped she sounded commanding and unafraid, but even she could hear the tremble in her voice.

Jacob walked ahead of them, but he stopped when he reached a clearing and indicated for the demons to let Deni stand. When her feet touched the ground, she yanked her arms away from the evil entities, but they held on far too strongly to let go.

"You're going to cut off my fucking blood supply," she snapped at them. Her head pounded. Her heart pounded. Adrenaline flooded through her, narrowing her world so she was only aware of Jacob and the demons.

Jacob smiled at her, a cold smile that didn't reach his eyes. "Do you remember me?" he asked. He sounded genuinely interested, as if he'd be surprised if she did.

She glowered at him. She remembered him giving her mother pills to pass on—tranquillizers to stop her opening doors when she tried to run away. Speed. Steroids. LSD. Heroin.

"I won't open *any* doors for you," she growled. "I can't anyway! You fucked me up so much that I don't even fucking work properly any more. I can open one or two and then I'm exhausted, so if you think I can do what you want me to, I'm afraid you're barking up the wrong tree."

"I can heal you," Jacob said. "I am far more powerful than you can imagine." He turned slightly and beckoned with his hand. "Come here, girl."

The warden, Tia, stepped out from the shadows of a fat-bodied oak and joined Jacob. She stood obediently by his side. Jacob placed his hand on the top of her head, almost fondly.

"Many of my children were ill when I took them in. I gave them new life. Watch."

Deni clenched her fists tightly and looked at Tia. Jacob had closed his eyes, his hand still resting on the girl's head. As she watched, a pink flush crept up Tia's neck.

"What are you doing to her?" Deni asked, frowning.

Tia's black eyes cleared and became human again, her irises a soft hazel colour. The girl's brow furrowed in confusion, then she coughed suddenly and clutched at her chest as her breathing shortened. "Help me," she gasped.

Deni tried to twist free. "What have you done to her? Stop it!"

"I have...cystic fibrosis," Tia managed, wheezing heavily. "I need...hospital..."

Jacob placed his hand once more on the top of Tia's head. She quietened down and straightened up, her eyes a soulless black. He waved her away.

"You see," he said, taking a step towards Deni. "I can heal you.

No more cravings. No more shakes. No more pain."

"You made me this way in the first place!" Deni yelled at him. "Fuck you!"

She fought frantically against the demons again, though they didn't even budge. Jacob approached her and placed a heavy hand on the top of her head. She jerked her head away and kicked out at him, but he simply reached for her again. "Humans could become so much more if they mixed with supernaturals. Look at you. You have immense power. Imagine what we could achieve together." She stopped struggling when a comforting warmth flowed through her body, though her mind told her to fight. It would be easier to sink deeper into it and forget everything, wouldn't it? All the little aches and pains that she barely paid any attention to any more faded away. The gnawing feeling in her stomach disappeared, and the itch left her palms. *Relax. Jacob will look after you.* Her memories clouded and fogged over until she felt nothing at all. The demons let go of her arms, and she straightened up and looked at Jacob as he removed his hand.

"Are you ready?" he asked.

Deni gazed at her palms, aware of a huge amount of energy coursing through her, begging to be used. "I am," she said. She offered Jacob a smile and felt for a door.

*

Max pulled Jack's van over to the side of the road and peered into the forest. He didn't like the colour of the sky much but figured Jacob would know what he was doing and really, who gave a fuck if the sky was grey, blue, or pink with green spots. He'd mentioned it to Jack, who told him it was a perfectly normal colour, and guessed only supernaturals could see what was really going on. He wondered if he'd have more incubi to compete with if the doors stayed open all the time. He hoped not.

"He's in there," he told Jack, waving a hand at the trees.

"Well, go and get him." Jack stank of beer and sweat and had a sour look on his face to match.

Max muttered curse words under his breath as he unbuckled his belt and got out of the van. If he could convince Jack to get off his arse and wander about in the forest, hopefully he'd end up killed by the demons. He sighed. It was probably best not to fuck with a mage, even a shit one like Jack.

He had no idea where Nick Lode was being kept, exactly, only that he was there somewhere and probably—hopefully—out cold. As he wandered deeper into the forest, he caught flashes of light from the depths and knew doors were opening. Black shapes whipped past him, whispering his name and taunting him until he snapped, grabbed one that came too close, and gripped its writhing mass in his hands.

"Where's the drus?" he asked. "Quickly, I haven't got all fucking day."

Cold burned his hands. The demon's red eyes flashed mockingly at him. "Incubus," it hissed.

"Yep. Demon, like you. Only I actually have a purpose." He squeezed harder as the demon attempted to pull away. "Here's what's gonna happen—I let you go, you lead me to the fairy, and then you piss off. Otherwise, we'll go to Jacob, and he can send you back to wherever the hell he dragged you up from. Deal?"

"Yes."

Max let go and the demon hovered in front of him, its form shifting until it had developed crude arms and legs. It smiled pointed teeth at Max and set off into the forest, its red eyes appearing in the back of its head briefly as it checked he was following.

Max scowled to himself as he walked. Some demons were so bloody weird. Why couldn't they stick to one form and be done with it? He *liked* looking human and he knew the ladies liked him looking human, too. Especially Sophie.

Get her out of your head. He slapped the side of his head with his palm in an attempt to dislodge the woman from his brain. The demon's eyes appeared in the back of its head again, so he gave it the finger and looked away.

That was when he spotted the immortal. God, he'd rather shag her, even though she looked a right bloody state. He paused and thought back to Jack's latest summoning. Had the marks scuffed enough for him to disobey his commands?

"Oi!" The demon had gone on ahead and Max had to jog to catch up with it again. He stomped after it until it hovered around a prone figure in a clearing. The drus was clearly out cold, though his wrists were manacled with iron to dampen his abilities should he happen to wake up, and several other demons flitted in and out of the trees nearby. Max had no idea why Jacob hadn't killed the bloody man—and his girlfriend and the immortal—instead of hanging on to them. Maybe he'd forgotten or maybe he just couldn't be arsed.

"Come on then," he said, walking into the clearing. "Let's get you to your brother." He hefted Nick awkwardly over his shoulder and headed back to the van.

*

Nick awoke with a start when the liquid splashed onto his face and neck. He grimaced and ran his hands over his skin, the smell of beer and the thick metal around his wrists soon waking him fully. Two figures loomed over him in the van and as he squinted upwards, he realised one was Jack.

"What are you doing?" he asked. "Help me!"

He looked at the other man and his eyes widened. His heart raced and he shuffled backwards until he hit back of the driver's seat. "No. Not you. No, no, no!"

Panic made him lose all sense of self and he kicked out at the demon as tears of fear sprung to his eyes. He couldn't get out of the van. He couldn't escape. But he had to! Not again. He couldn't go through that again.

Hands holding him down.

Jack would help him. "Jack...brother...please!"

"I am *not* your brother," Jack snapped. "I lost my real brother, and I lost my mother the day you arrived because she loved *you* more. You took her from me! You make me sick, you pathetic fucking fairy."

"Please, Jack, please!" He couldn't look at the demon—the man stood back with his arms folded. He could only cower in the corner and hold up his palms in the hope that they'd let him go.

"Do it then," Jack said. "Now!"

The incubus sniffed. "You know what, this isn't really doing it for me. Once was enough. Look at the bloke!"

Nick chanced a look up from beneath his hands, wondering what was going on. His heart pounded painfully hard.

Jack's face was red. "I *order* you to—"

"Won't work. See, the line smudged. Too much booze and not enough care, Jackie boy. I'm off."

The demon turned away and pulled the van doors open before jumping out. Nick scrabbled up and made a dash for the doors, but Jack grabbed him and slammed him back down into the corner. Pain barely registered.

"Jack, no!"

Jack stood over him, eyes wide and nostrils flaring, and

unbuckled the belt from his jeans. "I'm gonna teach you a lesson you won't forget in a hurry, fairy."

Nick backed into the corner and tried to protect himself with his arms. He cried out in horror as Jack unzipped himself. Then the van doors opened again, and a snarling mass of fur and teeth burst inside and pulled Jack violently backwards. It threw him from the van and into the forest. His head hit a tree trunk with an audible smack.

Nick doubled over and threw up, then retched until his stomach was empty. He sobbed and trembled until Esme, in her human form, returned to the van and clambered inside. She pulled him into her arms and held him tight.

"It's all right, baby, it's all right." She stroked his hair and rocked him gently in her arms.

He stared out of the van door into the gloom, just able to make out the twisted figure of his dead brother in the distance. He closed his eyes and held on to Esme.

*

Allery had given up pulling at the chains. She sat on her heels with her head bowed, ignoring the demons flitting in and out of the trees around her as blood dried on her face and clothes. Pain pulsed inside her skull, louder and harder than anywhere else in her body. The world was going to die. Deni was going to die. And she didn't know how to stop it.

The snap of a twig underfoot made her look up.

"What do you want?" she asked.

The incubus, Max, smirked at her. "In a word, you." He stepped closer to her, but she didn't retreat. If he came close enough, she'd throttle him with the chain. He scratched his cheek. "Can you even imagine how much power I could get from fucking an immortal? I could take you to death over and over. Maybe then I could take on Jacob, eh?"

"You're too much of a coward."

Max shrugged. Allery tightened her grip on the chain and mentally dared him to come closer. "Does Sophie know you're here?" she asked.

The incubus let out a snort of amusement. "You think she knows everything I do? Hey, maybe I should've brought her along to watch. I'm sure she would've got a kick out of me shagging her ex."

"You're sick in the head."

"I'm a *demon*."

"One of the greatest people I know is a demon," Allery said. "And she is *nothing* like you."

"She sounds boring as hell. Anyway, I'm done talking. I've never fucked a dyke before. Not that I'm aware of anyway. Reckon I could screw you straight?"

He grinned at her, and she screwed up her nose and braced herself for a fight, every muscle in her body tense. Without warning, Driscoll appeared behind Max, his face as dark as thunder, and he grabbed the incubus by the chin and drew a knife across his throat. Dark-red blood spurted from the jugular and air hissed and gurgled as Driscoll dropped Max to his knees. The demon clutched at his neck, eyes wide, and for a moment Allery thought he would recover. Then he fell to his side, blood pulsing out onto the forest floor.

Allery let go of the chains and threw her arms around the leprechaun's neck. Relief made her tremble, and she fought back tears. "I'm so glad to see you. I'm so sorry. I was so angry."

"No, I'm sorry," he mumbled into her hair. "I should've stayed with you, not run away. I was ashamed, I—"

"You had no choice!" She pulled back and held out her wrists to let Driscoll work the point of his blade into the cuff's lock. She didn't look at the body. Sophie was safe now. Sophie was safe and she needed to be able to say the same about Deni.

"I've been watching you guys lately," Driscoll said. "I knew you needed me. I've got something for you." He unbuckled Allery's scabbard from his belt and gave it to her. "We've got a hell of a lot of work to do, Al."

"I know." She pulled the sword free and stepped over the still-twitching body of the incubus as the demons began to swarm. "I'm ready."

Chapter Thirty-Eight

*K*ill *Jacob. Save Deni. Kill Jacob. Save Deni.*

Allery plunged her blade deep into another demon and pulled it out with a yell. With her right eye missing, she felt like she was working twice as hard to fight them off, that they were coming from all angles. She spun around and slashed across the chest of a dark figure, the sword slowing as it sank into black sludge. She was aware of Driscoll fighting by her side, appearing and disappearing from view. A howl in the distance made her heart leap as she realised Esme must be fighting, too.

"We're gonna need help!" she called to Driscoll.

"Look up, Al."

She kicked back an approaching demon and looked up through the canopy at the grey sky. Birds circled high above, just dark specks, barely recognisable until they came lower and she could make out the wings.

"Angels!" She grinned in triumph and ducked as a demon swung its arm at her. She dragged her blade across its stomach and drove it straight through the middle of the next one to come at her.

The forest glowed when the angels descended and several landed between the trees nearby. The demons withdrew and advanced again like startled fish. Allery didn't have chance to look for her father, but she had no doubt he'd be there somewhere.

Driscoll cried out on her blind side, and she turned to see him caught between two demons, the creatures pulling his arms as if to tear him apart. With a yell, she ran one of them through, giving Driscoll the chance to plunge his knife deep into the guts of the other, spilling oil-like blood over his hand and wrist. He cursed and Allery laughed.

"You're not worried about your watch, are you? It's not even a real Rolex."

Driscoll flashed her a smile, teeth white beneath his dark moustache. "So, I don't like demon blood. Sue me!"

They turned together and faced the next two demons that flew at them from the dark. Allery ducked as claws slashed wildly over her head.

"Hey, Al?" Driscoll called, sticking his knife in the demon's neck. "I forgot to mention, nice pyjamas!"

Allery rolled her eyes. She was about to retort that he was lucky she didn't sleep naked, when something struck her hard between the shoulder blades. She fell forward and rolled quickly onto her back. The demon leered at her. The one she had been fighting had turned its arms to spikes and she just had time to roll aside before it plunged one of the points into the earth. "Little help?" she called to Driscoll, snatching up her sword and scrabbling to her feet once more.

"They're never ending," Driscoll commented, standing by her side.

"We need to stop Deni opening doors. We need to kill Jacob and end this."

"Right," Driscoll agreed. He glanced at her. "Any idea how?"

Allery thrust with her sword, keeping the demons back. They hissed and advanced again. "We need to find them," she said. "Get ready to run."

*

Jack. The incubus. Nick had no time to digest what had happened other than to force the images down when they popped into his head. The earth shook beneath his feet as the roots danced to his command, impaling demons as easy as if he were threading a needle. His ancestors sang to him, but he ignored them, too. Out of the corner of his eye he spotted the wolf smash a writhing black mass into a tree trunk.

Jack's face flashed into his mind again.

He was never your brother.

"Esme!"

She had two demons on her back, clinging to her fur as she snarled and snapped and twisted to get away. Nick put his hands to an oak and made its roots burst forth and strike the creatures. Something bowled into him and landed on his chest as he hit the ground. An imp chattered pointed teeth at him, and he cried out and punched the thing in the face.

After he'd hurried to his feet, he drew the sword Driscoll had given him and slashed at the imp, but it squealed and ran off, disappearing deeper into the forest.

Nick cursed, loudly, and spun around again only to see another imp leap through the air towards his face. He cleaved it in half, grimacing when too-hot blood splashed his bare arms.

When Driscoll appeared by his side, it made him jump.

"Imps now, too?" the leprechaun said. "Jesus, it's all a pain in the arse, that's for sure."

A rush of footsteps and Allery arrived, breathing heavily and covered in blood. She doubled over for a moment, her hands on her knees, but when she straightened up, Nick's eyes widened.

Her eye!

Allery waved a hand, as if she knew what he was thinking. "No time. Nick, where's Deni?"

"Uh…" He reached out to the nearest tree, a beech, and closed his eyes to join with it, trusting his companions to watch his back. His awareness raced away into the forest and his ancestors pulled and tugged at him in their excitement. He ignored them. He saw Jacob and there, by his side, her eyes black and soulless as she tore open another door, was Deni.

He looked at Allery. "Sessile oak, about three hundred years old… Never mind, follow me!"

He ran, calling Esme to follow, knowing Driscoll and Allery were right behind him. Angel wingtips brushed his cheek, imps ran at him only to be snatched up in the wolf's jaws and tossed aside, and demons circled all around. And still his brother's face flashed into his mind.

*

Allery stopped when Nick did and nodded to say that she understood Jacob was just ahead. Pain throbbed in places she couldn't quite name though she told herself she was doing a pretty good job of ignoring it. She feared that if she let it take over, she wouldn't have the strength to continue, and she *needed* to carry on.

She gasped when somebody touched her shoulder, but as she

turned to lash out and saw her father instead, she relaxed and wrapped her arms around his neck.

"Allery," he said, his voice soft.

"I'm okay." She pulled back and offered him a smile. "I'm so glad you're here."

"Jacob's too powerful. I don't know if he can be stopped. He's killed two angels, Allery."

The words didn't affect her. Nobody could kill angels, not easily. It was like somebody had just told her she didn't exist when she knew she did because she was standing right there. The information wouldn't process. She lifted a hand to her head and rubbed her temple.

Her father peered at her. "The more doors Deni opens, the stronger he gets. He's feeding off the energy."

"You can stop Deni," Driscoll said. "We'll hold back the demons. You get to her, and you get her to stop. Then we'll tackle Jacob together."

Easy. She looked at Driscoll, then at Nick, and Esme—who'd changed back into her human form with the cuffs of her too-long pyjama bottoms covered in mud. Esme nodded.

"Right." Allery drew her sword once more. "Let's get me to Deni."

Esme changed, Driscoll disappeared, and Nick drew his own sword with a grim smile. Allery glanced at her father as he spread his wings, then she surged through the trees. Deni stood just ahead in a clearing, in the middle of opening a door of swirling yellow light. Demons circled her and dispersed to intercept Allery and her friends as they advanced.

Allery slashed at demons, taking her gaze from Deni long enough only to dispatch them. Her friends were a blur of activity around her; roots burst forth from the ground, the wolf snarled and snapped, Driscoll appeared once in front of her to take out an imp before he vanished again. She moved onward, determined to reach Deni.

Something came at her from her blind side and rugby tackled her to the ground. Pain jolted up her left side and she cried out and struggled with the demon, spitting curses as the creature leered at her and dug needle-fingers into her wounded shoulder. She elbowed it until it let go and awkwardly managed to grab her sword and swipe out. The demon backed off and hunched over like a startled cat, showing her pointed teeth and red eyes.

Allery stabbed at it, but it grabbed the blade and pulled her close so that she was face to face.

"*Allery,*" it whispered, its breath hot.

She grimaced and closed her eye. Her grip loosened on the sword.

"*Allery.*"

It was her mother's voice, and it was in her mind, and all she had to do was let go and she could be with her. Forever.

"*Allery.*"

Allery, that's it. Hold my hand, sweetie. Why don't you have a go on the slide? Don't be afraid, I'm here to catch you at the end. I'm here, my darling.

"Allery!" Her father's shout jerked her into wakefulness. She grasped the sword tight and pulled it from the demon's grip before pushing the blade through its middle with a yell. The demon jerked back and whizzed away, trailing black sludge as it went.

It passed Deni, and Allery realised there was nothing between the two of them to stop her. She ran to her, gripped her hands, and yanked her away from the door.

"Deni, listen to me!"

Deni looked at her, her eyes nothing but black orbs. Allery gasped.

"Deni. You need to stop this, close the doors. You can beat this, I know you can!"

Deni smiled. "I feel...powerful," she said, pulling her hands from Allery and looking at them. "Why would I want to stop this? I am so fucking powerful." She laughed.

"No, listen to me." Allery gripped her hands again and held them tight. "Listen. This isn't you; this is what Jacob's done to you. If you don't stop opening doors, you'll tear the world apart. You don't want that!"

"Why not? What has the world ever done for me? Fuck it. Fuck you." She jerked her hands back, but Allery held fast.

"No! You've got to come with me now. Come with me."

"I said no!"

Allery pulled her on, desperation giving her strength. Deni dug her heels into the ground like a spoilt child.

"Leave her alone." Jacob strode towards them, demons and imps scattering from his path. He had his hand out, ready to snatch Deni away.

Driscoll appeared between them, forcing Jacob to an abrupt halt. The leprechaun looked back at Allery. "Take Deni and go," he said. "Get out of here. Go!"

Allery tugged Deni a few paces farther until she pulled free and stepped back. She instantly reached out and began opening another door.

"You can't stop us!" Jacob cried. "You—"

Driscoll lunged at him, knife blade flashing in his hand. Jacob moved faster, grabbing the leprechaun around the throat and lifting him from the ground. The knife fell to the leaves.

"Driscoll!" Allery hesitated, torn between stopping Deni and going to her friend.

Jacob laughed and Driscoll choked. "You are a fool, Miss

Locke. Go home or be killed. There is nothing you can do!"

The ground trembled beneath her feet and for a moment, Allery thought Nick was doing something, until she noticed the earth split and crack as if there were an earthquake. Deni moved away from her open door and began peeling back another. All through the forest, doors blinked and flashed as demons and imps and other creatures now jumped through them and into the world. The crack in the earth ran between them all.

"Allery." Driscoll's voice was strangled, his face blue. "Stop her."

Allery didn't know how. She ran to Deni and grabbed her arm, pulling her back. Deni turned and swung her fist, catching Allery in the side of the jaw. She didn't say anything before turning back to the door again.

Allery gasped and held her face, though Deni's punch hadn't been particularly impressive. *It's not her.* The realisation caused her to bite back a sob. Deni had gone, just like Dillon had, her soul destroyed by Jacob. She wasn't *her* any more. She drew her sword from its scabbard with trembling hands. The demons and imps and angels and werewolves were nothing but a blur around the centre of her vision; in the middle was Deni, crystal clear.

She reached for her again, touching her shoulder. Deni swiped her away. "Just let it go, Allery. This is what's happening. When the world ends, we'll all be at peace." She laughed. "Even you."

Allery looked away from Deni towards Jacob. Driscoll's grip was loosening around the warden's wrists and slowly his hands fell to his sides. She turned back to Deni.

"I love you," she said. "Forgive me."

She screamed and thrust the sword through Deni's chest, under her ribcage and up into her heart. Deni's eyes widened with shock. Allery closed hers. Blood warmed her hand and Deni's weight fell forward, and Allery dropped with her to her knees.

She opened her eye when she heard an angry roar. Jacob had dropped Driscoll, who was alive still, though fallen and gasping for breath, and was storming towards her. All throughout the forest, doors snapped shut.

Allery carefully slid her sword free and laid Deni back on the ground. She stood to face Jacob.

"You will die," he told her, the words twisting his usually expressionless face. He raised his arm in one sudden movement, palm out, and the demons swarmed to him, then turned to Allery.

She ignored them. Angels swooped in, plucking them away, roots burst from the ground and dragged them into the earth, and the wolf clawed them aside to stop them from getting to her.

Allery's sword still dripped Deni's blood. Her hand was slick on its handle. "No," she shouted, thoroughly pissed off with the whole situation. "*You* will die."

She struck out at Jacob as soon as she reached him, but he twisted aside and moved within her reach, grabbing the tops of her arms and squeezing tight. She tried to catch him with the sword, but he'd clamped her arms to her sides. He laughed in her face.

"Fuck's sake," Allery said. And she kicked him in the balls, hard.

Jacob let her go and with one swift movement, Allery raised her hand and brought the sword down on the back of his neck. Then she struck him again, and again, until his head dropped from his body, and she collapsed to her knees in a trembling, sobbing mess.

Chapter Thirty-Nine

Somebody was hugging her. Allery opened her eye long enough to see that it was Esme through the tears.

"Where are they going?" Esme said. It took a moment for Allery to realise she wasn't speaking to her.

"Scarpering through the last few doors before they close for good." Driscoll's hoarse voice.

A pair of footsteps rustled the leaves. Nick said, "There's kids here, young wardens. They...they're waking up."

Allery opened her eye again as her father crouched by her side and gently touched her shoulder. She looked between him and Esme and her gaze fell on Deni's body.

"You did the right thing," her father said. "I'm so proud of you, Allery."

She extracted herself from Esme's embrace and got to her feet. "Dad, can you do me a favour?"

"Of course!"

"Take Deni back to Merrybell. I'll be there soon." She pulled her attention from Deni and looked at him. "I have to find Dillon now."

Her father frowned a little but didn't argue. He gave her hand a squeeze and turned away, and as he knelt beside Deni's body, Allery turned back to her friends.

"Help me find Dillon. Please. We need to take him back to his mum."

"Him and the other kids," Esme said.

"If he's even here," Driscoll added.

Nick removed his hand from the trunk of a young tree. "He's here," he said. "I know where."

They followed Nick through the forest, sparing the bodies of the fallen only a brief glance. Allery figured the old wardens were free to go where they pleased now and would soon come to clear up the aftermath. She wondered briefly if she should've left Deni there but wanted to get her out of Savernake.

She didn't know how long they trudged after Nick, but she snapped back into wakefulness when she heard shouting in the distance.

"*Help! Someone help!*"

"It's Dillon!" Allery ran towards him. She spotted Dillon crouched by another child and he looked up when he heard them approach, his eyes now blue and once more like a child's. He looked frightened.

"It's Tia," he said. "She can't breathe."

Tia was on her hands and knees, hacking wet-sounding coughs. Dillon had a hand to her back.

"Tia, listen to me." Allery knelt by the girl and rubbed her back. "You need to calm down, try to take slow, deep breaths. In through your nose and out through your mouth, okay? We're going to get you to a doctor, okay?"

Tia nodded. She took in some ragged breaths and coughed again.

"I'll fetch the van," Driscoll said. "I'll bring it to the road here. Carry her, okay?"

Allery nodded and Driscoll disappeared. She was about to lift Tia into her arms when Nick stepped in and lifted the girl. "I've got her," he muttered. "He's gone to get the van. My brother's van. My brother was here…"

Allery hadn't seen Jack and didn't particularly care if he was there or not. Esme came forward, put her hand to Nick's elbow, and offered soothing words. Allery reached for Dillon's hand again and relaxed a little when he took it.

"Will she be okay?" he asked, his voice small.

"Of course," Allery said. "And so will you. I'll take you back to your mum."

"What are we doing here?"

"You don't remember?"

Dillon shook his head. *Just as well.* Nick started off through the trees, in the direction of the road, so she squeezed Dillon's hand and followed him.

*

Nick sat in the passenger seat while Driscoll drove. Allery and Esme stayed in the back with the kids. He stared out of the window and said nothing, the van depressingly silent besides Tia's cough.

This is Jack's van.

There were empty beer cans in the footwell.

Jack's dead.

It was raining. Tiny drops beaded on the window, and he looked past them to a grey—a naturally grey—sky. What if the incubus came after him? Jack had orchestrated the whole thing. He hated him that much? He felt nothing.

"You all right?" Driscoll asked.

Nick pulled his gaze from the window. "Yeah." He turned to the back of the van and Esme smiled at him. "Yeah, I'm all right. Let's get the kids safe. It's been a mad day."

Driscoll chuckled. "No shit. But it's over now. It's over."

"It's over." Nick repeated the words, wondering whether he believed them. Jacob was dead. Jack was dead. Deni was dead. He looked out of the window again and watched the trees flash by.

*

"Allery."

The voice came from far away. A light touch brushed against her hand.

"Allery? Time to wake up."

She opened her eye and groaned a little at the pain in her body. The van doors were open, and Driscoll stood looking in. "We're at the hospital at Savernake," he said. "Esme's taken Tia in as she's the most presentable. I think you should see a doctor, too."

Allery lifted a hand to her head and sat up a little. "No, I can't," she muttered. Dillon sat opposite her, his arms wrapped around his knees. She had to get him home.

"Allery—"

"Just get Nick to fix me up. Can you fetch him whatever he needs? Please?"

Driscoll pursed his lips at her.

"Come on, I can't go in there. Can you imagine the questions? I've got a massive fucking hole in my face just...help me, please." She offered Dillon a half apologetic smile, aware she'd cursed in front of him. Driscoll nodded and retreated from the back of the van, so she sighed and leaned back to wait.

She didn't have to wait long before Nick climbed in beside her with a first aid kit and some clean clothes. He spoke to her but she barely listened; the pain almost sent her back to oblivion. Eventually, Nick pressed a couple of pills and a bottle of water into her hand and she swallowed them back. He'd tied a bandage around her head and eye, and she touched it tentatively. "How do I look?"

"We'll get you an eyepatch," Nick said. "You'll look like a pirate."

She smiled. She was just about to ask someone to fetch Esme so they could take Dillon home, when the boy muttered, "Whoa," and put a hand to his head.

"Dillon?"

He looked at her briefly, then clutched his chest, and a puzzled frown creased his brow. "I feel dizzy." He made to stand up, but Allery reached out to stop him, though the movement made her own head spin.

"I don't feel right," Dillon said. "I—"

His head slumped onto his chest and Allery realised he'd fainted. She scooped him up into her arms and clambered out of the van with him, ignoring Driscoll's calls for her to take it easy. She marched towards the glass-fronted main entrance, determined not to lose Dillon now that she was so close to reuniting him with his mother.

"I need help here!" she called, entering the building. "Someone help!" She'd barely taken another step when a nurse in a pale-blue tunic ran up to her. She passed the boy over and stood back.

"Allery?" Esme came to her, her eyes wide when she saw Dillon. "What happened?"

"I don't know. He fainted. I..." She ran a hand through her hair and watched as Dillon was taken away. "Is Tia...?"

"She's safe. She's being looked after. They want to contact her parents, Al, but I don't know who they are. They're asking questions I can't answer. I think they'll call the police."

Allery reached for Esme's hands and squeezed them to stop her from panicking. "The wardens will come. They'll deal with all that. Go and wait in the van with the others." She spotted a pay phone in the foyer and left Esme to go to it. Sophie's number still stuck in her memory, and she borrowed some coins from a friendly old lady who looked like she was about to launch into her life story before Allery shoved the coins in the phone and dialled Sophie's number.

"Pick up, pick up," she muttered. She drummed her fingers on the wall and listened to the ring. Her heart thumped and the world faded around her.

"Hello?"

"Sophie, it's me, it's Allery, don't hang up." She took a breath. "I've found Dillon."

There was silence on the line for what felt like longer than it probably was. Sophie said, "Where?"

"We're at Savernake hospital. He's okay—"

"I'm on my way. It'll take me a little while to get there, okay, just over an hour, but I'm on my way. Tell him Mummy's coming."

"I will do."

"Thank you, Al. Thank you."

The call ended. Allery put the phone back on the hook and sighed deeply. The little old lady placed her cold hand on Allery's and smiled up at her. "Is everything okay now?"

"Yes." Allery removed her hand, frowning a little. "Yes, thank you. It is."

Chapter Forty

Allery stepped back out of the way as a nurse pushed a wheelchair down the corridor. She waited a moment, then glanced in the window of the room where Sophie stood watching over Dillon. Nick and Esme had headed for home—Nick never coped too well with the overly sterile environment of a hospital and Esme, impatient as ever, wanted to get into some clean clothes and wash her hair. Driscoll had collected his car and waited outside.

Deni can wait. She's not going anywhere.

Still, she was itching to get back to her. She knocked on the door softly before opening it up and offering Sophie a smile.

"Hey." Sophie held her baby in her arms, rocking her distractedly as she watched Dillon.

"Hey. How is he?"

"Asleep." The baby grizzled and Sophie made soothing sounds for a moment before looking at Allery again. "They say it's congenital heart disease. He'll have to have a pacemaker or something.

My poor boy! How long has he needed me, and I've not been there?"

"You've been looking for him."

"I should've listened to you. I should've trusted you. Everything you've always said. Max..."

"Max is gone."

"She's his. I've called her Phoebe. Will she... I mean, is she like him? Or you? Is she a what d'you call it?"

"A supernatural?" Allery reached out and took Phoebe's tiny hand, smiling when the baby gripped her finger. She didn't know what had happened, but for some reason the child appeared human. "She's a mortal."

Sophie breathed an audible sigh of relief. "I mean, not that there's anything wrong with being a...what d'you call it—"

"Supernatural."

"Yeah. But I'm glad she's normal." She pointed a finger at Allery's bandage. "Will that heal?"

"It'll heal," Allery replied. "But my eye won't grow back." She glanced at Dillon again and moved back towards the door. "I have to go. Are you okay?"

Sophie had already turned away, back to the bed. "We'll be okay. Thanks, Al. For everything."

Allery nodded. She turned and left the room before heading back down the corridor and out of the building.

*

Nick sat on his mother's sofa and vaguely wondered if it'd ever feel like his. They should probably go out and buy a new sofa anyway. One that wasn't quite so floral. Esme leaned back against him as she painted her nails, the smell of the varnish now overpowering the coconut of her wet hair. He smiled and put an arm around her.

"I love you," he said.

"Hm? Oh! Love you, too, baby."

The clock on the wall ticked loudly. Nick looked at it before his gaze settled on an old school photo of him and Jack. They were both smiling.

"It'll be all right, you know," Esme said, and Nick frowned.

"What will?"

"Everything. You. Me. Us. Allery. Locke & Co." She screwed the lid back onto the bottle and blew on her nails. "I know you're thinking about Jack. What the wolf did...what *I* did—"

"You saved me," Nick said. "Don't you *ever* blame yourself. Jack was twisted. Something had gone wrong somewhere along the line, and I'd missed it. I should've been a better brother."

Esme turned around and straddled him, putting her arms around his neck. "I have some news."

"Oh yeah?"

"I wanted to wait and tell you when things had calmed down a little. I think they've calmed down enough now." She kissed him and broke out into a silly grin. "I'm pregnant!"

"Oh!" Nick's heart fluttered. "That's—" *Terrifying* "—great!"

Esme kissed him again and hugged him tight, and all he could do was stare over her shoulder at the picture of Jack smiling back at him.

*

Allery approached the door to the cottage with trepidation and looked back at Driscoll as he waited in the car at the bottom of the path. He waved her forward, so she turned, drew in a nerve-steadying breath, and opened the door. Her father stood in the kitchen, leaning back against the kitchen worktop with his hands wrapped around a mug. Deni's grandfather was in the lounge, crouched beside the sofa where Deni lay. Both of them looked up as she entered.

"What are you planning, Allery?" her father asked.

Allery didn't answer. She walked towards the sofa, gazing at Deni and marvelling at how still and calm she looked. She noted she'd been dressed in clean clothes, the wound in her chest presumably likewise taken care of.

Deni's grandfather nodded gravely and she noticed his Adam's apple bob as he swallowed. "Thank you," he said.

She bent to the sofa and lifted Deni awkwardly into her arms, not complaining or asking for help though Deni was a little too heavy for her. She stopped when she reached the door.

"Allery," her father said again. "Tell me what you're planning."

She looked at him briefly, then back at the door. "Open the door for me, please? I'm keeping a promise."

Her father frowned but he came to the door and opened it anyway. Both angels followed Allery outside and walked behind her down the path towards the car as if they were in a bizarre funeral procession.

Driscoll got out to help her settle Deni on the back seat and then he got back in and started the engine. Allery looked at the angels. "You can come," she said. "If you want to."

"We'll follow," her father said, flexing his wings. "Allery...am I going to like this?"

She smiled a little. "Probably not." She hugged him then, holding him tight. Then she released him and got into the passenger seat before buckling her seat belt.

"Ready?"

She looked over at Driscoll. "Ready."

They drove for what felt like an age through the countryside, down lanes too narrow for two vehicles to pass, until they reached a spot she could vaguely remember. Driscoll pulled the car over into a layby and they both got out to take Deni from the back.

The woodland beside the road was filled with spindly trees that creaked and moaned in the wind, and the air smelled of earth. It was the perfect spot for wardens.

Allery stepped beneath the canopy with Deni in her arms as the angels descended behind her. Ahead, she spotted a tree stump, and she headed for it. She'd not got very far before there was a flash of light and a door opened between two trees.

A warden walked towards her.

"Miss Locke," he said.

"I've brought you the key. As promised."

The warden reached her and raised his eyebrows at Deni in her arms. "It is a little too late."

Allery didn't want to let Deni go but she had to put her down. Carefully, she laid her on the ground at the warden's feet.

"I was told you could take my immortality. Take it. Give it to her."

"Allery, no!"

She ignored her father and waited for the warden. He didn't respond.

"Well?" she prompted.

"I cannot make her immortal."

"You have to do something! I have done *everything* for you people. I've stopped Jacob, I've killed Deni, it's your turn now! It can't end like this. It—"

The warden raised a hand to stop her speaking and she closed her mouth with a frown.

"I can only drain your life force and feed it into the body."

"Do it."

"Allery…"

She turned and looked at her dad. "I know what I'm doing. Please. Just...let me do this."

"You will both be mortal," the warden said. "Is that what you want?"

Allery nodded. A tear dribbled onto her cheek and she swiped it away. She'd beg if she had to. "Please," she whispered.

The warden took a step closer. He lifted one arm and placed his palm against Allery's chest; the other hand he settled above Deni. "Do not struggle. It may hurt."

She was about to answer when the pain hit her, sudden and sharp as if needles were being drawn from her body. She couldn't cry out or move. Her vision narrowed to a pin prick.

Just as suddenly as it started, it stopped, and she fell to her knees beside Deni. Gasping, she scooped Deni up into her arms and cradled her. "Please," she whispered. "Please. Please."

There is no jolt. Or shock. Or sudden, great intake of breath. Your eyes don't snap open. This is no rebirth. It's like waking up but not remembering the moment you were no longer asleep. You will hurt, depending on how you went, and you will scar, but you will live again. And that's all that matters.

Slowly, Deni opened her eyes.

About the Author

E.J. Tett has been writing stories since primary school, some of which still survive in notebooks in her dad's attic, and wanted to be an author as soon as she realised it was a possible career choice and "pony" and "ninja" weren't viable options.

Her first short story, *Club Freak*, about an anonymous woman's determination to find her husband's killer, was published by Park Publications' *Debut* magazine in May 2009. Since then, she has gone on to write many short stories and poems for various small presses and has achieved an honourable mention in the 2011 Writers of the Future competition. In 2014, writing as Emma Jane, she signed her first publishing contracts for not one, but two novels: *Otherworld*, formerly published by Torquere Press, and *Shuttered*, by Dreamspinner Press. She also has two novels published by NineStar Press, one a space opera and the other a contemporary romance.

Website
ejtett.weebly.com

Other NineStar books by this author as Emma Jane

Space Mac

Whitecott Manor

CONNECT WITH NINESTAR PRESS

WEBSITE: NineStarPress.com

FACEBOOK: NineStarPress

X: @ninestarpress

INSTAGRAM: NineStarPress

BLUESKY: NineStarPress

THREADS: @ninestarpress